Pride Publishing books by Jason Wrench

Single Books
Twelve Days of Murder
Till Death Do Us Wed

Up on the Farm
Finding a Farmer

I0663150

Up on the Farm

FINDING A FARMER

JASON WRENCH

Finding a Farmer
ISBN # 978-1-80250-973-1
©Copyright Jason Wrench 2022
Cover Art by Kelly Martin ©Copyright August 2022
Interior text design by Claire Siemaszkiewicz
Pride Publishing

FINDING A
FARMER

Dedication

This book is dedicated to my Friday reading group—Carol, Caytea, Nancy, Sarah, Stephanie and Susan. Thank you for your continued feedback and for helping this author feel less alone in the writing process.

Acknowledgements

First, I want to thank the team at Pride Publishing for once again helping me along my writing journey. Second, I also want to thank my Friday night Ninja Writers Reading Group. Your feedback on all my works, including this one, has been a godsend. Third, I want to thank all my colleagues at the Romance Writers of America. I continued to be awed by your dedication to the romance genre. Lastly, I want to thank all the readers. Your kind words during this journey have made this writer's heart sing.

Chapter One

I glanced down at the Rolex watch my granddad had given me when I had finished my MBA a few years earlier. It's not one of the crazy expensive ones. Of course, I'd had to google the price after he gave it to me. At the time, it was worth around ten grand — so, nothing to sneeze at, but still on the lower end of the Rolex scale. I've thought about upgrading it a couple of times but can't bring myself to do it. Sure, I can afford a more expensive one. Between my day job working on Wall Street and my trust fund, I can afford almost anything I want.

I guess I should say my 'former' job on Wall Street, since that's what I was celebrating — my getting fired. I wasn't fired for cause or anything. My firm had scrolled back its trading arm in the US to focus on overseas markets. Thankfully, Granddad had taught me to squirrel away money. I'd been taking my skills on the trading room floor of the Stock Exchange and turning them into my private nest egg. There was something satisfying about having an account with seven figures that hadn't been given to me by my family. At least the firm had waited until the Tuesday after Memorial Day to fire my ass. So, there I was on June first, drunk out of my mind.

I stared down at my empty glass, which was supposed to be filled with two shots of Belvedere Single Estate Lake Bartężek Vodka. I was about to raise my hand and order another one when I caught sight of my watch. I hadn't realized it was this late already.

"Dudes, it's ten-thirty," I said, looking at my two drinking companions.

On my left was my best friend in the universe, Grayson Jackson. Grayson and I had met when we were attending The Quad Preparatory School in Manhattan. And with a seventy-five-thousand-dollar-a-year price tag, The Quad opened the doors to go anywhere we wanted. We'd both ended up at Harvard, for the fun of it. After making it through our undergraduate years barely sober, I'd gone off to their MBA program, and Grayson had gone to law school. Now we were both single, hot, wealthy guys in their late twenties getting everything we ever wanted out of life. We'd lived by the 'work hard, play harder' motto our entire adult lives.

On my right was Avery Addington, my sort of on-again, off-again lover or fuck buddy. He's a couple of years younger than me. I had met him on a dating app and figured it would be a onetime hookup, but he'd ended up sticking around. I called him my 'on-again, off-again boyfriend' because I didn't know what the hell we are. Hell, I didn't know if we even *were* at that point. We weren't exclusive, that much I knew. God, the idea of being in a long-term relationship gave me heart palpitations — and not the good kind. I liked my freedom. I enjoyed doing what I wanted to do when I wanted to do it. If I found a hot guy at a bar and I wanted to fuck him senseless in the back room, then I took him into the back room, bent him over and showed him the best time of his life. And while I'm an admitted slut, I was on PREP and played safely…most of the time. And despite my use of protection, I got regular checkups to make sure I hadn't contracted anything. Shit happens.

"It's already ten-thirty?" Avery slurred. "How long have we been drinking?"

I found myself with my mouth open, on the verge of responding, but I honestly did not know what time we'd gotten there. I tilted my head to the side and glanced at Grayson, because I knew he'd know.

Grayson rolled his eyes. "You texted me about four, and I got here about five-thirty. You said you'd just gotten here, which I figured meant you had at least thirty minutes on me already. Based on this, you've been here drinking for six hours," he said with the emotion of a forensic accountant. Oh, I should have mentioned that Grayson had also gotten a master's in accounting after law school from NYU. He worked for the Manhattan District Attorney's Office in accounting crimes—or something like that. Honestly, when he talked about numbers, I daydreamed. I enjoyed making money and could tell you all about bulls and bears, but when it came to the day-to-day math part, I tuned out. I liked the game of making money, the strategy of making money—hence, why I have an accountant who handled my books.

"I don't feel drunk," I heard myself say right before I started touching my forehead. "But I can't feel my forehead."

"Okay," Grayson grumbled. "I hate to be the adult in the room, but I have work in the morning, so I've gotta get out of here. Can you two make it home?"

"Your place or mine?" I asked Avery.

"Yours. It's closer."

"We can call my car service." *No worries.*

Grayson shook his head and grabbed my phone off the table. "What are you doing?" I asked.

"I'm calling your car service."

"But we're not ready to leave yet," Avery whined.

"Yeah, I think you two are."

"But, Dad," I complained.

"I've gotta go," Grayson said flatly. "And I'm not leaving you two to your own devices. To keep my conscience clean, I'm putting you in a car and sending you on your way. What you do after that is up to you."

I thought about objecting, but I knew Grayson was right. I'd had my pity party and would have to get up and join the world of the unemployed the next morning. Thankfully, between my granddad's and my contacts, I was sure I wouldn't be unemployed for too long. Honestly, I didn't understand why some people stay unemployed. It's like, why don't they use their personal and family networks to get a new job? It's not like it's that difficult.

Grayson got up and put his suit coat back on.

"How can you wear a suit in this heat?" I questioned.

"Don't you wear a suit to the office?" Grayson asked.

"Oh yeah," I said, as I tried to stand and realized my eyes were going in and out of focus. Grayson reached out and steadied me until I got my feet firmly planted below me. "Whoa, maybe I've had too much to drink."

"You think?" Grayson asked.

Once I was fully standing and the lightheadedness had passed, I helped Avery to his feet and the three of us exited the bar and grill after paying our tabs. I didn't know how much this evening was going to cost me. I'd handed over my American Express Black Card and given my signature. I'd worry about the expense later.

Thankfully, my car service arrived right as Grayson's Uber did. I shuffled into the car, sliding over so Avery could get in. Once Avery closed the door, the driver took off. I put my arm around Avery and rested my head on his shoulder. I felt his arm sneak around and pat the side of my head as he leaned down and planted a kiss on the top of my head.

Why aren't we dating? I thought to myself, as I was almost on the verge of falling asleep.

"We're here," the driver said.

"Thanks. That was fast," I muttered as I untangled myself from Avery, who had fallen asleep.

"What?" Avery said as I jostled him awake.

"We're at my place."

"I must have fallen asleep."

"Well, duh," I said, reaching over him to open the door.

I nudged him out of the car and followed before gently closing the door. I stared up at my apartment building, noticing all the lights in the windows were turned on.

I walked into Twenty Exchange, where I have a two-bedroom apartment. For its location and proximity to Wall Street, Twenty Exchange is an ideal apartment complex for the up-and-coming business type in Manhattan. Not only is it in the heart of Wall Street, but it also caters to an exclusive tenant list. When I decided

I wanted to live there, I had my granddad pull a few strings to get me to the top of the list for a new two-bedroom apartment when one opened up, which wasn't often. But here I was, four years later and I'm still living here, paying my four-thousand-dollar-a-month rent. Maybe one day I'll break down and buy a condo in the city. But for the time being, I'm okay with renting. I've always liked the idea that I could choose to move at the end of my lease if I wanted to.

The doorman opened the door for us with a polite bow of his head. "Good evening, Mr. Devereaux."

"Good evening, Jack," I responded. "How are the kids?"

"They enter the first grade this year," the uniformed man responded. He had the look that all proud fathers get when they realize their kids are growing up much faster than expected.

"Wow! Already... I can't believe it," I said with a smile. "Well, good night."

"You, too, Mr. Deveraux."

Granddad had taught me early in life to always respect those people in service positions. He was a whiz at remembering names, birthdates, anniversaries and all kinds of other facts. Me? I was happy I could remember someone's first name and maybe one or two details about their lives, but I tried.

Avery and I made our way to the elevator banks. I pushed the button, then leaned against the wall to make the marble around me stop spinning. *I haven't been this wasted since my first year in college.*

I heard the ding of the door and sort of spun myself into the elevator then hit the button for the fifty-fifth floor. Avery was leaning against me by this point as the elevator doors slid shut.

The ride up was smooth and uneventful. When the elevator opened onto my floor, Avery and I stumbled out and made it the few feet to my door. I whipped out my key card and let myself into the apartment.

"I'm going to get a bottle of water." I asked Avery, "You want one?"

"Yeah, we should definitely hydrate after all this alcohol. I'm going to take a leak first."

I didn't watch him make his way to the bathroom, but I heard him as he bumped into one wall and tried to apologize to it.

I made my way into the kitchen, opened the fridge door and pulled out a bottle of Glacial Flow, a bottled water company that harvested water from fifteen-thousand-year-old glaciers. Each twenty-four-ounce bottle cost something like sixteen dollars, but I liked it and loved the conversation starter it provided me when I was drinking one at work. I could always talk about saving the planet and our melting icecaps while I was drinking one. Trust me, the irony wasn't lost on me.

I twisted off the top and took a swig, savoring the crisp taste before swallowing. I leaned against the fridge, took a second sip and noticed that my answering machine light was blinking. Okay, I know what you're thinking. Who has an answering machine in the twenty-first century? Well, I do. And it's connected to my home line. I know, who has one of those in this century?

I'd broken down and gotten myself a home line and answering machine when I had to work from home for six months during the pandemic. I could have done everything through my cell phone, but I figured having an actual phone with a headset attached was going to make my life easier while I stared at the four-monitor terminal I'd set up in the spare bedroom. I lived in the one bedroom, and the second one had become my home office. I figured the only people who ever stayed over with me slept in my bed, so I didn't need a spare room. Besides, a spare room seemed like an utter waste of space. Who needs to have a bedroom that is only used when they have company over? I don't get that. If someone is coming for a visit, I'll put them up in a luxurious hotel, not my apartment. Again, I liked my space.

I walked over to the flashing red light, put both water bottles on the island separating the kitchen from the dining area and pushed the button.

"Dale, it's your granddad. I heard through the grapevine that you were let go from your firm today. I'm sorry to hear that, but I think it's the perfect opportunity to talk to you about the family business. Why don't you show up at my office tomorrow morning at seven a.m. for breakfast?"

Well, fuck!

"How the hell does he already know?"

"Who knows what?" Avery asked, coming into the kitchen. I picked up one of the bottles of water and offered it to him. I turned around, leaned my hip against the island, unscrewed the cap on my bottle again and took another swig.

"My granddad. He already knows about my being let go today. I swear he has spies that watch my every move."

"You don't think he'd actually do that, do you?" Avery questioned, scrunching up his face in an expression I couldn't read.

"No. It's a figure of speech…or maybe hyperbole. In reality, Granddad knows too many people in this town.

I can't say that I'm too surprised, though, but I wish I'd been the one to tell him. You know?"

I glanced over at the clock on the microwave, and it read eleven-twenty p.m. "Dear God, I have to be up in five hours."

"Five hours?"

"If I'm going to get to his office by seven a.m., I'm going to have to get up at four-thirty to hit the gym."

"Why not skip tomorrow?"

"Because you don't look this amazing by skipping the gym," I said. I attempted to wink at Avery, but I'm sure my wink probably appeared more like some kind of facial spasm. "Let's just crash."

I grabbed Avery's hand and led him down the hall to my bedroom. I wished I could text my granddad and say I wouldn't be able to see him in the morning, but I knew that when you're summoned by my granddad, you show up—whether you like it or not.

* * * *

I was enjoying a pleasant dream that involved me and a team of cabana boys when the dance version of *I Am What I Am* roused me out of my sleep.

Next to me, I heard Avery grumble, "Dear God, you *are* gay."

"Shut it," I replied as I pulled myself from under the sheets and turned off the phone. "Go back to sleep."

I leaned over and kissed him once on the forehead before I put my legs over the side of the bed and started wiping the sleep from my eyes. *God, I hate mornings.* Okay, in reality, I hated being awake. I loved to sleep. If sleep were an Olympic event, I would absolutely get behind devoting my life to training for it. Sadly, our world doesn't work that way, so I planted my feet on the floor and walked over to my dresser. I rummaged around, quietly finding my workout clothes before grabbing my sneakers and slipping into the living room. I closed the door behind me so I wouldn't wake Avery again when I turned on the lights. Avery was already snoring away—not obnoxious snoring, just a gentle, even pattern that I found comforting and cute.

I went into the bathroom and relieved myself before slipping out of my night clothes and hanging them on the back of the bathroom door. Next, I put on my workout gear. I was wearing a night-blue tank top and a pair of two-in-one running shorts. I loved the shorts because they provided me the support for my junk with compression shorts stitched inside. One pair of shorts to rule them all… I went back into the living room and slipped into my sneakers.

I then grabbed a water bottle and glanced at myself in the mirror that I had hung in the hallway. *Dear God, pasty much?* I'm a white boy. And when I say white, I mean that I'm practically translucent because I'm so white. There are people out there who look at the sun and magically have a golden tan. I am *not* one of those guys. I can spend the entire summer slathered in olive oil on a beach and I would become a crispy critter reminiscent of a blackened lobster. I simply do *not* tan.

When I used to spend summers out in the Hamptons as a child, my friends would joke that my skinny white body blinded them next to the pool. They also joked when I applied the highest strength sunscreen possible. When I was in middle school, I spent the day at a friend's pool and didn't think about applying sunscreen to my feet. I couldn't wear shoes for a week because of how burned the tops of my feet had gotten that day. After that incident, I have always applied sunscreen liberally and often any time I had to be out in the sun.

I may not be able to control how white my skin is, but I can control how defined my abs are, which was why I grabbed my water, phone, AirPods and key card before heading off to the gym. I rode the elevator down to the nineteenth floor, where the gym and sun deck were located, then I let myself into the gym and flipped on the light switch. Although the gym was technically open twenty-four hours a day, no one was in there at four-fifty in the morning. I wished I didn't have to be.

Thankfully, the gym was state-of-the-art and contained a range of cardio machines, weight machines and free weights. I put my AirPods in and picked out a treadmill. Today was a chest day, so I needed to get warmed up. I would start with twenty minutes of running, followed by thirty minutes of chest pumping and another twenty minutes doing more cardio.

I opened my favorite music app and selected an appropriately upbeat dance station as I hopped on the treadmill and started running.

By six-fifteen when I was finally leaving the gym, there were probably a dozen other residents who were now exercising in the early morning hour. I'd forgotten to bring a towel with me, but I used the same paper towels that they used to clean the equipment to at least blot off the worst of my sweat. Thankfully, the gym was air conditioned, because even at this early hour, it was going to be hot and humid outside. *The joys of summer in New York.*

I rode back up to my apartment and let myself back inside. Since I'd left, Avery had gotten out of bed and let himself out. We may be friends and regular fuck buddies, but we were hardly joined at the hip. I wasn't surprised that he'd gone or that he hadn't left me a note. I figured I'd text him at some point later in the day.

I threw my gym clothes into the laundry. The cleaning lady who came in daily to care for my apartment would wash and fold my dirty clothes and have them sitting on my bed when I got home from work. *Probably need to decide whether that's an expense I need, now that I'm out of work. Nah, that's a decision for another day.*

Before jumping into the shower, I called my car service and asked to be picked up at six-forty-five. I hated doing this to my car service last minute, but they were always very accommodating. Sure, I could have used an Uber like Grayson does, but they were not as reliable as my service. And with my granddad expecting me at seven, I needed to make sure I was on time. With the car taken care of, I slipped into the bathroom and took a quick shower.

Finally feeling like a human, I slipped into a slim-fitting blue suit with a light blue button-down shirt and a gold tie. I liked how the blue made my hazel eyes pop in the mirror as I was tying the tie. Once I was in the suit, I put some product in my hair and got it to stand the way I liked it. I was going for a clean-cut but slightly tossed style. I knew my granddad hated my haircut, but it was what all the gorgeous guys on Wall Street were doing, and I loved to follow the latest trends in business wear and fashion. If I didn't look like I'd stepped out of a Tom Ford catalog, then I hadn't done my job in the morning. Half of being good in business was looking the part. I'd learned a long time ago that people who were hot and smart got much further in life than those that were just either hot *or* smart. And thanks to my gifted genetics and premier education, I was fucking gorgeous and a highly intelligent businessman.

After stare-fucking myself once more in the mirror, I smiled at what I saw and grabbed my attaché case before leaving the apartment. I glanced at my watch, and it was already six-forty, so it was time to head downstairs and catch my car.

The ride down was uneventful, and a couple of other residents joined me in the elevator. One guy was in his exercise clothes. I nodded in his direction.

"Going for a morning jog?"

"Yep, want to get out there before it's too crazy hot."

I smiled and nodded knowingly. *What is his name?* We had fucked once after seeing each other at a club — or had it been someone's party? *I honestly don't remember.*

I exited the elevator then walked to the front door. My car was pulling up as the doorman opened the door for me.

"Good morning, Mr. Jessup," I said, nodding to the doorman.

"Have a pleasant day, sir," the older gentleman said.

I walked to the curb and opened the door to the black sedan.

"Mr. Devereux," the driver said, recognizing me from previous trips. "Where am I taking you this morning?"

"I'm heading to the Bush Tower, Carl."

"Which entrance?"

"One-Hundred-Thirty-Second West and Forty-Second Street."

"Sure thing. We should be there in ten minutes."

I peeked down at my watch. It was already six-fifty. *Great, I'm going to be late.* "Any way you can shave a minute off the trip?"

"I know a couple bypass routes at this time of the morning. Shouldn't be a problem, sir."

"Great. I'm meeting with my granddad, and he is the king of punctuality." The driver nodded at me and kept his eyes on the road. I pulled out my iPhone to see if there was anything I needed to deal with.

Hey, D. Got home last night. Checking in to see if you're okay.

I quickly responded to Grayson.

Hey, G. All is good. Got summoned to G-Dad's this morning. He's already heard... Sigh... Will text after my seven a.m. meeting.

There was also a quick text from Avery.

Went home to get ready. Had fun last night. Totally need to do it again. Preferably some time when we aren't so wasted that all we do is pass out when we hit your bed.

I turned off my phone. *I'll text him later.* I leaned my head against the black cushion and closed my eyes for the rest of the ride.

* * * *

The black sedan slowed down, and I opened my eyes. We were pulling in right behind my granddad's black limo. *Perfect timing.*

"Thanks," I said as I opened the door. "I'll call the agency when I'm done. I don't know how long that will be."

"Not a problem. If it's not me, one of the other drivers will be glad to come get you, Mr. Devereux."

I put my foot on the curb, grabbed the inside door handle and hoisted myself into a standing position outside the vehicle. I closed the door and nodded goodbye to my driver, who wasted no time heading back into traffic.

I walked a few paces to my granddad's limo and rapped on the window three times lightly. The driver's side door opened, and Franklyn, Granddad's long-term chauffer, came out into the morning air.

"Good morning, Master Devereux."

"How many times am I going to have to tell you to call me Dale?"

"As many as you'd like, Master Devereux," the old man said with a sly smile.

We'd been playing this little game for years. Franklyn Jackson was an old-school chauffer. He was part driver, part body man, part confidant and probably filled more roles than my granddad's secretary did. They don't make them like him anymore. Admittedly, my generation preferred using car services instead of a single car and driver. It's easier to always have a car and person on standby whenever you need them.

There was a light rap on the inside of the window and Franklyn moved around me to open the door. With it opened, he reached one hand in to help my granddad out.

"I won't be needing you again until around one, so go do what it is you do when you're not driving me around this town," my granddad said to Franklyn.

"Will do, Mr. Deveraux. If you need me, have your secretary call and I'll be here in minutes."

With that and a nod to me, Granddad started walking toward the front door of the Bush Tower. My granddad's offices were on the fifteenth of the building's thirty floors.

My granddad isn't one for small talk, so we basically walked into the building then rode the elevator to the fifteenth floor in silence. The Devereux Farms corporate headquarters were simple by New York standards. They leased half the floor, and the other half was leased by a Chinese corporation, which was rarely seen on the floor. In fact, I'd only run into people from the Jīnróng Corporation twice in all the years my granddad had leased the space.

We walked into the primary office, which was still quiet at five minutes after seven. The rest of his workers wouldn't be in until eight-thirty or nine. My granddad liked this time before the rush of people came into the office to get a lot of work accomplished. He might not be a skilled conversationalist with me, but he was the epitome of the old IBM 'management by walking around'. He knew everyone who worked in the corporate offices and was known to drop by to see how things were going. In that respect, Granddad's ability to know his workers and know his business always amazed me.

I followed him into his primary office.

"Good morning, Mr. Devereux — and good morning, Dale. Well, isn't this a pleasant surprise?" The chipper voice from an older woman in a neat teal business suit came as I walked into the office. Molly Frone had been my granddad's personal assistant for as long as I'd been alive. She was one of the first people outside the immediate family who'd held me as a baby. For that reason, she always seemed way more like family than she did my granddad's assistant. "Let me get a look at you."

I did a little spin and a pose. "Well, if this business thing doesn't work out, you can always have a second job as a model. Shall I call a couple of modeling agencies and set up appointments? I have a few connections," she said with a wink.

"I don't think we're there yet," I said. "But trust me, after the day I had yesterday, I may be a couple of days away from taking you up on that offer."

"Oh, let me show you what your grandfather bought me for my birthday," Molly said, gesturing for me to come over to her desk. She looked from side to side conspiratorially before she opened the top drawer on her desk. Just inside, in the pencil tray, sat a two-inch toy gun.

"Okay?" I asked. "What am I looking at? He bought you a model gun?"

"Not a model," Granddad said, "but rather the Swiss Mini Gun."

"It is, it is," Molly said with glee. "I've always wanted one. The gun shoots real ammunition."

"I never knew you were a 'gun nut', Molly," I admitted.

"Oh, I'm not like one of those card-carrying crazy people or anything. I just love antique or interesting guns. I've been a collector for years. And your grandfather gets me a new and unique one every year for my birthday."

"Well, happy belated birthday. And don't go shooting your eye out with that thing."

"I would never!" Molly looked almost scandalized by the prospect of shooting herself, clearly missing my *A Christmas Story* reference.

"Well, we've got things to discuss, Molly," Granddad interjected. "Come into my office, Dale." He then turned to Molly. "Will you bring in breakfast in about ten minutes?"

"Yes, sir." Molly walked over to a phone and dialed a number. I heard her put in the order before leaving to go pick it up.

My granddad's office was old school—all dark cherry wood and a lush midnight-blue carpet. The carpet was something that should be in the Oval Office at the White House, except Granddad's carpet had the Devereux family crest embroidered into it.

"Just out of curiosity, how much does something like that cost?" I asked my granddad as I sat down in a leather chair on the opposite side of his desk.

"Roughly six-thousand Swiss francs."

"So essentially, sixty-five hundred US dollars, then," I replied after converting the sum in my head.

"Good to see your time on the floor of the New York Stock Exchange hasn't dulled your currency knowledge, my boy."

"And speaking of the stock market, I guess you heard about my being let go."

"Yes, yes, I did. I was sorry to hear about that."

"Not half as sorry as I was."

"If it's any consolation, their letting you go had nothing to do with your performance or perceived value to the firm itself."

I didn't bother asking my granddad how he knew that. I'd learned over the years that granddad had his fingers in so many pies and knew half the 'who's-who' of New York City. I wouldn't be surprised if he'd talked to the firm's CEO last night and given him a piece of his mind. He would never tell me he'd done that, though.

"Well, as much as I'm sure this is a blow to your ego, I don't think it's necessarily a bad thing."

That caught my attention. I hadn't expected him to say that. I had expected him to say many things, but that wasn't one of them. I had expected him to blame me for choosing the firm when he had been opposed to them. I had expected him to blame me for choosing to go to Harvard instead of Columbia. I had expected him to blame me for not being so indispensable at work that they'd fired everyone else first.

"How so?" was all I said.

"Well, I've done a lot of thinking about life and you in the past year. I think it's time we discuss what you want for your future."

"Granddad, I'm only twenty-nine. Can we have the future talk when I'm in my thirties—or maybe my forties?"

He cocked his head and eyed me for a second. I could tell he was trying to figure out how to make sense of what I'd said.

"It's just...I'm not ready to settle down yet. I don't know if I'm the getting married and having children type—"

"Oh, dear God," he said with a huff. "I'm not talking about that. I'm talking about your future with Devereux Farms."

My eyes grew with the realization at what he was saying. "Granddad, I don't know if I want to work for Devereux Farms." *Well fuck, that just flew out of my mouth.*

"Excuse me?"

"I want to make my own way in the world. I want to make my own decisions in business without knowing you're ten steps away, watching over me."

"And?"

"And I enjoy working on the stock market. I like the thrill of trading. I don't know if I'm meant to work in an office like this one."

"What's wrong with an office like this one?"

Fuck. "There's nothing wrong with your office. I don't know if I'm ready for a traditional nine-to-five office-type job yet. I like the interaction with people I get on the stock-room floor. I enjoy having more control and flexibility over my life and schedule."

I was about to continue listing all the reasons I couldn't work here in the corporate offices when a knock on the door interrupted me.

"Enter," Granddad said. He eyed me as Molly opened the door, rolled in a breakfast spread and started putting it out on the boardroom table my granddad kept in the corner of the room for important business meetings. I watched as Molly laid out placemats to prevent anything from scratching the wood's surface. I wonder if they'd ever removed the crayon artwork from under the table that I'd done when I'd been a kid?

As soon as Molly left the room, my granddad motioned to the table. I walked over with him. We both slipped out of our suit jackets and hung them on the backs of our chairs before sitting down. I placed the linen napkin in my lap, then removed the cover of the plated breakfast.

My granddad likes his hot breakfasts, so I wasn't surprised when I saw a plate of scrambled eggs, bacon, sausage links, toast and fresh fruit staring back at me. *Thank God I ran this morning.*

"Coffee?" I asked my granddad.

"Yes, please." I picked up the carafe, poured him a cup and handed it to him.

He took the cup of coffee, and as I poured my own, he said, "I have cancer."

Chapter Two

It took me a second to process what he'd said. I had the carafe still in my hands when he'd said the 'C' word. For a second, my brain kind of stopped, and I almost overfilled my coffee mug. Thankfully, I snapped out of it before I made a mess.

"Cancer?" I asked.

"Yes, cancer."

"What kind? What did the doctors say? Are they sure? What treatments do they recommend?" The questions started flowing out of my mouth quickly.

"Slow down, boy," my granddad said. "Give me a chance to answer the first question."

I took a deep breath and mindlessly stirred in some cream to my coffee as I asked my first question again. "What kind?"

"Prostate cancer. Thankfully, the doctor caught it during my annual checkup and sent me to an oncologist, who confirmed the diagnosis."

I grabbed my coffee cup and lifted it to my mouth to drink. I needed to think through what this meant. My brain was spinning in so many directions. I heard my Granddad talking at one point and forced myself to refocus.

"...ninety-nine percent at five years."

"What?" I blurted with a bit more emphasis than intended.

"The survival rate with treatment is ninety-nine percent at five years. So don't think this means you're getting rid of me yet."

"What now?"

"Well, I have a meeting with a radiation oncologist to start treatment in the next couple of weeks. My regular oncologist said that he sees no reason this can't be treated."

"I'm glad to hear that. You had me worried there for a moment. You hear the word 'cancer', and you think the world is collapsing around you."

"I get it, which is why I wanted to talk in person. I didn't think leaving a message saying, '*Hey, Dale. Got the cancer. Talk to you soon.*' would have been the best way to handle it."

I nodded, and once again focused my attention back on my breakfast. I was still trying to figure out where my granddad was going with this. He was holding his cards close to his chest. Sure, he has cancer, but it's apparently treatable, so that's good. I tried to come up with something to say, but, honestly, I was drawing a blank.

"So, now what?" was all I could come up with.

"Well, now we discuss your future. Although my cancer is treatable, it has given me pause."

"Okay," I said, drawing the word out as I gestured for him to continue.

"And, well, if something should happen to me that was more serious, I need to know that you're ready to take the reins of Devereux Farms."

And there it was. I knew this day would come eventually. Granddad had beaten around the bush so many times in the past. He'd never come right out and said he wanted me to work for Devereux Farms, but I always knew he hoped I would eventually decide to join the family business.

"I know nothing about farming."

"We can fix that."

I did my best not to roll my eyes before adding, "And I don't have any desire to learn. I don't like animals or plants or dirt. I don't even buy organic. Hell, depending on the day, I'm iffy about people."

"Dale," my granddad said, staring me down from the other end of the table. He had this stern look on his face, and he gestured with his coffee mug. Amazingly, none of the coffee sloshed out while he did. "You don't need to know about dirt or animals. We have people that do that for us. You need to know about business and how to run one. We're one of the top agricultural corporations on the East Coast. Personally, I haven't stepped foot on a farm in over a decade. I learned a long time ago that if you hire the right people, you don't need to oversee the day-to-day operations."

"Okay, but how can I run a business if I don't understand what it does?" I countered.

"Then, we need to get you an education in agri-business."

"And we're back to me playing in dirt and stepping in horseshit."

"Language!" Granddad huffed.

"Sorry," I said quickly, doing my best to look somewhat contrite, but I wasn't. "I'm a city boy through and through. I don't think I'm the right person."

"Who else is going to do it?" he asked with a grave expression on his face. For the first time, I realized how much distress this conversation caused my granddad. Ever since my father had died, my granddad had given me plenty of room to 'sow my oats', so to speak. I focused on him as I shoveled a forkful of scrambled eggs into my mouth. I could tell there was something he wasn't saying.

"What else?"

"What do you mean?"

"I can tell by looking at your face that you're holding something back. What aren't you telling me?"

"I am worried about you taking over when I die. Like you said, you don't have any experience farming. I kept hoping you'd decide to join the family business in your own time. Unfortunately, I can't wait for you to make up your mind any longer."

I didn't like the direction this conversation was heading, so I stared my granddad in the face and waited for the next shoe to drop.

"And since you no longer have a job on Wall Street, I think it's the perfect time for you to learn our business."

"I'm sure I won't be out of a job for very long. Like you said earlier, everyone knows that I'm exceptional at what I do. I'm sure another firm will hire me soon."

"Not if I don't want them to," Granddad said, looking at me with the intense stare I've only seen him give during board meetings when someone on the board was being uppity and my granddad wanted to put them in their place.

"You wouldn't," I challenged.

"I most certainly would," he responded, staring me down. I finally glanced at my plate as he continued talking. "You're used to our family connections benefiting you. My connections could easily work against you."

"So, you're planning on holding me hostage?"

"If that's how you have to think about this to sleep at night, then sure, I'm holding your career hostage. You're currently unemployed. Give me until the end of the year to teach you about Devereux Farms. If at the end of the year you want to move back into a job on Wall Street, I'll help you get a job at any firm where I have pull, which is most of them."

I sighed. Part of me wanted to tell him off and storm out of the room, but I knew I would look like a petulant child. I took in a deep breath and let it out of my nose as I sighed. I raised my hand and massaged the bridge of my nose as I muttered, "Okay."

"What did you say, boy?"

I jerked my head up and shot him the most defiant look I could muster and said it more firmly. "Okay."

"Good. Tomorrow you're going to be heading upstate to Devereux Farms–Upstate."

"Where is that?"

"Outside of Woodstock."

"Where the hippies are?"

"Were. Well, there are a few who stuck around the area, I guess. But no, for the most part, Woodstock is not a giant hippie commune. Devereux Farms owns a working farm up there, and you'll be overseeing it for the rest of the year."

"How am I going to oversee a farm? I don't know how to garden."

"Thankfully, like I already said, that's why it's important to hire the right people."

There was a knock on the door, and Molly stuck her head in. She looked over at my grandfather and asked, "Are you ready for him?"

"Thank you, Molly," Granddad said with a grin on his face. "Please, let him in."

* * * *

Talgat

I gazed up at the tall building. *God, I hate this place.* I'm a farm boy. I'm used to wide-open spaces, so being in the concrete jungle that is New York City makes me uncomfortable. I glanced from left to right and couldn't see a single tree in sight. *What am I doing here?*

My family has run Devereux Upstate for almost twenty years. I had been born in Nur-Sultan, Kazakhstan. My family had immigrated to the US when I was two, and we had ended up in Woodstock, New York, of all places. I think my parents had settled in Woodstock because of the famed music festival, but they had never admitted that. Thankfully, my parents had a background in farming and were hired on at Devereux Farms soon after we'd moved to the US. Before long, the farm manager had retired, and my parents had been asked to take over the farm's management. When my father had died a year ago, the CEO of Devereux Farms, Jameson Devereux, asked me to continue their legacy.

I already had my Bachelor of Science in Agricultural Business and had been finishing my Master of Science in sustainable food and farming from the University of Massachusetts, Amherst, so the timing was as perfect as it ever was going to be. Also, taking over the family business had meant I could keep my siblings, Ayala and Rasul, employed. Both of them had been born after my parents and I moved to Woodstock, so they were US citizens at birth. I hadn't been, but my parents had become naturalized citizens when I was thirteen, which meant I'd become a naturalized citizen, too.

I'd received a phone call the previous afternoon from Jameson Devereux to attend a meeting at the Devereux Farms Corporate Headquarters first thing in the morning. Thankfully, there'd been an early morning bus out of Kingston, New York, at four-twenty a.m., which had gotten me into the Port Authority Bus Terminal by six-thirty.

I had spent the next thirty minutes making my way from the Port Authority to the Bush Tower. It hadn't been a long walk, but the early morning heat and humidity had felt a bit oppressive already. If this meeting went according to plan, I'd be on a bus and back up in Woodstock long before the real heat of the day settled in over the city.

I scrutinized my khaki pants, button-down shirt and tennis shoes and felt like a fish out of water as I watched the corporate types around me walking into the building in their three-piece suits. I didn't own a tie, but I owned a blazer that I'd thrown on. I was already regretting that decision, as the early morning heat and humidity was getting to me. I could only imagine how much it was going to suck when I left here later.

I walked into the building and headed over to the security station. "I have a meeting with Devereux Farms," I told security.

"Name?" the guard asked without looking up.

"Talgat Kudaibergen."

I watched as the security guard dialed a number. "Yes, I have a Talbert Kuda-tobagon here for a meeting with Devereux Farms."

Part of me wanted to correct his butchering of my name, but sadly, I was used to people in the US being unable to pronounce it. For the record. it's Tal—*hey, I'm your pal*—Gat, *I've got your bat.* As for my last name, it's pronounced *Ku-Day-Burr-Gin*. It shouldn't be complicated, but people screw it up so often that I'm used to telling people how to say it phonetically.

I took the elevator up to the fifteenth floor, got off the elevator and walked into the office. It was a little after seven-twenty a.m. by the time I got there, and the place was still empty. Thankfully, Mr. Devereux's administrative assistant met me at the front door.

"It's good to see you again, Mr. Kudaibergen. You're a few minutes early for your seven-thirty meeting, so can I get you a coffee while you wait?"

"That would be amazing, Mrs. Frone."

"How do you take it?"

"Black is fine."

"Take a seat," she said, gesturing toward a chair in her office.

I sat down and pulled out my cell phone to see if there was anything I needed to catch up on from the thirty minutes it had taken me to walk from the bus to here.

I was keeping my fingers crossed that today would be the day that Mr. Devereux officially made me the farm manager. Since my father had died the past year, I'd been basically doing the work of the farm manager without getting the actual compensation. I felt the light vibration of my phone as a text came in. I swiped on the message and saw it was from my baby sister, Ayala.

You've got this!

She was sure I was getting the promotion.

"Here you go," Mrs. Frone said as she came back into the office and handed me a cup of coffee.

"Thanks."

"How are things upstate?" she asked.

"Things are doing well. The trees are looking great. If the weather keeps up, we may have an early and extended harvest this year."

Mrs. Frone walked over to the big door at the other end of her office and knocked before sticking her head inside and asking, "Are you ready for him?"

"Thank you, Molly," I heard Mr. Devereux say from inside his office. "Please, let him in."

She partially shut the door before turning to me and saying, "They're ready for you."

I grabbed my cup of coffee, walked over to the door, and Molly opened it for me as I walked inside.

Sitting at the table with Mr. Devereux was a face I'd never seen before. I put on my best fake smile.

"Mr. Kudaibergen," Mr. Devereux began, "thank you for making it down so early and on such short notice."

"Thanks for inviting me."

"I want to introduce you to my grandson, Dale," Mr. Devereux said, motioning to the young man sitting on the other side of the table.

"It's a pleasure to meet you, Mr. Devereux," I said politely to the younger man.

"Please, call me Dale," he said as he stood and extended his hand.

I gripped it and shook. I was immediately taken aback by how smooth the man's hand was. It's one of those things you notice as a farm worker. There are people who work with their hands and there are people who don't. Dale's hands hadn't seen an honest day's work in his entire life. *Ahh, what must it be like to live like a king?*

With the niceties out of the way, Devereux Senior motioned for me to take a seat opposite him and his grandson.

"I'm guessing you're wondering why I asked you here today?" Mr. Devereux inquired.

"Yes, sir."

"Well, as you know, Devereux Upstate has not been doing as well financially as it should be for a few years now."

"Yes, sir. I'm still not sure how that's possible."

"I'm sure your people at the farm are doing an amazing job on the farming front," Mr. Devereux replied, clearly trying to placate me.

I detest it when rich White people act like I'm a dumbass farmer. Most of them couldn't understand the math and science related to modern farming to save their lives, but they all seem to think all we do is dig in the ground and water things.

"I've asked my grandson here," Mr. Devereux continued as he motioned to Dale, "to come spend some time up on the farm."

I hoped I masked the shock that came over me, but I clearly didn't do it well, because Jameson tried to reassure me.

"Don't worry. You'll still be overseeing the day-to-day agricultural aspects of the farm. Dale will be handling the business parts."

"Okay?" I said, less a statement and more a question.

"I'm sure you and Dale will find a symbiotic working relationship. Between your agricultural knowledge and his business sense, I'm sure you'll have the farm producing record-breaking profits in no time."

"Sounds like a plan," I said, plastering on a thin-lipped smile.

"Don't worry, buddy," Dale said. "I don't want to be there any longer than I have to be. I'll be the first to admit I know nothing about farms and farming, so I'm going to be depending on you to get me acclimated quickly. The faster we get the farm running smoothly, the sooner I can get out of your hair."

Something about the way the young man stared at me made it very clear this wasn't his idea. *Dear God! I'm going to be babysitting a rich prick.*

* * * *

Dale

I sat on the opposite side of the table from Mr. Kudaibergen. From the moment he had walked into the office until he had started speaking, I would have expected him to be some kind of upstate trailer park trash. His clothes were from Sears. *Is that a thing anymore?* Maybe they were from Walmart? I'd gone to summer camp with one of the great-grandchildren of Sam Walton. Pleasant enough guy, but we didn't run in the same social circles.

While my granddad was speaking, I analyzed what I could see. There was a stain on the front of the man's pants, and there was a hole that had been patched on the guy's jacket. Why didn't he buy a new one? The tennis shoes with the outfit were a delectable touch. I wondered if this was what farm-chic looked like? *Note to self. I probably need to buy some L.L. Bean stuff online tonight.*

Mr. Kudaibergen was clearly decently built—not like the gym queens I know, but the type of build you get from lifting livestock or something. He was also pretty dark for an Asian guy. I wasn't sure if that was because he worked outside or because he was a specific flavor of Asian. I never considered myself a rice queen before, but I could definitely see how much fun it would be to roll around in the hay with a farmhand. *Dear God, I think I actually saw that porno once.*

I could tell from the conversation that Mr. Kudaibergen was not exactly happy that I was going to be coming up to the farm. So, I figured I'd be blunt about it.

"Don't worry, buddy," I said, taking in his dark brown eyes. "I don't want to be there any longer than I have to be. I'll be the first to admit I know nothing about farms and farming, so I'm going to be depending on you to get me acclimated quickly. The faster we get the farm running smoothly, the sooner I can get out of your hair."

I shot him one of my most winning smiles, but the man wasn't charmed by me at all. He seemed sourer now than he'd been a few minutes before. *I can't believe I'm being sent to a prison farm with this asshole.*

My granddad rambled on for the next twenty minutes. I smiled and pretended I was listening. What was I going to tell Avery? What about the rest of my summer plans? Well, fuck!

"When should we expect Dale to arrive?" Mr. Kudaibergen asked. When I heard my name, I snapped my attention back to the conversion.

"Tomorrow afternoon," Granddad said.

"What?" I blurted out.

"Don't worry, Dale. Molly has already taken care of the arrangements."

I sat there with my jaw practically on the table. My granddad clearly didn't care what I thought about this at all. If Molly had already made the arrangements, then Granddad had decided to do this before talking to me. I felt my anger simmering underneath the surface but did my best to keep it together.

"Well, then," Mr. Kudaibergen said. "We'll see you tomorrow. Need someone to pick you up at the bus station?"

"Bus station?" I asked.

"Unless you're driving yourself, the bus is the only way to get from here to Woodstock."

"Can't I fly?"

Mr. Kudaibergen barked out a laugh. Not like a 'ha' laugh, but a true full belly laugh, which only made me detest the man more.

"What?" I finally said.

"We don't have an airport."

"What's the closest airport then?"

"Newburgh."

"Okay, so I'll fly in there."

"You have no sense of New York State geography, do you?" the man asked again with a goofy grin on his face.

"That will be enough, Mr. Kudaibergen," Granddad said. Immediately, Mr. Kudaibergen looked admonished.

"I'm sorry," Mr. Kudaibergen said. "I shouldn't have laughed."

"Yeah. Sure. Whatever," I replied.

I sat there stewing and didn't bother standing up when Granddad showed Mr. Kudaibergen from the office. I'm sure I seemed like a spoiled, petulant child and I frankly didn't give a rat's ass.

Once Mr. Kudaibergen had closed the door, Granddad came back and sat down in his chair. "I thought I taught you to have better manners than that."

"What? He laughed at me."

"Maybe so, but you weren't exactly on your best behavior, either."

"So, what was so funny?"

My granddad let out an exasperated sigh. "Newburgh, New York, is about seventy miles north of the city, so flying isn't realistic."

"And Woodstock?"

"About another forty-five minutes north of that. Driving from Manhattan to Woodstock is about maybe a two-and-a-half-hour drive. It's probably more like three hours on the bus because of stops."

"And there's no airport?"

"No, Dale. Most small towns don't have airports. And those that have them aren't landing commercial planes."

"Couldn't I borrow the corporate jet, then?"

My granddad scrutinized me once again and sighed. "No. Newburgh is probably the closest airport where the corporate jet could land. The bus is your best bet. You could take Metro North to Poughkeepsie, but you'd still be forty-five minutes from Woodstock."

"And I couldn't Uber from Poughkeepsie to Woodstock?"

"No. Trust me. The bus up to Woodstock is a pleasant ride. You can take your laptop and do work or sleep. Heck, the bus has Wi-Fi these days, so you don't have to disconnect from your life on the trip."

Well, at least that was one thing going for the bus. I was rapidly bouncing my leg up and down on the ball of my left foot. I got like this when I was anxious or trying to keep my temper in check.

"Why are you banishing me like this?" I said, and quickly realized it sounded more like a whine than an actual question.

"I'm not banishing you. I want you to take over the corporation when I die. And to be ready for that moment, I need you to be well versed in how our business works. Think of this as a learning experience. It's no different from going to boarding school."

"It's boarding school in the middle of nowhere, with animals?"

"Actually, we don't have that many animals on the farm. Mostly, it's apple trees."

"Great. I'm going to become Johnny Appleseed," I muttered under my breath.

"Now," my granddad said, "go pack. According to Molly, the bus leaves at nine-fifteen, which will put you in Woodstock a little after noon."

With that, I stood up, put my suit coat back on and left his office. Once I was out, Molly stared at me. "Are you okay, Dale?"

"So, you knew about my exile, too?"

"I tried to talk him out of it, if that's any kind of consolation," Molly told me.

"Actually, it is. At least there's one sane person working in this office."

Molly tilted her head and shot me an unsettled look.

"Sorry," I said. "I shouldn't take my frustration out on you. I'm guessing you have a packet of stuff for me?"

"Yes. Your granddad had me put together an entire file for you to read. Your ticket for tomorrow's bus ride plus the number for the local taxi company is on top in the file. Also, your brand-new Devereux Farms corporate credit card is on top. Keep receipts. I'm sure you're used to keeping track of expenses with your old job, so get the receipts to me by the fifteenth of every month. Your granddad didn't put any limits on your spending, but if you're going to go crazy on a purchase, at least give me a heads-up."

My shoulders drooped as I accepted the small care package from Molly. "Thanks for this," I said genuinely. She put one arm around my shoulder and gave me a quick squeeze.

"You'll be fine."

I responded with a half-grin, but I'm sure my eyes had a lost puppy look in them. The Deveraux offices were filling up with workers, so I was glad to escape before their workday started in earnest. I wasn't in the mood to talk to anyone.

I got outside Bush Tower and realized I hadn't bothered calling for a pick-up from my car company. I thought about making the call right then, but a Starbucks across the street caught my attention, and I decided I needed to go smother my feelings in a Venti Mocha instead. After the morning I'd had, I was going to allow myself whipped cream.

Once I had the cup of mocha goodness, I sat down at a small table and pulled out my phone. I connected to Starbucks Wi-Fi and texted Grayson and Avery to let them know what my granddad had done to me.

The first response was from Avery.

You. On a farm! Ha! Send me pictures, farm boy!

And he was supposed to be my friend. *Little fucker!*
The text from Grayson was more muted.

Whoa. That will be a different change of pace for you. You up to this?

I ignored Avery for now and responded to Grayson.

I don't know. I've never been to hippy-dippy land. I didn't smoke pot as an undergrad. Tried some Molly and Oxy when I was in college. And I tried cocaine when I started on Wall Street because it was everywhere, and some guys swore it helped them stay on their game. Honestly, coke just made me want to clean my house repeatedly.

Bro, you're over sharing.

Sorry. I'm a bit out of sorts.

I put the phone down on the table and opened the packet Molly had given me. Sure enough, there was a bus ticket, information about a rental house they'd gotten me, a corporate credit card and a bunch of financial statements. I figured the paperwork would give me something to pore over in the morning while I was on the bus. I sat back and took another drink of my mocha.

Bzzz. My iPhone received another text message. I glanced down, and it was from Grayson again.

You're probably not going to want to hear this from me, but I think some time away from the city could give you some perspective. Think of this as a retreat. Take some time to figure out what you want the next chapter of your life to be. And don't worry, I'll definitely come visit.

That text made me feel better. And Grayson was right. I needed to stop with the self-pity already and see this as an opportunity to do something different. A time to grow. I wished it didn't have to happen in Woodstock.

Chapter Three

I didn't have any clue what time I needed to get up and get to the Port Authority to go through security before boarding the *bus* to Woodstock. *Do buses have first class? Will I have to share a seat with someone?* I tried to think back on my life, questioning if I'd ever been on a bus. I think I rode one once when I was on a ski vacation weekend at a chalet in Aspen. I prefer skiing in the Swiss Alps — *who doesn't?* — but a group of us chartered a plane when I was in college. Sure, there are ski resorts somewhere in New York, but they're not Aspen.

I got up and planned to be at the Port Authority at least forty-five minutes before the bus departed, to make sure I didn't have any problems. *I hope I don't need two hours like I do at the airport.*

I finished packing my bags and left a note for the cleaning service that they could cut down cleaning the condo to only once a week. I didn't need them coming by more often when I wasn't going to be there.

I completed a last-minute run-through of the things I needed immediately in my bags. Phone charger? Check. Microsoft Surface? Check. Kindle? Check. Jeans? Underwear? T-shirts? Button downs? Shorts? Slacks? Belts? Loafers? Suit? Tie? Cufflinks? All checks. Toiletries? Check. Condoms, just in case? Check. Lube? Check.

"I guess that's everything I need," I said aloud. "Who am I talking to?" I groused.

I grabbed a bottle of water from the fridge. I studied my Dior and Rimowa rolling trunk and my Ghurka Garrison No. 147 walnut-colored leather briefcase. *I sure hope they have bellhops, because the luggage is crazy heavy.* I might have over-packed, but what did one take to Woodstock? I felt like I needed to be prepared for a bit of everything. I slung my briefcase over my shoulder and rolled the trunk behind me as I left the condo, traveled down the elevator and left Twenty Exchange.

"Goodbye, old friend," I muttered as the doorman opened the door for me and I wheeled my bag through.

"Excuse me?" the doorman asked, clearly thinking I'd said something to him.

"Sorry, Bill," I said with a quick smile. "Talking to myself."

The doorman grinned and nodded. I checked the curb and saw my car and Carl waiting for me. As I walked closer, the driver went around to the trunk, opened the door and hefted the bag inside. I could tell he struggled with the luggage. Again, I may have over-packed...a bit.

Once my suitcase was secure, I got into the car, setting my briefcase on the seat next to me.

"I have you heading to the Port Authority this morning. Is that correct, Mr. Deveraux?" Carl asked.

"Yes," I said, trying not to let the dread sound too much in my voice.

"North or south building?"

"There's more than one?" I asked.

"Yep. Where are you headed?

"Woodstock."

"Okay, so that means you're going to be on Trailways, which goes out of the south building. I should have you there in fifteen minutes, depending on traffic." With that, Carl pulled out, and I settled into the back seat.

I pulled out my cell phone and saw texts from both Avery and Grayson. Avery was letting me know he'd miss me and would see me soon. Grayson wished me good luck with my new adventure. I hovered my fingers over the keyboard for a second, thinking about what I wanted to say to each of them, but I was at a loss. Instead, I put my phone back into my pocket, deciding I'd text them once I was on the road.

The ride through town was uneventful. Before long, the car pulled up to a massive square structure. The driver had passed the south building, turned onto Forty-first Street off Eighth Avenue and pulled up to the curb. He hopped out to get my trunk from the back as I got out and slung my bag over my shoulder.

I said thanks and gave Carl a fifty-dollar bill for his help, before asking, "Where do I go now?"

"Go back to Eighth and take a right. You'll see the main entrance. To get to Trailways' help desk, go through the food court toward the restrooms in the back. You'll see it on the left-hand side in the back."

I followed Carl's instructions and soon found myself in the hustle and bustle of the Port Authority. Honestly, it reminded me a bit of Grand Central Station. In retrospect, I think I'd been in the Port Authority before.

I didn't think there were buses running out of the complex. Who knew?

I saw my favorite juice bar in the food court, so I made a mental note to get one before boarding the bus, assuming they had a different food court after security. I quickly found the Trailways people in the back and approached.

"I'm checking in for the bus to Woodstock," I said to the middle-age Black woman sitting behind the plexiglass screen.

"All buses leave from the ground floor," she responded.

"Good to know, but I need to check in."

"And you'll do that when you get to the ground floor," the woman said without looking away from her computer.

"What about my luggage?"

"What about it?"

"Don't I need to check it?"

For the first time, she glanced up from her computer screen, looked at me and busted out laughing. Between her bouts of laughter, she wheezed out, "I'm sorry. I don't get many rich, pretty boys in here who've never taken a bus."

I wasn't sure how I was supposed to take that remark. I stood there, thin-lipped, before asking, "I feel like I'm the butt of a joke, and I don't get it at all."

"I'm sorry, dear." She smiled and shook her head. "Here's how this works. You're going to take your luggage and go down to the ground floor. It's two floors down from this one. Once there, ask for the bus you're looking for. They'll point you in the right direction to the line you'll stand in. Make sure you have your photo ID and ticket in hand. You have a ticket already?" I nodded yes, so she continued. "Your bus driver will take your ticket and ID, then you can load your suitcase under the bus. It's that simple."

"Okay," I said, feeling a bit out of sorts. "How do I get through security?"

"Security?" she asked, which led to another round of laughs. When she finally got herself under control, she continued, "We don't have security in the sense you're talking about. There are no metal detectors or required security screenings. It's like taking the subway in that respect. The Port Authority Police Department patrol the facility looking for suspicious behavior, but we don't have the TSA here."

Isn't that dangerous? I feel like they're asking for trouble. "So, are there people who can help me with my luggage?"

"Oh, honey," she chided. "Welcome to how the other half lives. You handle your own luggage until you get it on the bus." She glanced at my trunk and added, "I would recommend taking the elevator with that thing. It looks like it would be too much to handle on the escalators and stairs down to the ground floor."

I thanked her for her time and patience before heading back to get coffee. Thankfully, the line at Jamba Juice was fast moving, so I had thirty minutes before my bus left. I figured I should head down to the bus lines soon. I spent a few minutes looking for the elevator the Trailways representative had told me about but couldn't find it. I finally asked someone who looked official, and she pointed me in the right direction.

After exiting the elevator, I entered a dark tunnel with roped queues as far as the eye could see. There was a Trailways representative, and he pointed me in the direction of the line for Woodstock. Well, it was a bunch of towns I'd never heard of, and Woodstock was the end of the line. I sighed and stood behind the only other person in line.

I was a bit surprised that there were only two of us in line since the bus left in thirty minutes. I leaned against the wall, then straightened when I realized I did not know when the wall had last been cleaned. As we got closer and closer to the time the bus was supposed to leave, more and more people joined our line. I was a bit surprised by how many people showed up in the last few minutes before the bus driver started taking tickets.

I had my ticket and ID in hand, which the driver took, glanced at and motioned for me to go through. I walked the few steps and found a man standing there in a uniform. "Where you headed?"

"Woodstock," I responded. He nodded, grabbed my bag and slid it under the bus. He wasn't exactly gentle, so I was glad my suitcase had a hard exterior. I turned and walked up the stairs and onto the bus.

I walked down the narrow aisle past the guy who had been standing in front of me in the line. He'd chosen a seat right behind where the driver would sit. I didn't want to be near anyone at the moment, so I headed to the back half of the bus and found a window seat. I put my briefcase down on the seat next to me, hoping it would work as a barrier and prevent people from wanting to sit next to me. Over the next ten minutes, a variety of people entered the bus. By the time the bus driver closed the door and pulled the bus back from its parking space, the bus was only about half full, so I didn't have to share my seat with anyone. He quickly thanked us for joining him on the ride upstate and rattled off a list of towns the bus would go through before ending up in Woodstock.

The bus pulled out into the sunlight then we were zipping through the Lincoln Tunnel and I felt this sense of loss. It's hard to explain it. I hadn't been out of New York City in a few years. I'm a city guy. I don't know what else to say. As the bus pulled out of the Lincoln Tunnel and I realized I was in New Jersey, I leaned my head against the glass and wanted to cry, but I didn't let myself. I told myself to put on my big boy pants. So, I took a nap instead.

* * * *

Talgat

I used the spatula to move the scrambled eggs around the pan, making sure nothing ended up burned. In a different pan, the bacon sizzled. And I kept my eyes on the toaster, waiting for the timer to go off.

"Breakfast's almost ready," I yelled from my perch.

"Smells amazing," my sister Ayala said as she swung around the corner. She came over and gave me a quick peck on the cheek. "Have I told you yet how much I love you?"

"Nope," I replied with a quick wink. "Your brother up yet?"

"I heard movement. Take that for what it's worth."

I gestured to the spatula. "Can you take over?"

"Sure thing," Ayala said as she took the spatula from my hand.

I lifted the apron over my head, went around the corner out of the kitchen and walked upstairs to the house's second-floor landing. I walked down the hall and found Rasul's door shut. The poor door was plastered in stickers from his teen-angst years. Rasul's door was a time capsule of all the phases he'd gone through in his adolescence, if you knew what to look for. Power Rangers and Pokémon stickers had been scraped off, but remnants lingered from the death metal phase he'd gone through. Then there were the more contemporary rock bands he followed.

I raised my hand to knock on the door right as it was flung open. I almost knocked right on his nose as he barreled into me because he was still trying to put a shoe on.

"Dude, watch where you're going."

"Sorry, bro. Didn't see you standing there," he said, standing up to his full six-foot-four-inch height. At five-foot-seven-inches myself, I barely came to his chest. Where my younger brother was tall and lithe, I was shorter and built.

I'm only twenty-seven and Rasul is twenty, with Ayala sitting in between us at twenty-four. Sadly, since my father died last year and our mother a few years before that, I've been the man of the house. Unlike my sister and myself, Rasul didn't have any desire to get his undergraduate degree. At first, my father had been beyond pissed off, but he'd realized that Rasul was a hard worker and didn't shy away from work. So it wasn't that Rasul was lazy, just that he wasn't the book-learning sort.

"Come on," I said, nodding my head toward the stairs. "Ayala is finishing up breakfast right now."

I spun around and the two of us bounded down the stairs, rounded the corner and entered the kitchen to find three plates full of eggs, bacon and toast sitting on the table, waiting to be consumed.

"Morning, sis," Rasul said as he passed her and planted a quick peck on the top of her head. "Smells great."

"I slaved over it all morning," she replied as she shot me a grin.

I went over to the coffee pot and quickly poured us each a mug. All three of us liked our coffee black first thing in the morning. Rasul and I would stay with black coffee, but Ayala would eventually make her way to some kind of frou-frou coffee drink by mid-morning, once we got to the farm.

"What's on everyone's agenda for the day?" I asked once I sat down. We each ran down the list of what we needed to get accomplished that day on the farm. My father had started this tradition of the Kudaibergen family-slash-management meetings when he'd still been with us, so I kept the tradition going. These little powwows helped us to know what the other parts of the farm were doing.

Ayala had her degree in accounting from SUNY Albany and was working on her MBA during the school year, so she ran the office and handled the farm's books.

Rasul oversaw the day-to-day manual labor. Although he was a young guy to be in a management position, the other farmhands respected Rasul because he would never ask them to do something he wasn't willing to do himself.

Then there was me. I'm more of a big picture kind of guy. I'd always had a head for science, so I ended up studying genetics and genomics of apple-tree breeding. Basically, how do we breed tastier apples that can withstand different weather events and still flourish? Ever since researchers at Washington State University unraveled the DNA of an apple in 2010, the field of apple genetics and genomics has made an enormous impact on our overall industry. Before that, there had been a lot of trial and error, and it took a long time to make advances within the field. For example, when the honey crisp apple had been created at the University of Minnesota in 1960, it wasn't patented until 1988 and didn't go into commercial production until 1991. We're talking a thirty-year period from creation to market, which is not an efficient way to run a business in the twenty-first century.

Thankfully, with modern technology, I can work on breeding stronger, healthier apples and other fruit much faster. It's still slow going, but we're making strides all the time. When I wrote my master's thesis for my Masters in Sustainable Food and Farming, I focused on the impact of food deserts on rural communities in the Catskills, and how the local farm can be a bridge to fix this problem. Technically, a food desert is a place where someone lives over one mile from a supermarket, and many people who live in rural communities can live fifteen to thirty miles from one, which can make getting healthy, nutritious food difficult. Teaching people how to garden or having more pop-up farm stands becomes one way to bridge this gap.

"I've got to finish payroll," my sister said, snapping me back into the conversation.

"So, is the new *master* getting here today?" Rasul asked.

I'd told the two of them about the 'citidiot' coming up to run our farm last night at dinner. I may have slightly biased them against Mr. Devereux before he got here.

"I wonder if he'll go screeching back to the city the first time he gets dirt under his nails," Rasul continued, hints of both mirth and disgust coming out.

"Let's try to give him the benefit of the doubt," Ayala, ever the mediator, tried to caution. "Who knows? He could actually make things better. It's not like he could make things worse."

"Knock on wood," I said absently. "But you're right. We need to keep an open mind." I then narrowed my gaze on Rasul. "And please, do not go around using the word 'master' like that so flippantly. You know that word contains a lot of history — especially on farms."

"Sorry, bro," Rasul said, staring down at his breakfast. "I knew as soon as I said it that I should have kept my mouth shut. It was a damn stupid thing for me to say."

I used the last of my toast to wipe down the leftover scrambled eggs and bacon grease before popping it into my mouth. I then stood, walked over to the kitchen sink and rinsed the plate before placing it in the dishwasher.

"Wheels up in fifteen minutes. Anyone not ready to go," I said, looking specifically at Rasul, "can walk to the farm today."

* * * *

Dale

I opened my eyes as the voice over the loudspeaker told me the next stop was Woodstock. I did a quick stretch and arched my back in my chair. I peeked around the bus and noticed there were only a handful of us left.

As the bus slowed down, I stared out of the window to see what the bus station was like. *Where's the bus station?* We pulled up to the curb of the main drag in Woodstock, and the bus just stopped. At first, I thought this was some kind of joke, but the other people around me got up and pulled their belongings down from the tiny overhead bins. I stood up and followed the other people off the bus after slinging my briefcase over my shoulder.

The heat hit me like a punch to the gut when I exited. Thankfully, the air up here didn't seem to have the level of humidity we had in the city, so it wasn't as bad as it could have been. Still, this was not the weather anyone wanted to hang out in.

The bus driver had opened the undercarriage doors, and I watched another guy grab his rolling bag off the bus. I eyed the bus driver to make sure he wouldn't yell at the guy for doing his job, but since the bus driver didn't seem to be in any hurry to help with our luggage, I grabbed my bag off the coach. I hadn't had to lift the blasted thing yet. Damn, it was heavy.

Once we all had our luggage, the bus driver picked up a handful of passengers and was on his way. I looked around for a taxi. There wasn't one. I pulled up my Uber app. I put in my location and told it where I wanted to go and was quickly informed there were no available cars. *What the fuck?* I kind of stood there in a daze. *What the hell do I do now?*

I leaned against my rolling bag and tried Lyft instead. That didn't work, either. The honking of a horn right next to me caused me to jump, which caused the wheels on the bag to roll. Before I knew what had happened, both me and my bag were sprawling across the sidewalk. I lay there dazed for a moment. What I hadn't expected was the face that suddenly filled my view with a look of concern.

"Talgat?" I asked.

"Dude, sorry about that. I called your name twice before I honked."

Suddenly, the pieces were fit together. "That was you? You could have killed me!"

"I seriously doubt it," he said, extending a hand to help me up.

I swatted his hand away, pushed myself onto all fours, then stood. I dusted myself off and found my iPhone a few feet away from me. *Dammit! The screen is cracked!* I picked it up and pocketed it before asking, "What are you doing here?"

"Molly asked me to pick you up. She figured you wouldn't have a ride from the bus station." Without asking, Talgat grabbed my suitcase, easily lifted the thing and placed it into the back of his truck. *That's right, he has a pickup truck. Am I surprised? Obviously not. What country bumpkin wouldn't own a pickup truck?*

"She didn't let me know. I was trying to get an Uber or a Lyft."

"Yeah, those big city services don't always work up here. We have a local cab company, but you need to have their number, because they don't hang out waiting to take people places." I remembered then that Molly had given me the local cab company's number. I guess I'd forgotten that.

He walked around to the driver's side of the truck, and I climbed into the passenger side. And I mean climb, because damn that thing was high off the ground. "Sorry I wasn't here on time," Talgat continued. "Your bus was a few minutes early. That happens sometimes."

"It's okay," I said, as I sat in the truck.

"Buckle up," Talgat said.

"People actually do that up here?"

"Yes," he said, giving me a sideways glance. "It's the law."

"If you say so," I muttered as I fiddled with the seatbelt.

"You're not joking. You really don't wear seatbelts in the city?"

"Why would we? I wait for the cab or car service to pull up, then I slide in and sit. When I get where I'm going, I slide out. No one wears a seatbelt in those things. Hell, if you're in a cab, you do your best not to touch anything you don't have to."

"Interesting," he responded as he looked both ways before pulling into the nonexistent traffic. "Where to? The house you're renting or the farm?"

I thought about it for a second before I told him to take me to the farm. I might as well get the shock of the farm out of my system first. Along the way, Talgat pointed out various landmarks, and I did my best to smile and nod while I was completely ignoring him. *Is it rude? Sure. Do I care? Not really.* I was here to do a job, and that was it.

In a couple of minutes, we were pulling out of Woodstock and onto a country road. Once again, I was shocked by all the hills and trees around us. I couldn't see a damn thing for more than a thousand yards in any direction. I was almost feeling claustrophobic in all that open air.

He pulled off a dirt road and, in the distance, I saw the white farmhouse that was on the cover of the brochure Molly had given me in the stack of materials to review. I'd memorized the map, but I was quickly realizing that the map was nothing like the reality in front of me.

"Um, where's the lake? Where's the picnic table area? Where's the fucking Ferris wheel?"

"The *what*?" Talgat asked. "What weird-ass movie did you watch about farm life that led you to believe there was a Ferris wheel?"

Chapter Four

I opened my briefcase, grabbed the folder Molly had given me the day before and pulled out the brochure for Deveraux Upstate Farms as Talgat parked in front of an old trailer that was probably a set piece from *Deliverance*. As he turned off the engine, I thrust the brochure at Talgat, saying, "This is what this place is supposed to look like."

He accepted the brochure and looked at the cover before flipping it over and staring at the map. And he laughed. I'm not talking a giggle laugh. I'm talking a full-blown, belly laugh where he was trying to catch his breath between hysterics. I furrowed my brow and did my best to stare daggers at him.

"Wow," Talgat finally said after he'd caught his breath. "What fantasy land is this? I can't wait to show my siblings. We're going to need to make photocopies of this and hand it out to all the workers. Everyone will get a kick out of this."

"What's so funny?" I finally asked.

"This map looks nothing like the farm. Well, it kind of has the barn on it, but nothing else on this map is real. Molly gave this to you?"

"It was in the stack of materials she gave me to review."

"Was she pulling your leg?"

"I seriously doubt it," I responded, doing my best to keep my temper in check. I did not appreciate being the butt of Talgat's jokes. He needed to learn to respect me if this situation was going to work for both of us.

"All I can guess is that this brochure was a concept of what this place could be, but it doesn't resemble what's actually here at all. For example," he said, leaning toward me and pointing to a cute blue cottage-looking building that said 'office' on the map, "this building right here is this trailer in front of us."

I peeked down at the map's drawing then up at the dingy, yellowish trailer sitting outside the pickup truck, and my face fell. *What the hell have I gotten myself into?*

He got out of the truck, and I followed suit. I almost tripped when I got out because I'd forgotten how far from the ground it was. "Shouldn't we take my suitcase inside? I have some things in there that won't last too long in this heat."

"Dear God," Talgat said, as he grabbed the sides of his forehead. He looked like he had a migraine coming on. "It's probably cooler out here under that tree than it is in there," he said, pointing to the trailer.

He climbed up the three wooden steps to the door of the trailer and opened it. Inside it was a tiny office space. I say space, but it was one room with two desks. A young woman was hunched over a computer at the desk farthest from the door.

"Did you drop off His Majesty at the castle?" she asked.

Talgat grunted, quickly getting her attention. She glanced over in his direction and her eyes grew three sizes when she regarded me.

"I'm so sorry," she said. "I didn't mean... It's just—"

"What my sister is trying to say," Talgat said, "is that the place where you're staying kind of has a castle feel. The main bedroom is at the top of a turret."

"Well," I responded, trying to be as self-deprecating as I could muster, "I feel like I've been exiled to the Tower of London, so I guess it fits."

The young woman let out a polite laugh. She stood, walked over and extended her hand, introducing herself as Ayala Kudaibergen. I shook her hand and introduced myself as Dale Devereux, since we were being so formal.

"I'm betting you wish you'd gone to your house now, don't ya?" Talgat questioned.

I did a quick glance around the small office. The outside may give every appearance of being a horror movie set, but the Kudaibergens seemed to make the most of what they had.

"Have you guys asked for a newer trailer—or at least an AC unit for in here?" I asked.

"We have," Ayala said. "Every time we ask for anything, it gets shot down."

She didn't need to say was 'by your granddad' because it seemed implied. I wondered if Granddad knew how bad the working conditions were up here. This didn't seem like the Devereux Farms I grew up hearing about at all.

"Well, I'll see what I can do about that," I responded.

Looking to Talgat, I asked, "Where does one buy an air conditioner?"

"Around here? Probably easiest to head down into Kingston and go to Lowe's or something."

"Okay, then do it. You have my permission. If someone balks, tell them I told you to."

"Must be nice," Talgat muttered.

"What?"

"To have the ability to say what you want and get it." Talgat's eyes went wide, and he grimaced. "I'm so sorry. I shouldn't have said that."

"It's okay. That seems to be going around a lot up here," I said with a sigh.

"I wouldn't mind running down into Kingston and getting an AC unit," Talgat said, "but we don't have the money to pay for it. Everything we purchase gets routed through the office in NYC. We have a small petty cash box up here, but that's the cash we use for the cash registers."

I sighed, reached into my bag and pulled out my corporate credit card. "Can we order it online and you pick it up? That way we can charge it." I handed the card to Ayala and said, "Just make sure I get the receipts or Molly will kill me."

"Are you sure?" Ayala asked, clearly hesitant to accept the card from me.

"I'm sure. Besides, I was told by Grandad to use this card to do what was necessary—and I think AC is necessary," I said, pressing the card into her hand. "Go forth and get AC."

"Ayala, why don't you make the purchase? I'll take Mr. Devereux to his house then run into Kingston to pick it up."

"Sounds good," Ayala said as she headed back to her desk. She smiled and nodded at me as Talgat ushered me out of the trailer.

"You didn't need to do that," Talgat said as we got back in his truck. "It's nice and all, but you don't need to shower us with gifts to get us to like you."

"Trust me, this had nothing to do with you. I'm going to be working in that little building, too, and I don't do heat. Think of it as a purely selfish purchase, if it makes you feel better."

A small smile perked up one corner of his mouth.

* * * *

Talgat dropped me off at my rental house. And they were right, it looked like a castle — well, a cross between a log cabin and a castle. Part of the house was a giant log cabin with four bedrooms. Then there was the brick turret part where the main bedroom was located. Actually, that part of the house was three floors. The first floor was a giant wardrobe area, complete with lots of hanging racks, spare bedding and a place to store my shoes. The second floor was a bathroom. The entire floor was a bathroom. It had a freestanding tub and walk-in shower, large enough for a delightful little orgy. I've seen some apartments in the city that were smaller than that bathroom.

There was a spiral staircase that led up to the third floor, which was the main bedroom. The room was round, with a king-sized bed pushed against the only part of the wall that wasn't glass. There was a motorized curtain that opened and closed the curtains almost a full three-hundred-and-sixty-degrees. The views out of my window were breathtaking. As one who doesn't like nature, even I was impressed by the view. I could see a valley below me with its rolling green hills and trees. Admittedly, all I saw in any direction was green and trees. I didn't see another house anywhere near me.

I unpacked my stuff and put my clothing away on the first floor. When I finished with that, I took my bag of toiletries to the second floor and stored them in the bathroom.

I then headed back downstairs and into the main living space, which was marble tiled and very open. And by open, I mean it had a giant fireplace in the middle but there wasn't much in the realm of seating. There was a couch, two recliners and a coffee table, but that was about it. Thankfully, one of the smaller bedrooms in the house had been converted into an office, so I took up residence there. I pulled out my laptop and plugged it in. Molly had written the house's Wi-Fi password on a sticky note, so I got logged in with no problem. I was going to make a phone call, but I realized I had no service out there. Thankfully, I still could text and FaceTime through the Internet. I FaceTimed my granddad.

He picked up. "Hello," he said. All I saw was the ceiling.

"Granddad, it's Dale. Where are you?"

"In the office, why?"

"All I can see is the ceiling."

The camera moved around for a second, and I could see his nose hairs. "A little too close. Pull it back."

"There you are. Did you get upstate?"

"I did," I said. "How long has it been since you were up here?"

"A few years. Well, maybe twenty. Maybe longer, I don't remember. Why?"

"Well, the brochure we have and what the farm actually looks like are two very different things."

"Really?"

"Have you seen the brochure?"

"Of course. I often tell people about the Ferris wheel we have up there at the farm."

"Speaking of the Ferris wheel," I said, "do you realize there isn't one and never has been?"

"Excuse me?"

I spent the next twenty minutes telling Granddad about what I'd seen on the farm that afternoon. I didn't want to hide anything from him. Someone was trying to hide something, and I didn't know who or why.

"When did the Ferris wheel allegedly get installed?" I asked.

"A long time ago. Probably before the Kudaibergens took over. Maybe it fell into disrepair?"

"Maybe. I'll definitely check it out. I'm also going to modernize things up here once I get a better feel for the place."

"Sounds perfect. Let me know if you need anything. Well, tell Molly, and she'll get it done."

"She always does."

I was about to ask my granddad another question when the doorbell rang. "Hey, someone's at the front door. I'll talk to you soon."

"Sounds like a plan. I'm glad I have you up there, Dale. Have fun."

We said our goodbyes, and I ran through the living room to open the door in time to catch the fucking hot UPS driver on my doorstep. I think my jaw dropped and I may have salivated a bit. He was tall, broad, blond and had piercing blue eyes.

"Dale Deveraux?" the driver asked.

"Yes, that's me."

"Okay, great. I wanted to make sure before I left your packages here. I don't think I've delivered here in a long time."

"I'm renting for a while," I said, sending him my best smile. *I have a package I'd like to give you*, I thought as he turned back around, and I saw the ass of steel on the man as he walked back to his truck. I felt myself getting semi-erect looking at the man's assets. *Down, boy!*

He walked back with four boxes in his arms, and I hid my ever-increasing erection behind the door. I opened the door a bit wider and said, "You can set them right there."

I forgot about my growing appendage as I did. I saw him glance down, smile and walk into the house to set down the stack of boxes.

"I'll definitely look forward to dropping off your future packages," the man said as he narrowed his eyes and lightly licked his upper lip suggestively.

"How many more deliveries do you have today?"

"Actually, you were my last." He turned and looked at me. One of his hands was gripping the top of his belt. I could see I wasn't the only one raring for a good time. "So, what can 'brown' do for you?"

I kicked the door shut behind me before asking, took four steps in his direction and pressed my mouth against his as I breathed in his sweaty musk. Normally, I'm not really into blue-collar workers, but who didn't have a delivery guy fantasy? Our mouths danced as we made swift work of each other's clothes. I bit him on his lower lip and pulled on it slightly while I let my hands roam over his body.

He dropped to his knees and started teasing the head of my cock with his tongue. He licked around the head, paying a lot of attention to the urethra. Without warning, he sucked me down all the way to the base of my cock, making a gagging sound as he did. There's nothing quite so hot as hearing a guy gagging on you. It's like the ultimate affirmation of how large and powerful your cock is — not that I didn't already know that my cock was above average, generously above average.

He started pumping my cock with his mouth rhythmically. I let my head fall back as I moaned loudly. When I thought I was going to burst, I reached down, and pulled him off. I lifted him off his knees and brought him back up to his full height so I could attack his mouth with mine again. I licked the outline of his lips. I could still taste my pre-cum on him. I traced the line of his jaw with my tongue before heading for his ear. I started at the top of it and licked around the outside before taking his lobe gently into my mouth, sucking on it. He whimpered in my arms. *Good to know. Ears are a huge turn-on for him.* I whispered, "I want to fuck you so hard right now."

"Fuck me."

"Right answer. I'm on PREP. You?" He nodded his head in agreement. "Perfect. STI free?"

"Yep. Tested two weeks ago."

"Perfect," I said as I reached around and grabbed one of his ass cheeks. "Let me get a condom."

"Breed me?" he asked.

"Not when I've just met you," I responded. I slipped a finger inside of him to let him know I was still interested.

"Condom and lube in my shirt pocket," he said. *Why the hell does he have a condom and lube in his shirt pocket?* He gripped down on my knuckle with his ass. *Impressive.*

With my foot, I reached out, grabbed his shirt and lifted it knee high. With a flick I threw it in the air and grabbed it with my hand that wasn't buried inside him. I'm pretty amazing when my hormones dictate my skills. I had that condom out and on my cock in seconds. The lube took a bit more work. It was one of those single-use quarter-ounce packets you pick up at health departments or bars. I twisted off the top and applied the generous amount to myself and UPS guy's crack.

I led the guy over to the back of the couch and bent him over. I lined up behind him and hit my cock against his hole a few times to let him know I was there. He let out a whimper and started to push back against me. *Oh yeah, that ass is mine.* I shoved and kept shoving until I was buried balls deep in his ass. He moaned. And from the lack of resistance he supplied, I could tell I had a power bottom on my hands. I pulled out until the head was almost out of his ass then I shoved it in again. His back arched in appreciation, which only made me pull out and slam back in faster. I intertwined my fingers and laced them behind my neck as I fucked him…hard.

"I'm going to cum," he said suddenly.

That's all I needed before I let out a guttural sound and felt cum leaving my cock in spasmodic bursts. I apparently had a lot of pent-up sexual frustration, because I kept coming and coming. When I felt the last spasm, I slowly pulled out and rolled off him. I slid to the floor, collapsing in exhaustion.

"Damn," I said. I shook my head to clear the cobwebs. I looked up and found UPS Guy already putting back on his clothes. "Have to leave already?"

"Yep. I must get the truck returned." He shot me a smile as he buttoned up his shirt and tucked it back into his tight shorts. "We should definitely do this again." He bent over, gripped the side of my face and planted one last kiss on my lips.

"I'm Dale, by the way."

"I know. Remember… I delivered your packages."

"That's right," I replied with a half-smile.

"I'm Chad."

And like that, he left. No goodbyes. He was just gone. I moved from a sitting position to lying down on the ground. After a good twenty minutes, I decided to take my new shower for a spin. I needed to wash the cum and the bus ride off me.

Once I was clean, I headed down into the kitchen to see what food Molly had had delivered. When I started going through the refrigerator, I realized that I had assumed Molly had stocked the kitchen. I hadn't asked. She hadn't told me she had. I knew she would take care of things. She always took care of things. *I need to send her a thank you fruit basket.*

I threw a pizza into the oven because I felt the need to indulge. With the pizza heating, I went back to the office and ordered Molly a gift basket. With that taken care of, I started looking at temporary office buildings on a whim. I figured someone out here could build a small office for the farm rapidly. I found several companies that specialized in prefab buildings. I called a couple of them and talked about how quickly they could get one delivered. They were taken aback by my request. Most told me it would be three to four months, which I told them wasn't workable. I finally found an outfit out of Virginia that said they had one in stock, could get it on a truck and up to the farm by the beginning of the next week.

They promised to send out a survey team in the next couple of days and a team of engineers to work on the foundation over the weekend. They emailed me the contracts, and I emailed them back. I spent the rest of the afternoon working on the project. When it was all said and done, it was going to cost me a couple hundred thousand dollars, but I figured it was an investment in myself and the farm, so it was worth it. Besides, I could always write if off on my taxes as a business expense at the end of the year.

I was walking back through the house when I saw the boxes delivered that afternoon still standing where the UPS guy had placed them. *How could I forget the UPS guy?* I grabbed the boxes and set them on the island in the kitchen. I searched for a knife to cut them open and found a utility knife in a drawer. I cut through the tape and pulled out my haul from L.L. Bean. I'd had them overnight me a range of clothes for working on the farm. I stripped in the middle of the kitchen and started trying everything on. I found the one mirror on the first floor of the house and modeled for myself. I thought the clothes made me ready for the wilderness, and of course, I was pretty fucking hot in them. I tried on the pair of hiking slash work boots I'd ordered. They fit me perfectly. I was ready for the next day.

With my wardrobe ready, I headed to bed early. I lay down in bed and closed the curtain. I plugged in my iPhone and set the alarm. And that's when I noticed it. I hadn't noticed it before because I'd been busy doing things. But as I turned off the lights in the bedroom, I noticed that the place was quiet. I'm talking silent. I'm talking eerily silent. Even on the fifty-fifth floor of my building, I could still hear the noise of New York City around me. Here, I didn't hear a damn thing. The absolute silence freaked me out.

After a few minutes of lying in silent darkness, I turned on the light and downloaded a white noise app for my iPhone and played it. To the sound of white noise, I slipped into asleep.

Chapter Five

I opened my eyes as Arcade Fire's *Wake Up* played on my phone. This song and its guitar solo at the beginning always seemed to get me going. It was the right mix of guitar leading into a chorus of voices before the lead singer takes over singing. Of course, this morning, the lyrics seemed to resonate with me the most as I wiped the sleep from my eyes. I could only wish my summer in hell was being turned into dust.

As I still lay in bed and turned off the music, I shot my granddad a text.

Granddad, realized I'm probably going to need a car while I'm up here. Thinking about buying one that I can end up leaving with the farm when I come back to the city.

Granddad texted back almost immediately.

Makes sense to me. Get something big and sturdy. I'm sure Mr. Kudaibergen will have some ideas for you.

I should have realized he'd already be glued to his phone at this early hour. I don't know when he sleeps. I used to joke that I thought he was a vampire because he seems to need no sleep. I can't remember the last time I saw him out in the sun at any other time than the crack of dawn.

I rolled out of bed and did some basic calisthenics. I'd realized yesterday that the house had almost everything I needed, but it didn't have a gym or a treadmill. I would need to rectify that situation soon. But for now, I figured I'd have to survive on pushups and crunches before work. And since I didn't have a car or share-ride services out in the boonies, I would need to walk to work. It was the realization that I had no way to get to work that led me to the early morning text to granddad. I figured he wouldn't have a problem with me buying a vehicle, but I still wanted to run it by him.

With that taken care of, I rolled out and made up the bed. I sleep in boxers, so I didn't have to worry about pajamas. Thankfully, there was a good-sized hamper in the bathroom where I tossed my boxers before going through my morning routine. I made a mental note to check in with Molly about whether the maid service did laundry. I hadn't spotted a washer and dryer yet, but I wasn't exactly hunting for them, either. I knew how to do laundry, to a point. I'd done my own basic laundry when I had been in college and graduate school, but since then I'd always relied on either my house cleaners or a drycleaner to do that for me.

I completed the routine shit, shave and a shower before heading down into the wardrobe. I put on a pair of khaki-colored hiking pants from my L.L. Bean delivery. I checked out my ass in them and was surprised by how they made my glutes look amazing.

The pants also zipped off at the knee, so I figured the versatility could be very helpful if I needed to switch from pants to shorts at some point during the day. I topped off the ensemble with a light blue long-sleeved shirt that was supposed to be for the tropics. If it was good enough for Costa Rica, I figured it would work for a hot day on a farm, too. I then put on my new waterproof hiking boots before checking myself out one last time in the mirror. I was hot, yet outdoorsy. Of course, my actual version of 'outdoorsy' was a day at the beach, skiing or looking at ducks in Central Park. But most importantly, I didn't look like some kind of gay lumberjack, so I had that going for me.

I put my billfold into my back pocket, strapped on my watch, put my phone with the cracked screen in my shirt pocket and was ready to walk to work. I had used Google Maps the night before to map out how to get there. Thankfully, the farm was less than five miles from the house, which is like walking one-hundred blocks in NYC. I ran twice that on an average morning. I had once read that New Yorkers walk more and faster than in any other large city in the world, which was one reason we did our best to bypass tourist areas. Nothing pisses off a New Yorker faster than a tourist gawking at the buildings and standing in the middle of the sidewalk. I always wanted to make a sign that I could whip out in Times Square, 'If you're going to gawk, get to the edge of the sidewalk. Some of us have places to be.'

Knowing the pages of *GQ* would be proud of my appearance, I had a quick protein shake before running back upstairs to brush my teeth and floss. I then put on my Oakley's, grabbed my briefcase and was ready to face the world.

The route Google told me to take was crazy and had all these small streets with twists and turns. One of my L.L. Bean purchases had been a handheld GPS device that was supposedly military grade, so I put where I wanted to go in my handy-dandy GPS device and the map showed me how to get there. The route was direct. I walked up a little hill and felt my leg muscles stirring. *This is gonna be a hard workout after all.* I then entered a forested area. I didn't realize there were forest areas up here. I assumed it was all farms and apple groves. I kept walking. After about twenty minutes, I realized that the little red dot on the GPS device had barely moved. *What the fuck!?* I figured the satellites were having a hard time keeping up, but for only a five-mile trek, I quickly realized I had gotten in way over my head.

I heard a rustling off to the side and saw the cutest thing I'd ever seen. Rubbing its back against a tree was a teeny-tiny little black bear. It reminded me of the stuffed animals I had when I was a child. I wanted to go over, pick it up and give it a quick hug, but I'm not a complete moron. I knew that animals in nature were not tamed.

I heard a snort to my left and saw this giant monstrosity walking toward the baby. Without thinking, I let out the highest-pitched squeal or scream of my entire life. Mama bear swiveled her head in my direction, noticing me for the first time. She lifted her head into the air and sniffed. I kept screaming. I wasn't sure if I was supposed to run, climb a tree, play dead or do a River Dance to scare the thing away. I found myself with my back to a tree, propping myself up to keep myself from fainting.

The mama bear kept looking at me, and I kept screaming. Apparently, she decided the crazy gay man screaming his head off wasn't a threat or food because she grabbed the baby bear and headed off in the other direction.

I slid down the side of the tree when the bear was gone and rested my forehead on my folded arms. *What am I thinking?* I sat there for a moment trying to get my wits back. The forest was still and quiet around me. Apparently, no one had heard me scream. No one was going to come rescue me. I was nowhere near civilization. I wondered how long it would take them to find my corpse if something happened to me out here. *Okay, city boy. Time to get up and get moving. And note to self, getting a vehicle must be on the top of my list.*

Once I was fairly sure nothing in the forest was going to come eat me, I checked my GPS device and found the trail again. In what felt like another thousand years, I came to a clearing, and I saw a bunch of hills laid out in front of me. Away I went.

After I traversed my first hill, I glanced down at my watch and realized I'd already been hiking for ninety minutes. I was barely halfway to my destination, according to the GPS. The mid-morning heat was already bearing down on me. I wished I'd brought a baseball cap or something, but there was nothing I could do about that now.

I climbed up and down hills. They weren't long or tall, but there were so many of them. Another hour passed, and I was making steady progress, but my entire body ached. Running on a treadmill had not prepared me for this type of physical exertion. I was also quickly realizing that walking forty blocks in the city is nothing like hiking through hills in nature. *What was I thinking?*

After another forty-five minutes, my body was on the verge of giving out. I finally saw a building in front of me. I checked my GPS device, and the device told me the white speck in front of me was the farm. I've heard stories of people hiking through deserts and seeing mirages in front of them, so I was glad it wasn't one of those.

Of course, a tiny white speck in front of you is much farther away than one would guess. I was a hot, sweaty mess. My mouth was so dry. It felt like a scorching desert in my mouth. I could feel the dried-out ridges on the top part of my mouth. My tongue was so dry that it was hard to move. My lips were sticking to my teeth. For the first time since my run-in with the bear, I was worried that I'd done something deadly idiotic.

I kept pushing on. I knew that if I collapsed out here, no one would find me. Sure, they could search for my cell phone. But it's not like I had service out here, so finding my cell was probably not going to happen. I took a deep breath, said a quick prayer to any deity who would listen and help. I pushed forward.

About twenty minutes later, I came over the last hill and saw the farmhouse and the small trailer in front of me. I was almost there. I kept pushing. My legs were jelly. I could barely feel them as I kept putting them one leg in front of the other.

As I drew close to the trailer, I saw Talgat's truck sitting in front. I was about a hundred yards from the trailer when the front door opened, and Ayala stepped outside. She glanced my way and yelled. Realizing I was going to be okay, I let gravity take hold as I collapsed to the ground and slipped into black.

* * * *

Talgat

I was off in the barn looking at an experiment. I'd been working on grafting two different fruits together. There's a farm up in Washington State that created an apple that tastes like a grape. They call it a Grāpple. I wanted to see if we could create something similar at the farm to put the place on the map. I'd tried combining apples with cherries, bananas, peaches and many other ideas. Some came close to a fun and interesting taste, but some ended up tasting like dirt.

I was about to taste the flavor of one of my latest creations when I heard Ayala scream. I tore out of the barn and ran into Rasul, who was also running toward a screaming Ayala. I found her kneeling in front of a crumpled form on the ground.

"Dear God, what happened?" I asked as I realized it was Dale Devereux on the ground.

"I was leaving the office to come find you, and he came down the road and collapsed," Ayala said, clearly trying not to freak out herself.

I motioned for Rasul to help me pick up the limp form and carry him into the trailer. The cool breeze of the newly installed air conditioning unit greeted us as we laid Dale's body on the small couch we had in the back. I grabbed a bottle of water from our mini-fridge and pressed it against his forehead.

"What do we do?" Ayala asked, hovering behind me.

"Give me a second to think," I said, a bit more sharply than I intended. "Sorry... I didn't mean to snap at you." I turned and gave her a reassuring smile.

I heard a grumbling sound from Dale, so I swung my attention back to him. His head was moving side to side, clearly trying to wake up. Finally, after what seemed like forever, his eyes fluttered open.

"Where am I?" he questioned as his eyes opened but clearly weren't focused on anything.

"You're safe," I said. I put my hand on his forehead and could tell that his temperature was already dropping. "When you're ready to sit up, we need to get some water into you. Ayala, call nine-one-one. I'm afraid he's seriously dehydrated."

"No paramedics," Dale grumbled. "I'll be fine. Give me a second."

"You are most definitely *not* fine," Rasul said from behind me. "Dude, what were you thinking?"

I swiveled my head in Rasul's direction and shot him a death stare. He took a step back and said nothing else.

Dale stirred a bit more, then he hoisted himself into a sitting position. I thought he was about to pass out again from the woozy look that flashed across his face. I watched as he blinked a few times and shook his head, as if trying to shake out the cobwebs.

"Here," I said. "Drink this. You need to get water into you." I opened the bottle of water and handed it to Dale, who immediately started gulping the water down. "Slow down there, cowboy. Sip the water. Don't gulp. If you try to drink too fast, you're likely to throw it all back up."

I watched as he took my advice, which made things easier because I didn't have to fight with him. I was so not in the mood to clean up his vomit.

"I think we're okay here," I said to Rasul. "You can go back to doing what you were doing. If I need you, I'll yell."

Rasul narrowed his eyes at me, but he didn't fight me on it. Instead, he turned around and left the trailer.

Dale took the cold bottle of water and placed it to his head. He was getting some color back into him. Admittedly, some of that color was probably going to be a sunburn from the looks of things.

"What happened?" Ayala finally asked, as Dale seemed to get more stable.

"I checked my GPS and it said this place was only like five miles from the house, so I figured I could walk here. I run twice that every day. I didn't realize how different running on a treadmill and hiking up and down hills was going to be."

I let out an exasperated sigh. "This is the country, not the city. Things are different here. You've got to be more careful."

"Yeah, I realized that when I had a run-in with a bear."

"When you *what*?" I asked, as Ayala gasped behind me.

I sat transfixed as Dale regaled us with the tale of his entire morning hike. The longer I listened, the more I was glad he'd survived, despite his absolute stupidity.

"I think you should go back to your house and take it easy. You need to rest and rehydrate. Also, you're going to have a nasty burn. Do you have any aloe at your home?"

"Aloe?"

"You know, the stuff you put on your sunburn to keep it from getting too bad and blistering?"

Dale shrugged.

"I'm going to take you home. We'll swing by Hannaford's and pick up a few things you're probably going to need. If you don't take care of yourself today, you're going to be in much worse shape tomorrow."

Dale regarded me with a sheepish smile. I took a long, slow breath in and out of my nose. "And tomorrow, I'll come by to pick you up."

"Can we go buy me a car tomorrow?" Dale asked. "Granddad told me to get to get a vehicle. He had recommended asking you what I should buy."

I shook my head. "Do you have a driver's license?"

"Believe it or not," Dale answered, "I do. I don't need it very often, but I keep it current. I've rented a Zip car here and there with friends."

What am I going to do with you? I helped Dale stand. His legs were wobbly, so I threw myself under one of his shoulders to help him walk.

"Thanks," Dale said.

"Don't mention it," I responded.

* * * *

Dale

Talgat pulled into the parking lot of a large grocery store. I hadn't seen one of these since I was up in Boston. In Manhattan, we have grocery stores, but they're not giant boxes with large parking lots. You won't find many parking lots in New York City to begin with. A friend of mine has a condo and owns a BMW. He pays more for his parking space than he does on the condo and car payment combined. I'd thought about buying a car a few times, but honestly, paying for my car service each month was cheaper. Sure, I may own nothing, but I also didn't have any of the upkeep responsibility, either.

After Talgat threw the truck into park, we both got out. He peeked over at me as I rounded the back of the vehicle. "Are you sure you should be up and walking?"

I gave him a half-smile. "I'm almost afraid that if I don't move right now, my muscles are going to rebel, and I won't be able to move for a month."

"Epsom salts."

"Excuse me?"

"I'm mentally adding Epsom salt to the list of things to get you while we're here. You should take an Epsom salt bath. It will help your muscles and your feet. I'm almost scared to find out how bad your feet are going to be."

"Why do you say that?" I asked.

"You hiked up and down mountains in brand-new boots before they were broken in. Your feet will not like you tomorrow. In fact, you may need to stay off them for a couple of days."

"You need to break in shoes?" I asked, before realizing how absolutely stupid that sounded. "Of course, you have to break in shoes. What a fucking moron I've been. You'd think I'd never been out of the city. I promise, I have. I went to camp as a kid up in Vermont and everything."

"Come on," Talgat replied, and we headed into the grocery store.

Talgat grabbed a cart and steered it straight ahead where the pharmacy section of the grocery store stood. We walked up and down the aisles. He'd recommend I put something in my cart, and I would do it. I was putty in his hands. Thankfully, he let me push the cart, which gave me something to lean on. As we pushed by the pharmacy, Talgat motioned for me to stop as he walked over to the pharmacist.

"Hey, Phil," Talgat said.

A guy in his mid-to-late thirties peered up from what he was doing and gave a slight scowl at Talgat. *I wonder what that is about?* I did my best to pretend not to listen.

"What do you want?" the Phil guy asked. I glanced at Phil's nametag and saw his full name was 'Philip Tucker, PharmD'. Phil caught me staring at him, and his mouth twitched as his forehead puckered. Phil then lowered his voice. "New boyfriend? I thought you didn't want to date anyone," he said to Talgat.

"Not that it's any of your business," Talgat said matter-of-factly, "but that's my boss, Dale Deveraux—as in Devereux Farms, Devereux."

"Whatever," Phil responded. "What do you want?"

Talgat clenched and unclenched his fists. Whatever the history between him and Phil was, it clearly wasn't very pretty at all. *And 'boyfriend'? How did I not know Talgat was gay? What's wrong with my gaydar?*

"As I was saying, Mr. Devereux went on a little adventure this morning. He's burned to a crisp, probably has blisters on his feet, his muscles are going to be hurting and he passed out because of dehydration."

"Damn," Phil said. "Why isn't he in the ER?"

"Because I'm stubborn," I said, breaking into the conversation. I was tired of being talked about as if I weren't even there. I stood up from the cart, settled my weight over my legs, walked over to the man and stuck out my hand. "Dale Devereux." He shook my hand, and I immediately noticed him eyeing my watch. If this were the city, I would have said "Yes, it's real," but I didn't think that was probably the right thing to say up here.

"What did you do?" Phil asked, after letting go of my hand.

"I thought I could take a simple five-mile hike to the farm."

"He's staying out at the castle," Talgat said. *Clearly, everyone knows what 'the castle' is around this town.* "Dale hiked to the farm this morning."

"You hiked *that*?" Phil asked incredulously.

"It seemed easy enough on GPS," I said flatly. "But anyway, as Mr. Kudaibergen noted, I'm a royal fucking mess right now. So, what suggestions do you have?" I tried to keep the impatience out of my voice, but my legs were turning to jelly again, and I needed to get home.

Phil didn't seem to notice the tone in my voice, thankfully. He rattled off a list of things we should probably purchase. He asked me if I had anything at the house, to which I responded, "Let's assume I don't."

Before I knew it, we had a cart full of items and instructions from Phil to go to the hospital or at least an urgent care if things were worse tomorrow. I smiled and nodded.

"Oh...and Gatorade," Phil said before going back to his work. "I'm betting he needs the electrolytes, so the Gatorade will help. Avoid eating anything with salt or caffeine for the rest of the day. You need to let yourself rehydrate, slowly."

I gave him a little salute and thanked him for his time. With supplies in hand, Talgat and I walked to the front of the grocery store and stood in line. After my supplies were on the conveyor belt, he put down one of the little plastic barriers and placed down a Coke and a Snickers bar.

He saw me eye them. "I want a snack."

"Get rid of that plastic thing," I said, as I put the divider behind his purchases for the next customer in line. "The least I can do is buy that for you. After what you've put up with for the past two days, you deserve a lot more than that."

"Thanks," he said.

"No. Thank *you*," I responded. "Honestly, if it weren't for you and your family, I'm not sure what would have happened to me today."

The clerk was already ringing up the items, and a bag person at the end of the checkout line placed our purchases into a paper bag. With the purchase made, we left the grocery store and headed back to 'the castle'.

Talgat was ever the gentleman and helped me get my bags into the house. I could tell from his eyes that he was taking the place in.

"Want a tour?" I asked.

He hesitated for a moment before saying, "I should head back to the farm and make sure everything is going smoothly there."

"Come on. It'll take ten minutes. As your *boss*, I give you permission to take a tour."

"Oh," Talgat said, looking insecure for the first time since I'd met him. "You heard that when I was talking to Phil?"

"Yeah. He wasn't exactly subtle."

Talgat barked out a quick laugh. "Phil doesn't do subtle."

"He's your ex?" I asked.

"He wants to be my ex," Talgat said.

I leaned against the large marble island in the middle of the kitchen before saying, "Do tell. Gotta love gay drama," I said with as much sarcasm as I could muster.

Talgat opened the fridge and grabbed me a Gatorade, twisted the top off and handed it to me. He then closed the door and leaned against the fridge.

"Nothing to tell. I am not interested in him. Honestly, I'm not interested in anyone. I have too much on my plate for a relationship. This last year has been rough. Between losing my father, seeing after my siblings and taking care of the farm, I don't have time for a social life."

"Well, hopefully, now that I'm here, maybe we can release some of the burden off your shoulders. I admit I know jack shit about farming, but I do know a thing or two about business. Let's figure out a way to divide and conquer...just not today." I pushed myself off the island with my Gatorade in hand and said, "Come on. Let me show you around."

I spent the next fifteen minutes giving Talgat a quick tour of the house. I thought I was going to pass out when I tried to walk up the stairs. Talgat was especially impressed by the three floors in the turret. I had to admit it was interesting and had creative architecture. After the tour, he said his goodbyes, and I promised to take a couple of Epsom salt baths, smear my body with aloe and do a whole bunch of nothing for the rest of the day.

Once Talgat was gone, I grabbed the Epsom salt and headed upstairs. I took off my clothes and put them in the hamper while the bathtub was filling with warm water. Once it was filled to my liking, I put in the Epsom salt before lowering my body into the tub.

I lay there and let my body soak. It was only early afternoon, but it could have been three a.m., because I was beyond exhausted. Off in the distance, I heard my cell phone ring. Normally, I would have jumped out of the tub to get it. Today, I didn't give a fuck. *Let it go to voice mail.*

Chapter Six

Talgat

The next morning, I pulled up to Dale's house after I dropped Ayala and Rasul at the farm. I honked the horn, and he opened the door and came outside. He didn't look as bad as I'd feared he would. After yesterday, I was worried he would look like death warmed over. He was bright pink, but his burn could have been a lot worse.

"How are you feeling today?" I asked, as he opened the door to the truck.

"My body still feels like it ran the New York Marathon a couple of times, but it's better than it would have been if I hadn't followed your instructions last night, doctor."

I grinned and rolled my eyes. "So, what now? The farm?"

"Actually, let's get me a car, truck, van, bus or something that runs so I don't have to depend on you for a ride or go hiking through the wilderness to work."

"What are you looking for?" I asked.

"I was thinking a truck or an SUV. I figure that when I'm no longer up here, the car or truck will end up staying here on the farm, so which of those would be the most useful for you in the long run?"

I thought about it for a few moments as I put the truck in gear and headed toward Kingston, which would be the nearest place to buy a new vehicle. "I would go with a Nissan SUV... Maybe a Pathfinder. Sound okay to you?"

"Sure," Dale said, like he was along for the ride.

The drive down the mountain into Kingston was uneventful. He asked me questions about the farm and my family. He didn't appear any worse off than he had the previous evening, which was good. I'd been worried about dropping him off at home. I'd almost gone to check in on him last night. Ayala had reminded me that he wasn't our friend, he was our boss.

As we pulled into the dealership, I asked, "Do you want me to come in and help you?"

"I'm buying a car. If there's one thing I'm *actually* good at, it's buying things," he joked.

"I'll see you at the farm then," I replied. I watched as he headed into the dealership office. I started pulling out when I caught sight of my friend Carly Chisholm, so I rolled down the window.

"Please tell me you're finally trading in this garbage heap?" Carly asked.

"You wish. My baby is still running fine, thanks to you."

Carly and I had gone to school together and had been best friends. Most had assumed the two of us were dating. No one had seemed to catch on that we were both gay. Having each other when we were both in the closet had made life easier, because the other could run interference if someone got too nosey.

"Nah. My friend Dale needed a new vehicle, so I drove him down here."

"Dale?"

"I say 'friend', but he's kind of my new boss out at the farm. He's Jameson Devereux's grandson." Carly had heard me talk about Devereux senior several times, so I didn't have to explain.

"That was kind of you," Carly said.

"Yeah, I kind of feel bad for the guy. He's a total fish out of water up here." I spent a couple minutes running down what had happened to Dale the previous day. Carly laughed out loud when I got to the part when he met Phil.

"Oh, I wish I could have seen Phil's face."

"It was admittedly kind of funny." I saw Dale out with a salesperson walking through the aisles. "That's him…over there," I said as I pointed in Dale's direction.

"He's hot!" Carly said. "I'd tap that ass."

"With what?" I said, as I rolled my eyes. "Besides, wouldn't your girlfriend get jealous?"

"Which one?" Carly said with a sly smirk. "Where's he staying?"

"Out at the castle."

"Oh-h…he's the new gay guy in the castle," Carly said. Something about how she drew out the word 'Oh' let me know she wasn't telling me anything.

"Spill it," I said.

"What?" she asked, feigning innocence.

"I know you're hiding something, so out with it."

"Okay," she said doing a quick about face. "I saw Chad Powell hanging out at Hole in the Wall, and he mentioned he fucked around with some hottie who had moved up here from the city. That guy has more notches in his belt." I thought that was all she was going to say before she added, "Aren't you one of them?"

I may have growled in that moment, but only lightly. "Yes, I admit it. I slept with Chad Powell…me and most of the other guys in the county."

"Yeah, it's like who needs 'six degrees of Kevin Bacon' — except you gay guys play 'two degrees of Chad'."

"He's hot," was all I said in my defense.

Carly rolled her eyes. "You gays are so predictable." She leaned in a little closer before adding, "I heard he gave Phil crabs last year."

"Crabs?"

"Yep."

"I didn't know pubic lice were still a thing."

"Probably picked them up from a bathhouse up in Albany or down in the city. As I said, Chad gets around — a lot."

I furrowed my brow and wondered if I should say something to Dale. I mean, it's not like his sex life is my business, but I also don't want him to get an extra special delivery from the UPS guy.

"Anyway, I best get back to the garage," Carly said, breaking me out of my thoughts. "There's a carburetor with my name on it that needs to be rebuilt."

"Have fun," I said as I put the truck back into drive and headed out of the parking lot.

I stopped at a convenience store and got myself a huge iced coffee and a Snickers bar before driving back to Woodstock. The drive was completely uneventful. I was on autopilot the whole way. Before I realized it, I was pulling into my spot in front of the trailer.

There was a group of men with surveyor equipment milling around the property. I was about to head over and ask them what was going on, but figured I'd get a faster answer from Ayala, so I entered the trailer.

"What's going on out there?" I asked before I'd even seen if Ayala was in the trailer. I was surprised to find Rasul hanging inside.

"Hey, bro," he said, giving me a slight head jerk.

"How is Dale?" Ayala asked. "His granddad called, and he's worried. Mr. Devereaux called Dale yesterday evening, and he still hasn't returned the phone call. Mr. Devereux was not thrilled when I told him what happened yesterday."

"Ah, for fuck's sake," I let out without meaning to.

"Don't worry. He doesn't blame us, though it sounded like he's questioning his decision to send Dale here. Maybe this will work out for all of us," she said with a grin. "As for what's going on out there, from what they told Rasul and me, Dale ordered a new office building online."

"You can order an office building *online*?" I questioned.

"Apparently," Rasul said. "Must be nice to have that kind of spending power."

"Hey," I said. "We have everything we need. We may not have everything we want, but all our needs are met. Our parents made sure of that."

"I meant nothing by it, bro," Rasul said. "But come on. Can you imagine what it must be like to order an office building online because you can?"

"No, I can't," I admitted. "But can you imagine being so thick-headed that you practically kill yourself hiking up and down hills? He's not better than us. He's…different."

"If you say so," Ayala said as she glanced sideways at Rasul.

I let out a short huff before asking, "What can you tell me about this new office building?"

Ayala jumped up from her computer and brought me over a stack of computer printouts. I flipped through the blueprints. I had to admit, the building was nice. It was an all-glass structure that was solar friendly, so it would fit right in here at the farm. The building was modern but not tacky.

"How long is it going to take to build?" I asked.

"Well, they're doing the survey today. They're going to file paperwork with the city tomorrow. They plan on completing the foundation over the weekend. And the building will be delivered next week. The foreman said everything should be up and running sometime mid-to-late next week."

My jaw dropped and I must have given every indication of having seen Bigfoot, Godzilla and King Kong from Ayala's amused expression.

"Yep, Dale doesn't mess around. When he decides to do something, he does it. And from these blueprints, he likes to go big."

"I'm beginning to see that," I admitted.

* * * *

Dale

By the middle of the next week, the new office building I'd ordered online had showed up and been installed. Frankly, I had been darn impressed with how quickly they'd laid the foundation and got the prefab building up and running when it arrived. I had that eyesore of an old trailer carted away once we'd moved everything into the new building. As part of the grand opening, I had worked with Ayala and Talgat to get new office furniture and computers to make sure everything was professional.

We had a christening party for the building, and all the farm hands were invited to a little soiree. I invited Granddad, but he couldn't come because of a pre-existing conflict. Thankfully, Granddad hadn't freaked out when he'd heard what I'd done. As a whole, he was hands-off so far, which allowed me to get my feet wet.

Over the next few weeks, I had done my best to learn the ins and outs of the farm business. In fact, I had spent at least one day shadowing everyone who worked on the farm. I had wanted to see how everything worked. If I was going to figure out how to make this farm profitable, I needed to see what was happening firsthand.

"Hey, Rasul," I said one afternoon, "I wanted to shadow one of your workers. Any suggestions?"

Rasul squinted his eyes against the sun as he scrunched his forehead. "Why don't you shadow Jordan? Have you met Jordan yet?"

"Not formally. I've seen him in passing but have never been introduced."

"Well, there's no time like the present."

Rasul walked me through one of the apple orchards, where we found Jordan spraying a tree. Jordan was a younger guy in his early twenties. He was currently enrolled at Ulster County Community College, from what I'd learned through the grapevine.

"Jordan," Rasul said, "Mr. Devereux is going to shadow you this afternoon."

Jordan put down the canister of spray and removed his face mask as he extended his hand. "Nice to finally meet you, sir."

"Please, call me Dale."

"Well, if you're going to shadow me, we need to get you some safety equipment first," Jordan said.

"Sure. I'll go back with Rasul, get suited up, then I'll come back. You going to be in this area for a while?"

"Should be. If I'm not, just yell," Jordan said. "Out here...there's not too much happening, so you should be able to find me quickly."

Rasul led me back to the barn and equipped me with standard safety equipment and my own spray bottle to help Jordan.

"What's this spray?" I asked Rasul.

"It's an organic formula Talgat created to prevent bugs from eating our trees. Since we started using it a couple of years ago, it has cut down on fruit loss because of bugs."

"Are we using it on any of the other farms in the system?"

"I seriously doubt it. I know we've talked to some of the other farm managers, but most are still happy using the chemicals that exist on the market."

"Well, that's definitely something to keep in the back of my mind," I said. I wondered why some of the other farm managers were resistant to using Talgat's formula. I planned to investigate that when I got a chance.

I said my goodbyes to Rasul and set out to work with Jordan in the orchard. I spent the rest of the afternoon spraying trees. I won't lie, spraying trees is one of the most tedious jobs I've ever done. I know it's important work, but it's mind-numbing. Thankfully, I got to know Jordan, which was kind of cool.

After the afternoon, I put the equipment up and headed back to the office building. I entered and was glad to feel the rush of cool air after having been in the sun all day.

"Hey there," Talgat said as I walked in.

"What's up?"

"So, Rasul told me you shadowed Jordan today. How'd that go?"

"I think it went well. I learned a lot from Jordan about the day-to-day work that goes on around here. And Rasul told me about the spray that you're using on the trees."

"He did, did he?" There was something in Talgat's voice that gave me pause.

"Should he not have done that?" I asked.

Talgat sighed and motioned to the lobby couches. I sat down on one and Talgat sat on the other.

"Did he also tell you I tried to get the company to use it broadly, but no one would pay attention to me?"

"He did," I admitted. "What happened?"

"We had an annual farm manager's meeting, and I discussed the formula and the increase in crop yield. But the older farm managers smiled and nodded, then ignored me completely. I'll admit, it was slightly frustrating. I wasn't surprised, but it was exasperating."

"I'm sorry to hear that." I was a bit befuddled, because I didn't know why the results hadn't spoken for themselves. *Note to self, follow up on this.*

"Anyway...I'm glad you got to shadow Jordan. He's a great guy. I took him under my wing when he was in high school. He didn't have the best home life. I'd gone to school with his older sister. She was concerned that he was becoming increasingly isolated, so she hooked the two of us up as her own personal 'big brother' project."

"Well, he seems like a perfectly pleasant young man now. Dear God, I called him a young man. I'm not that much older than him." Talgat's lips curled upward as I spoke. "So, when do you think we'll open up for apple picking?" I asked, shifting topics suddenly.

Talgat caught up with my topic shift. "Well, it definitely looks like we'll be up and running by mid-August."

"Can we go ahead and set a date for our grand opening?"

"I would recommend against it right now."

"Why?" I asked.

"It's still a bit too early to know how large the yield is going to be. Sure, everything looks great today, but what happens if in two weeks we have a giant hailstorm that decimates the orchard? We don't want to get ahead of ourselves."

I thought about it for a moment and could clearly see Talgat's logic in waiting. But something nagged at the back of my brain. "Is there ever a good time, though? I mean, with weather, we could always be in a bad spot at any moment." Although it wasn't exactly a question, the way my voice rose at the end implied that it was.

"I guess I learned to be conservative with this stuff from my father. And you're right, weather happens. Severe weather at any time of the year can be detrimental to our crops. But bad weather earlier in the season could do more damage. For example, if we had a freak freeze in late April or early May, the entire East

Coast could have lost billions in profits. People don't realize how important climate stability is to farming."

I put the base of my palm to my forehead. I wasn't sure what I wanted to say, but I ended up going with, "Worrying about how weather could make or break the company is something I only thought about in terms of stock prices. I never thought about how it impacted the real lives of people on farms. When I first started at the Stock Exchange, I spent a lot of time trading farm futures. To me, it was dollar signs and a game."

"To those of us who live out here in rural America, it's most definitely *not* a game. It's our lives. One drought, ice storm or hurricane can cause a family farm to go bankrupt. Thankfully, we belong to Devereux Farms. If something happened to us, the other farms can pick up the slack. If something happens to one of the other farms, we can pick up the slack. All our resources are pooled together. Your average family farmer doesn't have that luxury."

I thought about it for a minute. Part of me wanted to debate the importance of the stock market for the farming industry, but I also saw how the market could be a nasty beast to tame — especially for the little farmer who was so dependent on stockbroker valuations of their products each year.

Chapter Seven

By the time early August rolled around, I was getting comfortable working on the farm. And when I wasn't working on the farm, Chad, the UPS Guy, dropped by periodically to make *special* deliveries. All-in-all, things were looking up.

I'd also been working with Ayala on the books, and I wasn't sure what the problem was. For the past few years, the farm's books were perfectly fine. Ayala was meticulous beyond belief, so thank God for that.

"Dude, what are you doing?" Talgat asked, leaning against the door frame of my office.

"Writing in my journal."

"You have a diary?"

"It's not a diary," I said, narrowing my eyes at him. "It's a journal. I've been writing about all my experiences here at the farm. Who knows? Maybe one day I'll write a book."

"You could title it, *City Mouse, Country Mouse*? Or maybe *The Socialite and Nature.* Or better yet, *From Finance to Farming – How I Changed My Career.*"

I shot Talgat a look and rolled my eyes before saying, "Anyway…what can I do for you?"

"I'm heading to the back part of the farm to fix some fencing. There's no one else around, so I thought I'd see if you'd be interested in going out to work with me."

I thought about it for a second. I had some work that I needed to get done, but this sounded like a new adventure, so I nodded yes.

"Let me throw on my work clothes."

"I'll be downstairs." Talgat closed the doors to my room as he exited.

Since I'd been working on various parts of the farm, I had started keeping a set of clothes in my office that I could get dirty and roughed up. I walked over to the closed door and shut the blinds on the glass window. I stripped out of my dress slacks and button-down shirt. I'd dumped the ties and jackets, but I still felt the need to dress somewhat professionally in the office.

I put on a pair of jeans, a light T-shirt, some sunscreen and a baseball cap. I hung up my dress clothes and put them on a hanger behind my door. I then sat down and tied up my work boots, which were worn in finally after that horrible incident the first time I'd worn them. I picked up my sunglasses and the bottle of sunscreen, just in case. The last thing I needed to do was blister again this summer. I'd learned my lesson the hard way.

I put my wallet and keys in my desktop drawer and powered down my computer. *I doubt I'll do any more work after this.* With everything squared away in my office, I left it and bounded down the stairs to find Talgat lounging on one of the couches, waiting for me. He had two bottles of water sitting in front of him. As he stood, he tossed one of them to me. I tried to catch it, but I must have appeared like a Tyrannosaurus Rex trying to play volleyball. The bottle eventually hit the ground, and Talgat threw his head back, laughing.

"You should have seen yourself. I wish I had recorded that. It was gold!"

"I'm sorry. I'm not used to things flying at my face."

"Well, there goes your social life."

I paused for a second, "Did you just make a *Clueless* reference?"

"I may work on a farm, but I'm still gay. What? You think only city dwellers watch movies?" he chastised me.

"That's not what I meant," I said, realizing that I had thrown on my pouty face. "It's just, I don't think I've ever heard you using any kind of pop culture reference since we met—let alone a classic gay one."

"Well, maybe you should hang out with me more often," Talgat said, as he walked toward the front door. "I'm full of surprises."

Of that, I am definitely sure.

I followed him outside and walked over to his truck. I glanced in the truck bed and noticed some wooden poles, shovels and other building supplies. *What did I agree to?* I consider myself a fairly handy person. I know how to hang a picture. I can even accurately locate a stud in a wall, like seventy-five percent of the time. I've learned to make sure the paintings I've hung hide the extra holes I've created.

Oh, who the hell am I kidding, I'm not handy at all.

I climbed into the truck and leaned back into the seat as I fastened my seatbelt. Talgat got in and buckled up before putting the truck in reverse, then pulled out onto one of the farm roads. He drove for about six minutes, and I think we hit every bump possible. The truck was vibrating so much that I felt like I was in one of those vibrating chairs you see on TV.

Before long, Talgat pulled up to a stretch of fence that had clearly seen better days. The posting was old and weathered, which made it seem like it would fall down any second. On top of that, the wires that ran between the wooden poles were drooping, and anyone or anything could walk right over them.

* * * *

Talgat threw the truck into park, opened his door and headed to the back of the truck without saying a word. I scrambled out, following him. I was getting used to climbing in and out of his truck, so I didn't look like a tall teenage boy going through puberty trying to get his gangly arms and legs to cooperate. I felt the ground firm and solid beneath my feet when I landed and headed to the back of the truck myself.

"Okay. How can I help?"

"Grab a shovel," Talgat said, pointing to one in the back of his truck. "We need to dig out these four poles. Then we're going to put new ones into the ground and rewire everything. Let me cut the wires first."

"Out of curiosity," I said, grabbing a shovel, "if this fence is so far back here, what's its purpose?"

"Basically, the fence is a small deterrent for larger animals—your deer and bears primarily. Don't get me wrong, they could still get over or come crashing through, but it tends to deter them from coming onto the farm and munching on the apples."

I nodded. Talgat walked over to one pole, which was still in excellent shape, and cut the connecting wires. He tied them off, then made speedy work on the wires.

When they were taken care of, he motioned for me to get digging. I put on a pair of leather gloves, angled the round part of the shovel to the ground and stepped on the top, pushing my weight down until the shovel broke through the dirt around the pole. My first attempt was pitiful. I barely got any dirt to come up at all.

"Dude, I wouldn't do that if I were you," Talgat said from where he was digging.

"Do what?"

"Bend your back like that. You will not be able to stand up tomorrow if you keep that up." He leaned his shovel against the post he was digging around and came over to me before saying, "Let me show you proper technique. First, don't bend at the back." He leaned over like an old man and showed me what he was talking about.

"I wasn't that far over," I shot back.

"You were closer than you might think. As tall as you are, you bend over quite a bit."

"What should I do then?" I said, handing Talgat my shovel.

"Bend from the knees. Like you're picking up something." Talgat bent his knees and bounced a little to add emphasis. "And since we have a lot to shovel here, put your arms like this." He rested his arms on his thighs. "Use your thighs as a fulcrum to help you lift. Then scoop up the dirt using your fulcrum and your thighs to lift the dirt." He demonstrated his dirt-digging technique. He then handed me the shovel back. "Your turn."

I followed the motion for a second and tried to dig into the ground. His way was easier, but I still wasn't making much headway on the dirt. I felt Talgat come behind me, invading my personal space.

"Also, when you're breaking into the ground, don't do it with your arms. Do it with your hips to add more momentum behind your shovel."

He put his arms around me as he showed me how to use my hips to make the shovel slice into the ground. I felt Talgat's body heat against my back as he ran me through a couple of attempts at digging. I've admittedly had a lot of guys behind me in a position similar to this one, but this definitely was more innocent and intimate at the same time. Without a warning, I felt something stirring down below. *Thank God my shirt is covering my crotch.*

Talgat pulled back and watched me dig out a few more mounds of dirt before saying, "There you go. Now you're digging like a champ. Keep it up."

I continued to dig as I watched Talgat walk back to his post and go to work. He followed his own advice on digging, and I instinctively started watching him a bit more intently than I should have.

I'm sorry, but if you put a hot-looking guy in front of me with his bent-over ass pointed in my direction, I'm going to peek. I know I shouldn't. *Dear God, he's your employee. Down, boy. Down!*

I shook my head and focused on the pole in front of me and I dug...and I dug. About twenty minutes later, I finished digging out my first pole. Of course, in the same amount of time, Talgat had already dug out two. Within forty minutes, we'd gotten all the poles out. He'd dug out four to my measly two. But who's counting?

I wiped the sweat off my brow after I wrangled my second pole loose from the earth, I turned to Talgat. "Now what?"

"Now, we use the pole digger."

"The *what*?"

"The pole digger shovel." He pointed at a different shovel in the back of the pickup. "It allows you to dig holes specifically for poles. It will make things more secure around the new poles before we pack in the surrounding dirt. If this were a taller fence, I'd dig a hole and put cement in to make it stay put. But for this fence, we're going to dig a slightly deeper hole, then push back the dirt back in around the new poles."

Talgat walked over to the truck bed and put his shovel in the back and motioned for me to do the same. "I only have one, so I'll dig the holes out really fast. Get some water in you."

I didn't need to be told twice. I was a hot, sweaty mess. I glanced over as Talgat removed his T-shirt before digging again. *Damn!* Talgat was shredded. I know muscle queens who would kill to have his definition. He put his sweat-soaked T-shirt into his back pocket. I stared down out at my shirt and thought, *When in Rome…* I took off my shirt and grabbed my sunscreen from the pickup. I squeezed out a generous amount of sunscreen and applied an additional layer on my face, neck and arms before getting more sunscreen to apply to my chest. I kneaded the sunscreen into my skin as best as I could.

"Need help with that?" Talgat asked.

I looked up to see him staring at me. "Huh?" was all I let my lips say.

"With the sunscreen?" Talgat asked. "You can't get your back, and it's kind of pointless to lather up the front part of your body if your back is going to turn into a lobster."

"Yeah," I responded, shaking the fog out of my head. "Thanks."

He walked over to me and gently leaned the pole digger against the side of the truck before taking off his gloves. I handed him the sunscreen and turned my back to him.

I heard the squishing sound as the sunscreen exited the tube, then I could feel Talgat's callused fingertips spreading the sunscreen into my back. I could have melted into his arms right then and there, but the application of sunscreen was quick and professional.

"All done," he said. I turned around, and he handed the sunscreen back to me. "Hang your shirt over the side of the truck. The sun will help dry it before we drive back."

"Thanks," I said as he turned around, hanging his own shirt over the side of the truck. Talgat grabbed his shovel and started digging again.

I let out a long breath and tried to focus on anything else for fear that my junior self would decide to pop its head up and make things awkward between us. I stared over the hill and green landscape in the opposite direction from Talgat.

"Can you grab a pole?" Talgat asked.

What did he say?

I shook my head, getting it out of the gutter before pushing myself off the truck saying, "Sure." I got up from my perch and left my water bottle resting on the side. I reached in, grabbed a pole and walked it over to Talgat.

"Here's what I'm going to need you to do," Talgat instructed. "You're going to stand there looking all pretty and make sure you hold the pole upright. Don't let it tilt. I'm going to pack the dirt in around it."

"You think I'm pretty?" I shot back before I could stop myself.

"It's an expression," Talgat said with a laugh. "Don't worry, boss. I'm not trying to sexually harass you," he said as he rolled his eyes.

"I didn't think you were," I said with a sheepish grin. "Trying to be funny," I said, trying to cover my outburst. "Guess that joked failed."

Talgat

I smiled at Dale's attempt at humor before dumping the dirt back into the hole. We repeated the process for all six poles. I asked Dale to tamp the dirt, and the utter confusion that crossed his face told me he had no idea what I was talking about.

"It's basically a metal square on a stick, but it helps pound the dirt flat," I said, as I grabbed it from the truck and showed him how to use it. I watched as Dale started tamping. From the furious way he started, I think he was taking out his frustration on the poor dirt. Dale tamped, and I wired the fence posts back together. In minutes, we had a new piece of fence. I put the equipment back into the truck before walking around to grab my water bottle from the cab. With my water in hand, I motioned for Dale to sit on the truck's tailgate.

"Can it hold us?" Dale asked.

"It can hold up to six-hundred pounds, so I think we're okay, unless you have an extra two-hundred-and-fifty pounds hidden on you somewhere."

"Look at me," Dale responded, twirling himself around like a model on a catwalk. "Do I look like I'm hiding that much weight anywhere?" he said with a laugh.

"Not at all. You clearly spend a lot of time in a gym."

"So do you," Dale said. "And you're right. At least five days a week I hit the gym. It was one of the first things I purchased for the house after I moved in. I needed to have a treadmill and weights. Gotta keep myself looking hot if I'm going to snag a husband someday."

"Yeah, I don't think you're going to have a problem there," I said, before taking a swig out of my bottle. "As for me, I don't hit the gym at all. I did. For years, I did. But I've found that working the farm keeps me in shape."

"Even in the winter?"

I shot Dale a big, toothy grin. "I may become a bit like a bear hibernating in the winter, but any belly fat I gain quickly disappears once the spring hits and I'm back at getting the farm ready."

"Well, here's to farm bods," he said, raising his bottle in a mock toast.

"To farm bods!"

We sat there on the back of his truck in comfortable silence.

After taking in nature and letting our bodies rest, I said, "Let's see if our shirts are dry." I pushed myself off the back of the truck and walked around to where both shirts were drying in the sun. I ran my hand over my shirt first and saw it was dry. I then felt Dale's shirt, and it was also dry, so I balled it up and tossed it over to him, saying, "They're dry." After Dale's earlier performance trying to catch the water bottle, I was impressed that he didn't let his shirt fall to the ground. I slipped into mine and watched as Dale did the same before he hopped off the back of the tailback. I brushed past him and slammed the tailgate shut.

And like that, our afternoon putting up the fence was over. I had other jobs that needed tending to around the farm, but I could tell that Dale was ready to call it a night. As much as he was trying—and he *was* trying to do farm work—Dale was a city boy. He would be nothing other than a city boy playing farmer.

I lifted myself into the cab of the truck, fastened my seatbelt and put the key into the ignition before making sure Dale was securely fastened inside the vehicle. At least Dale was now buckling his seatbelt without being asked to do so.

I had to admit to myself that Dale was gorgeous—but gorgeous in the way a marble statue is gorgeous. He might as well be Michelangelo's David. He appeared chiseled out of marble and just as out of reach.

I put the car into drive and took us back to the front office. Before long, I pulled up in front and saw Ayala and Rasul standing there. I glanced down at my watch and realized it was four-forty-five. I threw the truck into park.

"Sorry, guys. I lost track of time. We rebuilt that fence in the back part of the orchard."

"About time someone got around to doing that," Rasul said.

"Weren't you supposed to do it last week?" I asked, shooting him a sideways glance.

Rasul smiled and said, "Who, me?" before bursting into a fit of laughter. "Want me to help you with those?" Rasul said, as he gestured to the tools in the back of the truck.

"Sure," I said, before turning my attention back to Dale. "I'll see you tomorrow. Have a great evening."

I heard Dale mutter, "You, too," or something along those lines as I went back to the tailgate and started grabbing the shovels. Rasul grabbed the other supplies I'd taken out.

"So, you and the boss out in the back?" Rasul said with a mischievous glint in his eye. "Do I need to be worried about the two of you?" he said as he bumped me with his hip.

"Little Bro," I said, trying not to sound too exasperated, "we're colleagues. He's my boss and I'm his... Hell, I don't know what I am. His farming sensei?" I shot Rasul a look as he exaggeratedly rolled his eyes.

"Come on. You're hot, and he's hot. Why not?"

"Because you don't shit where you eat," I said. "Besides, I hear he's messing around with Chad Powell."

"The UPS driver? Didn't you mess around with him, too?" A hint of judgment came through my brother's voice.

"Don't you dare become all judgy," I reprimanded. "Shall I list the number of women you've slept with in the last six months?"

"Bro, I'm giving you a hard time. Chill out," he said, putting his full hands up in mock surrender. "I'm fucking with you. But Dale's messing around with Chad?"

"That's what the gay gossip mill in Woodstock is saying."

"I wonder if he knows how much Chad gets around delivering..." Rasul let his voice drag out the word 'delivering' to make sure I understood he was talking about fucking as if I needed help understanding his insinuation.

"Who knows? Not my job. I'm not his parent, and I'm not his boyfriend. I'm basically no one to him other than the guy who works at his farm."

"Dude, you don't think you're at least a bit more than that?" Rasul asked.

"Not really. I went to school with his type—rich, privileged, stuck up... They're all the same. Even if we rolled around in the hay, which we won't, I'd be nothing more than a farm fling. And I've done that. I'm too old to do it again."

Rasul was about to object, but he caught my grimace and apparently decided the conversation was over. We quickly put the tools and supplies where they needed to be before heading back to the office building. Ayala was already in the truck's cab. I glanced over to see if Dale's SUV was still there, but it was gone.

I'm sure he has a fuck date with Chad!

Chapter Eight

Dale

The next couple of weeks flew by in a fury of activity as the farm got itself ready for the forthcoming opening weekend. I had ordered what amounted to a small festival, which included a range of amusement park rides and activities to entertain the guests. I had hired a new advertising firm down in the city to create a simple campaign to draw in opening weekend traffic. I had contacted Trailways to give them a heads up about the influx of bus traffic. They had worked with me to set up a series of buses that would leave directly from the Port Authority Bus Terminal and drop off customers at the farm.

The night before our grand opening, I called a meeting with all the farmhands and seasonal workers we'd hired to make things run smoothly. I had ordered a full-on barbecue dinner from a local eatery, and we held our picnic in the barn. Once everyone was fat and happy, I took my chance to address the crowd.

"Can I have your attention?" I asked, but people kept on talking and didn't seem to realize that I was even speaking. Suddenly, there was a loud whistle from the back of the audience. I scanned over to see Talgat with his fingers in his mouth.

"Our fearless leader is trying to talk," he shouted, getting everyone's attention.

"Thanks!" I said, nodding in Talgat's direction. "I wanted to take a moment to say thank you to everyone for all your hard work over these past couple of weeks to get this place in tip-top condition for our grand opening tomorrow. I talked to Trailways today, and they're going to be running buses every hour from seven-thirty a.m. until one p.m. from the city, because they have that many reservations. It's a two-hour trip, so the first bus will arrive at nine-thirty. The last bus going back to the city will depart here at five p.m. It's going to be a madhouse. I'm probably not going to get the opportunity to thank each of you tomorrow, so I wanted to make sure I did that tonight. Talgat, do you want to say anything?"

I'd clearly caught Talgat off guard, but he did his best to roll with the punches.

"I know all of you are amazing workers. And things tomorrow are going to be crazy. Let's do our best to show all our guests a great time. If you run into any problems, please find Dale, Ayala, Rasul or me to run interference for you. And, as a reminder, Dale is overseeing the broader picture tomorrow, so you can go to him with any problems. If he can't handle them, he'll point you in the right direction. If there are questions related to sales, find Ayala. If there are questions related to the orchard and apple picking, direct them to Rasul. If there are logistics questions, find me. It's going to be a crazy day, like Dale said, so make sure you get some serious rest. We'll see everyone here at eight-thirty tomorrow morning, so we can start welcoming visitors."

"Thanks," I said, nodding my head in Talgat's direction. "On that note, enjoy the rest of your evening, and we'll see you in the morning to open the farm and have everything ready for the first bus load… Oh, and one more thing, I have brand new T-shirts, polos and name tags in the office, so please go grab yours before going home."

There was a polite round of applause, then people went back to their dinner conversations. I wormed my way through the barn to where the Kudaibergen siblings were standing.

"When did you order new shirts?" Talgat asked as I approached.

"It was a little secret your sister and I cooked up a couple of weeks ago," I said with a wink in Ayala's direction.

"Yep," Ayala said. "See? I can keep secrets. It was fun to see the shock on your face, big brother."

The party went on for another hour, and I went to help Ayala distribute the shirts and nametags as people left. Once the last of the workers departed, I said my goodbyes to the siblings and headed home to get an early night's rest myself.

* * * *

The first bus rolled into the parking lot at nine-thirty. Thankfully, everyone was there and raring to go. We showed the first bus load of customers right onto the farm. By mid-morning, things were going crazy. I was running around like a chicken with my head cut-off. Thankfully, my newly acquired golf cart made my life much easier. I zipped around the farm — well, as fast as a golf cart can zip anywhere. I finished switching out the staff in the parking area so they could have lunch when I heard my name being yelled from somewhere off to the right.

I studied the crowd and my jaw practically dropped when I saw Avery and Grayson making their way through the crowd toward me.

I ran up to them and embraced them both in great big bear hugs.

"I didn't know you two were coming."

"What and miss your grand opening?" Grayson said. "We rented a car and everything. Hope you don't mind. We planned on staying overnight with you."

"Of course, I don't mind. *Mi casa es su casa*. Let me give you a tour," I said, throwing my arms around Grayson.

"Dear God," Avery finally said after I'd embraced him, too. "You're a gay Grizzly Adams." He tilted his head and narrowed his eyes before adding, "It's kind of hot."

I laughed. "Yeah, farm life is definitely a bit more rugged than life in the city." It was only then that I took in both Avery and Grayson and the outfits they'd put together. They seemed like a pair of hipsters who went camping. It was only after a few seconds that I realized they were pretty much dressed how I had been when I'd first come to the farm. *Did I look this out of place when I got here?* I did my best not to chuckle at the sight of the two fish out of water.

I spent the next twenty minutes walking Avery and Grayson around the farm's chief attractions. It felt good to have a piece of home on the farm with me. I'd forgotten how much I loved these guys.

"Mr. Devereux." A voice drew me out of my tour.

I spun around to take in the twenty-something blonde woman wearing her polo with a name tag that read *Ainsley Kelloway.*

"How can I help you, Ainsley?"

"How do you know my name?" she asked, her eyes growing wide in shock.

"Your nametag," I said with a gentle smile.

"Oh, right!" She let out a loud giggle. "Duh! I have my blonde moments."

"Don't we all…and I'm not blond. Anyway, how can I help you?"

"There's a problem in the market, and I was told to find you."

"Okay. I'll be right over." I then turned to Avery and Grayson and said, "Duty calls." I glanced around for a brief second, caught sight of Jordan Floyd and called out his name.

"What's up, boss?" Jordan said as he approached.

"Do you have a few minutes to show my friends here," I said, nodding my head in Avery and Grayson's direction, "how to pick apples?"

"Sure," Jordan said, taking in the two men standing beside me. "Should be an experience for them."

"Perfect," I said, trying not to appear too amused. I turned back to my friends. "Avery and Grayson, this is Jordan. Jordan, Avery and Grayson." I waited as the three exchanged handshakes. "I'm going to leave you two in Jordan's very capable hands." With that, I wormed my way through the crowd to the market.

* * * *

Thankfully, the afternoon flew by ridiculously fast. By the time we closed at five p.m., I was exhausted. At some point, I'd directed Avery and Grayson to the office building so they could get out of the heat. Once things were wrapping up and the last customers of the day were checked out, I headed to the office building myself.

I opened the door and found the Kudaibergen siblings sitting with Avery and Grayson as I walked in.

"Then there was the time Dale practically threw a hissy fit when his granddad forced him to take a car service out to the Hamptons instead of renting a helicopter," Grayson said as I entered.

I watched as the Kudaibergen family snickered at my expense.

"Shoot me now," I groused as I settled in the only empty chair in the office. "Do we have to tell that story? I was fifteen."

"A ridiculously spoiled fifteen," Grayson responded with a grin.

"Dare I ask what other stories you've been telling?"

"Just the good ones," Avery said with a wink.

"I don't want to know," I said. I turned to Ayala and changed the subject. "What do the preliminary totals look like?"

"I won't know anything official until I get to run the financial statements early next week, but this was by far the best opening day the farm has ever had," Ayala let the group know. "I'm betting we'll still outdo any of our previous opening weekends, even after we deduct the expenses of the new shirts, name tags and advertising."

"That's good to hear," I let her know. "I would be lying if I said I wasn't worried."

"Well," Talgat said, "we should probably go get some rest. We have a repeat performance tomorrow. Thankfully, Sunday will be a little less chaotic, but not by much."

"Sounds like a plan to me," I said. "Wanna see my office?" I said, looking at Avery and Grayson.

"Sure," Grayson said.

The three of us stood, and I walked upstairs and showed them the office while telling them the story about how I'd ordered the building online.

"You can order a building online?" Avery asked. "Who knew?"

"You can order almost anything online these days," Grayson said.

"So, what's the deal with that hot little number, Jordan?" Avery asked out of nowhere.

"He's a great kid finishing a degree at the local community college," I said.

"Oh, come on," Avery said, rolling his eyes and leaning his head to the side. "You're telling me you haven't tried to get in his pants at least once?"

"Whoa," I said, completely taken aback. "That would be beyond inappropriate."

"Yeah," Grayson said, his brows furrowing. "That's what we call sexual harassment in the legal profession."

"Party poopers," Avery said. "I've seen enough porn involving hot guys on a farm. I know how you guys get jiggy with it in the barn."

I was a bit flummoxed. I didn't know how to respond. I mean, how does one respond to something so out-there?

"Beyond the fact that it would be completely unethical, not to mention illegal, the dude's straight."

"Are you sure about that?" Avery asked. "My gaydar was totally going off as he was showing us around."

"It's not like I've discussed his sexuality with him," I admitted. "But I have no reason to believe that he's anything but a cis-gender straight guy. Sorry, but your farmhand fantasy will have to be lived out another day."

Avery sighed and rolled his eyes, as if saying he was placating me and letting this conversation end — for the moment.

I ushered the two out of my office. Talgat was exiting his. "Give us a second," I said to Avery and Grayson. "I'll be right down."

I watched as Avery and Grayson walked down the stairs before turning to Talgat. "I wanted to thank you for all your hard work today. Without you, I don't think today would have been remotely possible."

"Thanks," Talgat said. He turned to walk down the stairs and I saw a hesitancy in his steps. He turned back around and said, "There's a group of us meeting up at Hole in the Wall, the local gay bar, tonight. You and your friends should meet us there."

"Sounds like fun. I didn't know there was a gay bar here."

"Well, it's more a bar that's been adopted by gay people and allies. It's a laid-back place. Besides, it will give you an opportunity to get to know Jordan a bit more informally," Talgat said as he flashed his eyebrows.

Without waiting to see my reaction, he left me standing in the hall speechless as he bounded down the stairs.

* * * *

The Hole in the Wall definitely lived up to its name. Avery, Grayson and I walked into the bar and felt as if every head in there immediately turned to stare at the three new strangers who'd walked in. It almost seemed like the start of a joke. *A playboy, a lawyer and a trust fund kid walk into a bar…*

I took in the ambiance, and this place was like no bar I'd ever been to down in the city. This place was maybe one-thousand square feet of actual space. There wasn't a proper dance floor to speak of, but there was a space and a couple of couples were out there swinging to the music, nonetheless. One thing that immediately surprised me was that there wasn't anyone on the door checking IDs. But then, it seemed like everyone in the place already knew everyone else, so it shouldn't surprise me too much that they didn't need to check.

I peered over into the far corner and saw Talgat and Jordan sitting at a table already with a couple of bottles of beer in front of them.

"I'm going to get a drink," Avery said. "What do you two want?"

"Vodka on the rocks," I said, as I started walking over to Jordan and Talgat. I didn't wait to hear what Avery said. I knew he'd get me whatever constituted top shelf in this place.

"Good evening, gents," I said as I approached the table.

"Glad you and your entourage could make it," Talgat said. "We saved you seats." He gestured to the three empty chairs around the table.

"Thanks."

"So," Jordan said, a mischievous look crossing his face, "Talgat tells me your gaydar never went off with me."

I shot Talgat a quick glance as I furrowed my brow. "Did you have to tell him that?"

"Sorry," Talgat responded, raising his hands in mock surrender. "It was too good not to share."

I let out a quick huff before looking at Jordan. "I hate to admit it, but my gaydar is clearly not tuned in to non-city guys."

"Yeah, you citidiots don't get what it's like to be gay outside the city."

"Citidiots?" I questioned.

"Oops, sorry," Jordan apologized. "It's a term we use for the lot of you who come upstate from the city to see what nature looks like."

"Hey, after my first few days here," I admitted, "I felt like an idiot through and through."

"I'll never forget when you hiked to work," Talgat said as he tried to stifle a laugh. "I was scared out of my mind. The last thing I wanted to have to do was call your granddad and let him know we killed you on your first day."

"But look at me now," I joked.

"Yep," Jordan said. "You've gone from regular weekend warrior to Danush farmer."

"What?" I asked, having never heard the word 'Danush' used before.

"It's not a real thing," Talgat said, rolling his eyes.

"Yes, it is," Jordan said. "I read it on urban dictionary, so it's gotta be real. It means 'hottie in the field.'"

I couldn't help myself but smile. "Well, thank you for the compliment—though I would recommend not flirting with your boss."

"Oh, please," Jordan said, rolling his eyes. "We're in a gay bar. What happens in the Hole in the Wall stays in the Hole in the Wall."

"Except for the diseases people catch in the bathroom," Talgat said. Something about his facial expression said that I should avoid the bathroom here.

"Anyway, I'm going to get another beer." Jordan stood up and added, "Be right back. You kids be good now."

"Whoa," I said. "Definitely not the Jordan I'm used to dealing with at work."

"Yeah," Talgat admitted, "he's a bit of a lightweight. He's still young and finding himself."

"And my gaydar must be totally out of whack. I still can't get over me not knowing he was gay."

"Well, you have city-boy gaydar. Being gay up here isn't the same as being gay down in the city."

"A lot of homophobia?" I asked, trying to put on a sympathetic face.

"Not especially," Talgat responded. "Come on. This is Woodstock. That's not to say there aren't some backward places in upstate New York, but this area is progressive...mostly. It's just the local gays rarely see being gay as a central part of their lives. It's a part of their lives, but not a central part."

"Being gay isn't a central part of my life in the city," I balked.

"Oh really?" Talgat asked. There was a brief silence, so I gestured for him to continue. "How many straight people do you hang out with?"

"Grayson," I said.

"So, you hang out with one straight person?"

"I know a ton of straight people."

"True, but when you think of your immediate social circle, what's the percentage of gays versus straights in it?"

"I prefer hanging out with the gays," I said, sensing my frustration rising. "What about you? How many straight things do you do?"

"Well, in the winter, there's the bowling team I'm on."

"I didn't know bowling teams were a real thing outside *Married with Children* reruns," I shot out before my head could stop me.

Talgat scrunched his face and shook his head. "I also play pickup sports with a bunch of straight guys when I have the time in the fall and spring. Summer's different, because there's always so much going on at the farm. So, beyond the occasional trip in here, I don't hang out with many gays at all. And most of the gay guys I know up here function the same way."

I took all this in, trying to process it. "So, why don't you do more gay things?"

"Well, we don't live in a place where there are a lot of gay things to do. We have a couple of gay bars within an hour of here. There's the LGBTQ Center in Kingston, but it's mostly young, like high-school-age kids, or the more seasoned and retired crowd. There's no drag brunch, drag bingo, drag-anything. The closest we get to a drag queen up here is *RuPaul's Drag Race*," Talgat said.

"Oh, so you want to be a drag queen?" I joked.

"I would be one scary-looking dude in a dress," Talgat smirked, as he picked up his bottle of beer and took a swig. "So, how's Chad?" Talgat asked.

"Who?" I asked.

"Chad. You know, the guy you've been sleeping with who works for UPS?"

You know that moment in *The Grinch Who Stole Christmas* where they say his "*heart grew three sizes that day*?" I think my eyes did the same thing when Talgat asked me that question.

"How did you—?"

"Heard it through the gay grapevine. We do not have a huge gay community up here, but trust me, it talks. Dear God, how it talks."

"So, I take it you and Chad—"

"Fucked? Years ago. I think I hooked up with him when I was an undergrad. Let's say that Chad has provided more special deliveries when he's off the clock than when he's on the clock."

"Oh really?" I said narrowing my eyes at Talgat. "Jealous?"

"Of Chad? God, no," Talgat said as he chuckled.

"I take it you don't like him."

"It's not a matter of liking or not liking. He is who he is. And as long as you're aware that you aren't the only one getting inside those brown shorts of his, it's all good. Besides, I'm sure you've already figured out that all those muscles of his are overcompensating for a lack of something else."

I had to snicker at that because it was true. Chad had a micro-penis, not that there was anything wrong with that. Thankfully, he's more of a bottom. He had tried to fuck me once. I think after the third for fourth time he asked me, "Am I in?" I had lied and let him hump me like a neutered dog with a stuffed animal.

"Anyway," I drew out as I rolled my eyes, "I'm getting what I want out of him. Sometimes, you need a warm body and a release."

Talgat didn't respond to that. I narrowed my eyes at him, wishing I could burrow into his head and see what he was thinking.

"So, yeah, the gay community here isn't big or active," Talgat said. "But as you now know, everyone knows everyone. It's part of life in a small community. On the plus side, it's hard for people to hide their dirty laundry from you for very long, because it always comes out to dry."

I hadn't paid attention to the lack of gay things to do in this area, but it was true. In the city, I could do something gay every day of the week if I wanted to. I could go to one of the fifty-plus gay bars in the city. There were gay book clubs and gay bookstores. There was the Gay Men's Chorus. There was Broadway, and we all know how gay that place is. There was even the bathhouse or sex clubs...if one was feeling less social and a bit more primal.

"Dude! Get the fuck off me!" The words were followed by the sound of a crash.

Chapter Nine

I spun my head to see what was going on and saw a very red-faced and angry-looking Jordan towering over a cowering Avery, who was sprawled out on the ground. Avery started to stand, and Talgat got there as Jordan was about to punch Avery in the head. Talgat hooked his arm around Jordan's, catching his fist in midair.

I sat frozen in my chair. I don't think I'd ever seen an actual bar fight before. Grayson was standing there with two drinks in his hands. His eyes were enormous, and his eyebrows were raised so high they were practically off his head. I finally got my wits about me and pushed back from the table.

As I made my way over, I watched Talgat diffuse the situation, but the woman behind the bar did not appear happy at all.

"All of you, out of my bar or I'm calling the cops. I will not put up with this gay drama shit." I didn't know if the woman had a gun under the bar, but she was the type to pack some serious heat.

Talgat was physically dragging Jordan out when I got over there. Grayson had set the drinks on the bar and was helping Avery stand.

"What happened?" I asked as Avery brushed bar guck from the back of his slacks.

"The little farm boy happened. That's what happened!" Avery exploded. He then turned to me and growled, "Fire him!"

"What?" I asked, because it was the first thing that came to mind.

"I. Said. Fire. Him."

"Back up. What the hell happened?" I could tell that I wouldn't get an answer out of Avery, so I stared at Grayson for some kind of information.

"I was ordering drinks. I don't know what happened," Grayson said, still in shock. I'm guessing it was the first bar fight Grayson had seen, too. You don't see too many bar fights at wine and martini bars.

I glanced over at the woman behind the bar and mouthed, "I'm sorry," before flanking Avery and heading to the door.

When we got outside, Jordan wasn't anywhere around, but I saw Talgat leaning against my SUV, waiting in the parking lot.

When we got near, Talgat zeroed in on Avery. The fury that crossed Talgat's face caused me to halt in my steps. I was afraid he was going to deck Avery.

Talgat took two steps and got right up into Avery's face. "What you did in there was sexual assault," he said. The veins on Talgat's forehead popped and his neck muscles clinched. Even though the lighting wasn't great, I could see Talgat's knuckles were turning a shade lighter because they were clamped so tightly into balled-up fists.

"Whoa," I heard myself say. "What happened?"

Talgat's head popped in my direction. "He didn't tell you?" His head jerked slightly to glare at Avery, who was a deer caught in headlights. I half expected Avery to break down into tears.

"Not really," I admitted.

"Well, your *friend* here groped Jordan. When Jordan asked him to stop, he grabbed his dick and tried to force his tongue down his throat, which was when Jordan shoved this asshole. From what Jordan said, your friend here tripped over a bar stool, which landed him on his ass."

I wanted to defend Avery, but I couldn't. I hadn't seen this specific altercation, but I knew Avery well enough to know what Talgat was telling me was well within his normal behavioral patterns.

"I was flirting with him," Avery finally spat. "I'm sorry if you two-bit hicks don't like to be flirted with."

"That's not flirting," Talgat said, knitting his brows. "You assaulted him. You laid a hand on his dick without his permission."

"Whatever," Avery said, as if that was some kind of defense.

"Listen to me, you dumbass, mother-fucking, douchecanoe," Talgat said, pointing a single finger right into Avery's face. "If you'd done that to me, you'd still be seeing black. I would have laid you out so hard and so fast you wouldn't be out of a hospital bed for a week."

I peeked at Grayson and we both mouthed 'douchecanoe?' at the same time.

Talgat finally turned and glowered at me. "I get this one is a friend of yours, but I don't think he should ever come back to the farm." He paused for a second before adding, "For his own safety." With that, Talgat sidestepped our little group and headed toward his truck.

* * * *

Talgat

I did everything within my power not to put my fist through that motherfucker. I admit I'm probably a bit more protective of Jordan than I should be, but that dude had no right to sexually assault him the way he did. I think the only thing that made me pause was the fear that had washed over Dale when I got up in Avery's face to give him a piece of my mind. Thankfully, I didn't lay a finger on the prick. I wanted to. God knows, I wanted to, but I didn't do it.

By the time I got home, showered again and got to sleep a couple of hours later, I had calmed down, somewhat. I tossed and turned most of the night and was ready to drag myself out of bed when the alarm finally went off. *Day two of opening weekend.* I got up, put on some deodorant and threw on my new Devereux Farms T-shirt. I topped it off with my Devereux Farms baseball cap and name tag. I glanced down and took in the getup. *I'm some kind of warped cast member working at Disney.*

I left my bedroom and knocked on Rasul's room as I was heading downstairs to make sure he was up and moving. He said nothing when I knocked, but he grunted acknowledgment, which is more than he usually does before his first cup of coffee. I found Ayala in the kitchen making pancakes for breakfast, along with scrambled eggs and sausage links.

"Morning," I said, heading over to the coffeepot and pouring myself a cup. Ayala had already set out three mugs, so I didn't need to go fishing for one.

"You were in early last night," Ayala said, as she sat a full plate down on the kitchen table for me.

"This looks amazing. Thanks!" I picked up the syrup and drizzled it over everything on the plate but the eggs. "As for last night, there was an incident at the Hole in the Wall."

She was putting together a plate right as Rasul walked in, grabbed coffee and sat down at the table. He muttered a thanks without looking up from his coffee mug.

"An incident?" Ayala asked.

I spent the next few minutes detailing what had happened.

"How's Jordan?" Ayala questioned when I finished with the story.

"I texted him before I went to bed. He's back to his usual chill self. He wasn't ready to be sexually molested at the bar last night."

"How did Dale react?" Rasul asked between bites. I glanced over at him and watched as he shoveled two more mouthfuls of pancake in rapid succession. I didn't know if he chewed the food or if it naturally slipped down his throat like a snake.

"He basically didn't," I said. "He had his back to the whole thing when it happened, then stood there slack-jawed when I went off on his friend in the parking lot. He didn't defend him. I think he was still trying to figure out what happened." The three of us sat there, quietly eating. All lost in our own thoughts, I guess.

"So, how slammed do you think we'll be today?" Rasul asked, changing the subject.

"It's Sunday, so it won't be as busy as yesterday, but it's still going to be busy. We still have the buses running up from the city, but only till noon."

After breakfast, I helped Ayala with the dishes as Rasul ran back upstairs to put his shoes on. We were out of the house and on the farm by eight-thirty. When I got there, Dale's SUV was already pulled in in front of the admin building, which didn't surprise me. What did surprise me was that Jordan's truck was also parked out front. I pulled in next to Jordan's. Ayala walked into the building and headed to her office, and Rasul headed to the barn, where a couple of dayworkers were already milling around.

I locked up the truck and headed into the building myself. I walked up the stairs to see what was going on and partially to grab some information on the bus schedules from my desk. I didn't want to eavesdrop necessarily, but I wanted to make sure Jordan was okay. I leaned up against the wall next to Dale's office, which was cracked open.

"It's okay," I heard Jordan say. "You're not the one who should be apologizing."

"I know. I know," Dale replied. "It's just... I just wanted to make sure you were okay and things between us were okay. What happened last night was completely off the hook on so many levels. None of them were your fault."

"It's cool. You can't be responsible for your friends."

"But I am. He's my friend, so I can't not feel some responsibility. Just know, he won't be back up here anytime soon—if ever."

"Can I go now?" Jordan asked. "Assuming there isn't anything else you need from me."

"Nah, get out of here. Have fun today."

Jordan slid back the chair, so I pushed off the wall and walked over to my office door and let myself inside before Jordan had exited. He went down the stairs, so I left my office and walked over to Dale's.

"Morning, boss," I said.

"When are you going to stop calling me that?" Dale asked, his lips forming a thin line in his face. "Call me Dale—not *boss*, not Mr. Devereux. You can still call me Your Majesty, but only on special occasions." The corner of his lips curled up when he said the last one.

"About last night," I said, which caused Dale's smile to disappear.

"Sorry about that. I was apologizing to Jordan for Avery. What Avery did was beyond fucked up. He's always been a bit of a loose cannon, but I've never seen him outright grope a guy who hadn't asked for it before. I don't know what the hell got into him." I started to say something, but Dale held up a hand and kept going. "And don't worry. I made it very clear that Avery is not welcome up here. In fact, Avery was so incensed I didn't take his side that he demanded Grayson drive him back to the city last night. Thankfully, it was still relatively early, and Grayson didn't mind. Honestly, I don't know if I would have slept if Avery had been in the house."

"How did you get Jordan here so early?" I asked.

"I texted him around midnight and asked if I could see him at eight-twenty this morning. He was still up and said he would come in," Dale replied. "Yeah, he's still young. He can run on a few hours of sleep. Me? I need at least six to eight hours."

"You and me both," I admitted. "I don't get to look this hot without my beauty rest," I added. Dale looked at me, shot me a quick smile and shook his head.

"What am I going to do with you?" Dale joked.

"'Look… If you want to torture me, spank me, lick me, do it. But if this poetry shit continues, shoot me now, please.'"

"Whoa, a *Tank Girl* reference. You are trying to keep your gay card current this morning."

The expression on his face at my queer cinema knowledge made me laugh as I turned around and headed down the stairs to go check on the parking lot. Today was going to be another long, busy day.

* * * *

Dale

I was beyond livid with Avery. I knew he was a cocky sonofabitch, but I'd never known him to actually try to force himself on someone. I don't know what was going through that thick skull of his. Then he had thrown his little tantrum and demanded Grayson take him home. Grayson had been magnanimous, as always, and hadn't minded driving Avery. I had made him promise to text me as soon as they reached the city, which he'd done.

Grayson told me Avery had stewed in silence most of the way back, so Grayson listened to his audiobook as if he were alone in the car. I had thanked Grayson for getting Avery away from me. I couldn't deal with Avery's bullshit anymore.

When I knew Grayson had made it home to the city, I had texted Jordan to make sure he was fine. He'd said he was, but I asked to see him first thing in the morning to make sure to apologize for Avery's abhorrent behavior.

After talking to Jordan, I felt better. That kid was beyond chill. At first, he'd tried to apologize to me for pushing Avery. I had quickly dispelled the need for him to do so and promised him that Avery would not be back to Woodstock.

By the middle of the afternoon, I hadn't received a text from Avery, which didn't surprise me. I'd been contemplating my on-again, off-again relationship with him for a while, anyway. I thought the previous night might have been the last straw. It was time the cut that cord. I didn't need him in my life. He was fun to play with for a time, but I don't think he was necessarily good for me — kind of like UPS Guy. *What was his name?*

I didn't have time to dwell on the unfortunate incident from the night before because the farm was once again very busy. Before I knew it, I was pitching in here and there all over the place. Finally, the afternoon rolled around, and I was helping get customers on the last bus down to the city when Talgat came around in his golf cart, carrying an older woman.

"She couldn't walk here fast enough, so I offered to give her a ride," Talgat said as he pulled up next to me. He offered his hand to the woman, who grabbed it and thanked him for his help.

"Everyone accounted for, Bos— Dale."

I shot him a quick smirk before telling him, "Yep. I think there's one more person we're waiting for, but I know where she is." I hooked a thumb at the public restroom behind us. "Once she's out, this bus can get on the road."

Talgat stood next to me as we waited. After what seemed like forever, the woman exited the restroom and boarded the bus.

"She's the last customer. You have everyone now," I told the bus driver, who nodded and closed the door. The bus started pulling away, kicking up a bit of dust. Both Talgat and I stepped back to get out of the immediate dust plume.

"I wanted to see if you and your family would join me for dinner," I said.

"When?" Talgat asked.

"Tonight?"

"Sure. I'll double-check with them. Say seven-ish?"

"Sounds great. And to make sure, are there any dietary needs I need to know about?"

"None. Just know that Rasul will try to eat you out of house and home if you let him. That boy can pack away food. I don't know where it goes, half the time."

"Great. I'll see you at seven-ish." I then nodded toward his golf cart and my golf cart. "Race you back to the barn," I said quickly before jumping into my cart and taking off.

I heard the roar of Talgat's little engine behind me as I left. It wasn't a long ride, and thankfully there were no more tourists hanging out, so I didn't run into anyone. By the time I pulled up to the barn, ready to enjoy my victory, I found Talgat leaning against his cart already.

"How'd you?" I asked, slack-jawed.

"Back road," he said with a wink as the corner of his lip tilted upward. "See you at seven-ish."

Chapter Ten

Talgat

With the promise of free food and a look inside the castle, Ayala and Rasul jumped at the chance to have dinner with Dale. We showed up at seven-fifteen. I debated with Ayala what seven-ish meant. She had thought it meant we should be there at seven-thirty. I had thought it meant we should arrive at seven. Rasul had laughed at Ayala's and my disagreement and was no help at all. We had split the difference and showed up at seven-fifteen.

I knocked and waited a few seconds before Dale opened the front door. He was wearing a pair of khaki pants and a white dress shirt that was unbuttoned enough that the muscle definition in his chest could be seen under the shirt. When we walked in and the light hit his shirt just right, it was practically see-through, but only for a second. I wondered if my brain was playing tricks on me, but then he walked under a different light and the same bare back could be seen under his white shirt.

"Who wants a tour?" Dale asked, spinning around.

We all looked at each other and shrugged. I knew Ayala and Rasul were trying to play it cool. I'd told them about my previous visit, so I knew they were itching to see it for themselves. This was one of those houses in Woodstock that everyone knew about but few had gone inside. Dale led off, showing everyone the downstairs areas. He then motioned to the spiraling staircase before taking us into the turret.

"The first floor is basically a giant closet," Dale said, motioning around once we'd gathered inside the round room.

"This is the largest closet I've ever seen," Ayala said. "And you're barely using any of it. For that matter, you're barely using half the house right now."

"Yeah," Dale admitted. "It's a bit much, but apparently my granddad's secretary got a great deal to rent it out of season. More people seem to want to come up here in the winter."

"I could see that," Rasul said, "what with that giant fireplace and all."

Dale walked over to the spiral staircase and started walking up. "Up here is the master bathroom."

Ayala, Rasul and I followed him up the stairs, and my siblings were pretty slack-jawed as they stared at the bathroom with the giant tub in the corner. The separate shower was large enough to house an orgy. *I wonder if he's ever had one in there?* This bathroom could easily be the size of six normal-sized ones.

He led us up the next flight of stairs to the main bedroom, which was equally amazing. He showed us how the curtains could open automatically, which was admittedly impressive. I loved how the whole thing was set up to allow the sunlight in in the morning, and the moonlight in in the evening, if that's what you wanted. And the view from Dale's bedroom was breathtaking. Now, our family home is a good-sized one, but this place was amazing.

I peeked over to see what book Dale had on his bedside table and noticed the bottle of lube sitting there instead. I looked up quickly, catching Dale's eyes as he tracked where my eyes had been. I didn't know it was possible for a white guy to turn that red without being sun burned.

I did my best to hide my grin before asking, "What's for dinner?"

Dale led us downstairs and into the kitchen.

"It's a make-your-own-taco bar," he said with a bit too much enthusiasm. Thankfully, he didn't try to say it with an accent, so I'd give him that.

I caught Rasul looking at the sheer amount of food and he immediately started salivating. Dale handed him a plate, saying, "Go for it."

Rasul didn't need to be told twice. He was quickly filling it then sat down at the giant round dining room table.

"What would you like to drink?" Dale asked everyone.

"What do you have?" I asked.

"I have sodas, bottled water and all kinds of alcohol. What would you like?"

"Whatever you're having," I responded.

"I was thinking of opening a bottle of Albariño I picked up from a winery in Galicia, Spain, a while back. Not the most expensive wine, but it's damn good."

And there it was, the first mention of the cost of something that evening. Dale turned everything and every conversation into one about money. I didn't think he knew he did it.

"Sounds good," I responded, picking up my plate and started putting food on it.

Before long, all four of us were sitting around the table. It was a bit more table than four people needed. It kind of reminded me of that scene in *Batman* where Kim Bassinger is at one end of a crazy-long table and Michael Keaton's sitting at the opposite. Again, not as ridiculous, but it seemed needlessly large.

Conversation around the table was genial. I think having this kind of interaction with Dale off the farm was good for my siblings. They still put a bit of a distance between themselves and Dale. They didn't understand why I was becoming increasingly chummy with him, either. Honestly, as much as I tried to dislike the guy, I couldn't. Sure, he was a spoiled rich kid to the nth degree, but it's not like that was his fault. He'd grown up in a completely different universe than we did—one so far away from planet Earth he didn't understand what it was like where the rest of us lived. But he was at least open to learning.

After dinner, we sat around in the living room. He'd started a small fire, even though the air conditioner was going full blast. The irony of doing this was clearly lost on Dale. If he wanted a fire, there should be a fire. Just cool the place down until you're comfortable with a fire. Again, he's from another universe.

After about forty-five minutes, I saw Rasul getting antsy. He was pulling out his iPhone every couple of minutes and checking his messages. He was bouncing his foot up and down so fast that I was amazed he hadn't bounced his sister off the couch they were sitting on together.

"Well," I finally said, "I guess we should get home. We have a long day tomorrow."

"Yep," Ayala but in. "I can't wait to see and digest the financial statements."

Rasul jumped up off the couch, saying, "It's been fun. Thanks for having us over. And let's do it again," in rapid succession.

I almost busted out laughing, but I kept it together. Ayala patted Rasul's shoulder, saying, "Calm the fuck down. You look like you downed a six-pack of energy drinks."

"Sorry," Rasul said, snapping out of it. He then turned to gaze at Dale. "I am totally ADHD. So, sitting in one place for long periods of time is hard for me."

"That's how you're able to eat all that food. You just keep moving," Dale joked. "I wish I had your metabolism."

"Yeah, I've never had to exercise because I'm kind of always in motion, unless I'm sleeping, which is why college was not in the cards for me. I barely got through high school. And that's only because I had parents, an older sister and an older brother who would have beaten the crap out of me if I didn't."

"Damn right! Well, let's get this train moving," I said, making a scooching motion with my arms toward my siblings. "Thanks for having us over, Dale. It was much appreciated."

"Next time, we'll have to have you over to our place for a home-cooked meal," Ayala suggested. "Talgat and I are talented chefs. Maybe not Michelin Five Star like you're used to, but we're okay."

"I didn't know Talgat could cook," Dale said, shooting a glance in my direction. "Any specialty dishes?"

"He's excellent with Italian and Mediterranean food, but he shines when he makes some of our mom's old Kazakh dishes we grew up with."

"What is Kazakh food like?"

"Well, traditional Kazakh cuisine is a combination of mutton, horse and milk." I saw Dale's face blanch when I said 'horse', so I added quickly, "Don't worry. We use beef in the US and not horse."

"His beshbarmak is to die for," Rasul added.

"Bes-what?" Dale asked.

"Bish-bar-mark," I said phonetically. "It's a popular Kazakh dish and translates roughly to five fingers. But don't worry, there are no fingers involved in the dish's making. It has mutton, beef, onion and rolled-out dough. Kind of like noodles, but not the same as Italian noodles. You can buy the rolled-out dough in some specialty places, but it's so much easier to make it and roll it out yourself."

"I'll take your word for it," Dale said with a slight giggle as he stared at me.

"What?" I asked. "Do I have something on my face?"

"No, it's just that I've never seen you get passionate about anything but farming. It's nice to know you're more well-rounded than I originally thought."

"I think that was meant as a compliment."

"It was," Dale said with a smile. I'd seen Dale's smile many times, but it was the first time I think a genuine smile had been directly pointed at me. I stared at his perfect teeth in all their whiteness. He had huge dimple crevices on either side of his cheeks. Heck, even his chin had dimples when he smiled.

"Well," Ayala said suddenly, "I guess we should be going."

I caught my breath, reached my hands into my pocket and pulled out the truck keys in response. "Yep, we should get going so Dale can get some sleep. Are you sure you don't need help cleaning?"

"I'm fine. I can handle the basics. My cleaning service comes tomorrow. They'll handle the heavy lifting."

And there it was again, his 'cleaning service'. It was like in one moment I saw Dale as just another gorgeous gay guy, then in the next he was the prince and I was the pauper, only we looked nothing alike. Oh well!

I headed toward the front door and opened it, holding it open for Ayala and Rasul to pass in front of me.

"I'm glad you came over," Dale said. "You and your family."

"Thanks for inviting us," I said. Without thinking, I put my hand on his chest, then tapped his pec twice with my fingers before saying, "This has been fun. See you tomorrow."

It took all my mental concentration not to jump the man and rip off that white shirt. But my siblings were watching, so I walked over to the truck and got in.

As I pulled away, I watched Dale framed by the light in his doorway. He started waving at us and went a bit spastic. It took me a second to realize he was trying to swat some insect intent on invading his house. And from the looks of it, Dale was losing the battle.

I laughed as I watched him scramble into his house in my rearview mirror.

* * * *

Dale

Feeling Talgat's hand on my chest made me want to bend him over the doorway and fuck him right there — or have him bend me over, I didn't care. I was trying to play it cool when I stood looking sexy in the doorway until this fucking huge moth attacked. Trust me, this thing was big enough to be 'mothman'. I'm sure I looked like I was having some kind of seizure, the way my arms went flailing about while I was defending myself from the winged intruder. Sadly, by the time I got the door shut, Talgat and his clan were already distant red lights down the long drive.

I glanced at my cell phone lying in the kitchen. I walked over it to and flipped through until I saw 'UPS Guy'. *His name is Chad or is it Chuck? Maybe it's Phil? No, Phil is the pharmacist.* My finger hovered over the call button. I knew that if I hit send, UPS Guy would be here with a special delivery in under thirty minutes, which is faster than pizza delivery around here. But my finger still hovered. I couldn't bring myself to hit the button. I didn't want the UPS guy. And I couldn't want Talgat because HR policies at the company would not approve.

Devereux Farms had a strict anti-fraternization policy to protect the laborers on our farms from undue influence. *I wonder how that policy actually reads?* Instead of calling UPS Guy, I slunk back to the living room couch and scoured the corporate website to check out policies. I never had a traditional onboarding, so it's not like I was given any specific training from HR. I knew that having an office romance was never a good idea. All the Kudaibergens had worked on the farm, which one would think would be against HR policies, too.

I found the employee section of the website and scrolled through until I saw the policies on employee dating. Basically, the policy talked about people in farm management positions having concealed relationships with employees. And there was a zero-tolerance policy for romantic entanglements between full-time employees and seasonal help. I guess the company wanted to make sure we kept all our employment decisions as above-board as humanly possible. One line of the policy caught my eye, "*Consensual personal relationships between full-time employees at Devereux Farms are not prohibited by this policy. However, in cases where employees are at different pay levels within the company, it is the senior-ranking person in the relationship's job to disclose the relationship to HR. HR will then ask the partners within a relationship to sign a love contract. The contract stipulates the individuals signing the love contract do so willingly and Devereux Farms cannot be held accountable for any problems after the fact.*"

What the hell is 'a love contract'? I conducted a quick Google search and found a few examples online. Most of them said the same thing. Basically, I wouldn't hold the company responsible if our relationship went south, which had to be signed and witnessed. *I wonder how many people fill these things out?*

I tossed my iPhone onto the coffee table and lay back on the couch, placing my left forearm over my eyes as I hung my right arm off the side. Besides, I was putting the cart way before the horse. One, I didn't know if Talgat was interested in me or interested in someone like me. Second, if he was interested, our lives were too different. He lived up here and ran the farm. I couldn't wait to get back to the city. I thought about it for a moment, though. Third, did I want to go back to the city? I was kind of liking it up here, true, but would I still like it up here in the dead of winter—or even next summer?

I went back and forth, debating myself for the next hour before I slipped into sleep. Around three a.m., I woke up and realized I was still on the couch. I stood up and stretched. I grabbed my phone and checked on my texts. There was a text from Avery. I didn't feel like reading it, so I clicked off my phone again. I found the charging cable I'd set up in the kitchen and plugged it in while I put away the taco party leftovers. *I'm going to be eating tacos for a week.* I'd clearly purchased enough for a small army. Once the leftovers were in the fridge, I grabbed my phone off the kitchen charger. I slipped out of my clothes and put them in the hamper before climbing the stairs to my bedroom. I set the alarm on my phone before plugging it into the charger up there before pulling back the covers and climbing in.

I was asleep in a matter of minutes.

* * * *

The next morning, I dragged myself out of bed and hit my home gym before heading into the office. I pulled into the drive leading up to the farm right as the Kudaibergens were pulling in. I trailed them down the short drive until we both veered off to the right and parked in front of the administrative building. I was trying to get everyone to call it that, but I knew at least a couple of workers who referred to it as 'the Devereux Castle' or 'Dale's Château'.

"Good morning," I said to Rasul, who exited first before heading off to the barn.

"Morning," Rasul yelled, his back to me as he walked away.

"Where's he off to in a hurry?" I asked Ayala as she exited the truck.

"Oh, he's in a hurry to get the barn organized after yesterday. Things were a bit out of sorts when we left here yesterday, and it's been wearing on him all morning."

Well, things with the Kudaibergen clan never ceased to amaze me. Finally, Talgat climbed out, and he was dressed a bit more laid-back than I was used to seeing him. He was wearing a pair of cargo shorts and a white knit polo. Talgat lifted his sunglasses, resting them on the top of his head.

"Morning, Dale. Get some sleep last night?" he asked.

"I did. Passed out on the couch shortly after you left, then dragged myself upstairs at like three or something. I guess I was more exhausted after the last two days than I'd imagined."

"That can happen. Weekends around here can be brutal. Generally, I encourage employees to take Mondays off, because it's a good time for everyone to rest up, and we still have the rest of the week to get ready for the next weekend."

"I wish I would have known," I admitted. "I would have been perfectly happy staying curled up under my comforter this morning."

"You and me both." Talgat headed toward the front door to the admin building. Ayala stood there with the door open to usher the two of us in.

After passing Ayala in the entryway, I turned around and asked her, "When do you think you'll have preliminary numbers for me?"

"I should have them by early afternoon. Want me to run comparison numbers for opening last year?"

"That would be amazing."

With that, I headed upstairs to my office to complete a bunch of paperwork. The rest of the morning flew by. I found myself buried in emails and spreadsheets from Granddad when there was a light knock on my door.

"Come in," I said without looking up from my computer.

"You ready to talk numbers?" Ayala said, entering the room with a couple of stacks of papers.

"Sure," I said, finally looking up from my computer. I glanced at the clock on the monitor and said, "Geez, I didn't realize it was noon yet. The morning flew by."

"I wish mine had flown by, but I was at least busy." She walked over and handed me a stack of papers. "I figure I'll walk you through the report, unless you want to read it first." I gestured for her to go ahead. "Okay, let's start on page one," she said as she flipped open the document.

We spent the next forty-five minutes going through the details from the weekend line-by-line and compared them to what we had done the previous year. Thankfully, the return on investment for all the advertising had paid off. We were up five-hundred percent in sales from the previous opening weekend, which was freaking amazing. Ayala swiftly dove into a lot more detail regarding the financial situation of the farm and compared it to where they had been at this point the past year. All-in-all, the farm was in good financial shape heading into the weekend, so I wasn't sure what the problem was that my granddad had mentioned when I'd first come there.

When Ayala finished covering all forty-five pages of the document, she asked me if I had questions. "Not really," I told her. "I'm going to take some time to digest this further. If I run into questions along the way, I will let you know. Thanks for your hard work on putting this together this morning. You're impressive."

"I know," Ayala replied with a quirk of a smile and a wink. "Well, I'm going to have lunch now. You should probably get something in you, too. I think my brothers are in the breakroom. You should join us."

"I'm not much of a lunch person while working, but I brought a protein shake. It's in the fridge in the breakroom. I can come hang out for a few minutes," I said, pushing myself away from my desk. I followed Ayala out of my office and shut the door.

I walked in to find Talgat eating a microwave meal. He looked up as Ayala and I walked in.

"Where's Rasul?" Ayala asked.

"You just missed him," Talgat responded between bites. "You know how he is. He shovels the food into his mouth without chewing and is out of the door before you can say Beetlejuice three times."

I walked over, opened the fridge and grabbed my pre-made protein shake. I kept it open for Ayala as she grabbed her box lunch. She walked over to the microwave and heated it up while I sat down at the small table. Although the breakroom was open to all employees, the Kudaibergens and I were the only ones who ever seemed to use it. I was hoping that as other workers got used to being around me and the new admin building, we'd see more use of it by a broader range of people. Admittedly, there was already a small cooking and sitting area in the barn, which was where most of the farmhands gathered.

"So, how were the numbers?" Talgat asked, looking between Ayala and me.

"We're up five-hundred percent from last year's opening weekend," Ayala said. "Dale's advertising more than paid for itself. Now, can we keep up this momentum for the rest of the season?"

"I'm sure we can," I admitted. "I think this weekend was the start to a very fruitful season. I can't wait to see how we blow the other farms out of the water this year." I couldn't help but smile. I trusted my team. The Kudaibergens were a well-oiled machine before I'd gotten involved, so I had a sneaking suspicion we were going to be make some records this summer.

"Well, what's everyone up to this afternoon?" Talgat asked. "I'm going to work in the lab a bit. I'm still trying to get my own Grāpple. None of the flavors are turning out the way I want them to so far, though."

I took a swig of my protein drink as the microwave dinged, letting Ayala know her meal was ready. I watched her as she pulled out the plastic tray and peeled off the plastic topper as steam billowed up from the food. From the smell of it, she was having Italian. She threw away the cardboard box and plastic wrap before walking over to the table and sitting down.

"That smells delicious," I told her. "What it is?"

"It's some kind of ravioli I picked up when I was at Hannaford's." She cut a piece and watched as more steam came out. She put her fork down, clearly deciding to wait for the meal to cool off. "I'm going to finish up the reports and send them down to corporate. I also need to complete the wire transfer."

"How does that work exactly?" I asked.

"It's simple. Every Monday or Tuesday, I complete a basic report letting them know our sales figures and profits and losses. I then make sure that an exact wire transfer is sent down to your granddad for the weekend, minus any recorded expenses. We all use the same bank, so it makes shifting funds from one account to the next very easy."

"What types of expenses do you report?"

"Everything," Ayala said, shaking her head. "Everything from a pen purchased to personnel expenses, I track it all."

"And you handle the purchasing?" I asked.

"I put forward invoices for purchasing. But someone down in the corporate office conducts all purchasing. I keep track of everything, but corporate handles all the money. Beyond transferring funds from our local account to the corporate account, the farm doesn't have much of a connection to the actual money."

"How do we handle cash purchases?" I asked.

"Well, we reconcile all cash registers daily. Then we make deposits on Saturdays, Mondays and Wednesdays. We keep two thousand dollars in physical currency for making change at the start of each day. We then pull it out again before reconciling the cash registers at the end of each day. When it's not in a cash register being used, it's locked in the safe in my office."

"Seems like the system is fool-proof," I said.

"We've been using this system for so long that I can hardly imagine working any other way."

"Good to know," I said, nodding.

Chapter Eleven

Before I knew it, we were well into September and quickly approaching October when I was called down for a quarterly finance meeting with my granddad. I hadn't visited the city since I'd moved to Woodstock, so I felt a bit of trepidation going down. But at the last minute, Granddad had to be out of the state and couldn't be there for an in-person meeting, so we ended up Zooming instead. I'd gotten used to using Zoom during the pandemic, but my granddad always had Molly in his office to help him.

It was blatantly clear that he did not know what he was doing when I said for what had to be the fourteenth time, "Granddad, you're muted. You need to push the audio icon on the lower left-hand side of your screen. Right now, it has a slash through it. You don't want that slash."

"Mr. Devereux," Molly added, "if you need me to walk you through it, you can call me on the phone. I'm sitting at my desk."

My granddad's face was turning a deeper shade of red with each passing second. "Do you want me to share my screen with you and show you how to do it?" I offered.

" —ckity, fuck!"

"Well, you're unmuted now," I said, my eyebrows raising and stifling a giggle. I stared at the screen Molly was on and couldn't hold it back anymore. Her mouth was in a giant surprised 'O', responding to Granddad's series of expletives. Both Molly and Granddad are old school, so they don't cuss nearly as much as the drunken sailors in my generation.

"Jameson! Watch that tongue of yours. Well, I never—"

"Sorry, Molly," Granddad said, his eye downcast, having been sufficiently chastised by Molly. "I let my anger get the best of me. But this convoluted technology is going to drive me to an early grave."

I stifled another laugh.

"And you, Dale… Don't think I didn't notice you laughing. You," Molly said, staring at me through the screen in a way that made me feel like I was five again, "are incorrigible. What am I going to do with the both of you?"

"Sorry, Molly," I replied.

Granddad cleared his throat, getting the meeting on track. "Well, as you know, I like to talk to the farm managers at least once a quarter to see how things are doing on their farms. Dale, how are things up in Woodstock?"

"Well, as you know, the brochures we'd been handing out about Devereux Upstate were a far cry from what was the actual reality on the ground. Don't get me wrong, the farm part was running well. It's just that the touristy parts were nonexistent, as was the infrastructure alleged in the brochures. I've spent a bit of money—" My granddad's eyes narrowed through the camera. "Don't worry," I quickly added. "I used my own personal funds on a couple of improvement projects."

"I'd heard through the grapevine that you'd done that," my granddad said. "Might I ask why?"

"I had the money and felt that the improvements were going to benefit me directly. And it was faster to use some of my money than get everything approved for a large expense. Apparently, the farm had asked for some of these upgrades previously and had gotten locked up in red tape for a couple of years."

"Interesting," my granddad responded. He then gestured for me to go on.

"I also invested in a new advertising campaign, which has already paid for itself and had a return on investment that far outpaced our expectations. Overall, I would say the farm is in great shape, and I'm proud of where things are standing right now."

Granddad read some of his notes. I had expected him to congratulate me on a job well done with a quick pat on the back.

"I see that you're still underperforming," Granddad said when he finally stared into the camera.

"Excuse me?" I blurted before I could stop myself. "I mean, I don't see how we could be underperforming at this point."

"I know that you're new to the farm business, so let me put it to you simply. When I compare your farm's current profitability to other farms in the system, you are simply not making as much money."

"Does that consider differences in local and state taxes?" I questioned.

"Yes," Molly added, "along with differences in cost-of-living in different parts of the country and pricing structures at the farms themselves."

"Take, for example, your opening weekend," Granddad said. "Your opening weekend was about half of what was done over at Devereux Lake Erie." The Lake Erie farm was near the Great Lake. And since it was in Pennsylvania, it was the closest farm to Devereux Upstate.

"So, you're telling me they pulled in almost two-hundred-thousand-dollars on opening weekend?" I didn't try to mask the skepticism I had.

"Well, of course not," Granddad said, clearly missing the point.

"We averaged fifty-thousand-dollars on both Saturday and Sunday that weekend, which puts our opening weekend total around one-hundred-thousand dollars, which was a tremendous change from the previous year. Even when you take out the sixteen-thousand-dollar investment in advertising we made, we still had a return on investment that was over five hundred percent. I'm not seeing the problem from my vantage point." I did my best not to let my frustration boil too hot in front of Granddad.

"Say that again?" Granddad asked.

"Which part?"

"How much did the farm make on opening weekend?"

"When we deducted costs, including advertising, personnel and other expenses, which may have totaled twenty-five-thousand-dollars, we still netted around seventy-five-thousand-dollars."

"Well, that is interesting," Granddad said, looking down at the stack of notes he had sitting in front of him. "That number doesn't come close to what I see on the spreadsheets in front of me. Are you sure your information is accurate?"

"Yes," I said, furrowing my brow in confusion. "I checked the numbers with Ayala on Monday after opening weekend. We went through the information line-by-line. I double-checked the accounting, and it was accurate."

"Hmm…" Granddad responded, clearly pondering what he wanted to say next. "Is there any way some of the money could have gone missing?"

"If you're suggesting that Ayala Kudaibergen somehow misappropriated the money, it's not possible. The checks and balances in the system prevent her from tapping into the accounts once they are in the bank. All she can do is shift funds from Devereux Upstate to the central Devereux Corporate accounts. Beyond the cash we keep on hand for making change, the local farm has zero control over its finances."

"Really?" Granddad said in confusion. "It was my understanding that each farm had autonomy over its own banking."

"If I may be so bold," Molly cut in. Granddad gestured with his hand, showing Molly that she should continue. "We centralized accounting about fifteen years ago to streamline the process. Dale is correct. The local accountants have little contact with the actual money, beyond making cash deposits. And those deposits must match cash register receipts, which are submitted electronically."

"Indeed," Granddad said, steepling his hands beneath his chin. "Molly, I want you to examine this for me while I'm gone. Something fishy is going on here, and I need someone I can trust to get to the bottom of it."

"Yes, Mr. Devereux," Molly responded.

"Thank you for your time and insight this afternoon, Molly. I want to talk to Dale on my own for a few minutes."

"Of course, sir." Molly's window disappeared from the Zoom call.

"What do you want to talk about, Granddad?"

"How are things on the farm? I mean, how are you getting along up there? Good working relationship with the Kudaibergens?"

"I won't lie. Things were rough to begin with. Let's face it. I didn't know a farm from a farmers' market when I came up here. I've already learned so much about how the farming industry works. As for the Kudaibergens, they're an amazing family. All of them are such hard workers. Honestly, I'm amazed every day by their work ethic."

"The kids sound exactly like their parents, which, I guess, doesn't surprise me too much."

"What were their parents like? Other than mentioning them in passing, we haven't discussed their folks in much detail."

My granddad leaned back in the hotel room chair, relaxing for the first time since we'd gotten on Zoom.

"They were some of the most upright people I ever knew. And for years, their farm was always one of the top producers in the company. I was genuinely surprised when their numbers started slipping. Now I'm wondering if something else isn't going on there." Granddad's voice trailed off as he furrowed his brow in concentration. "Well, I'm sure we'll sort this out,"

Granddad said, determination flashing across his face. I'd seen that look a few times in my life, and it meant he was now like a dog with a bone, and he'd get to the bottom of this.

We hung up on Zoom. I debated whether I should tell Talgat, but I didn't feel like I could keep this from him, so I got up from my desk, left my office and went to find him.

I ran into Ayala and asked if she knew where her brother was. She pointed me toward his lab.

I meandered my way across the farm and into the barn. Now, we call it a barn, but it was a lot more than a barn these days. On the outside, the barn appeared rustic, but the inside was completely modern—from the gift store and farmstand that stood in the center, to several rooms where equipment was stored and where Talgat kept his lab.

I knocked lightly before opening the door. "So, this is where the mad scientist lives?"

Talgat let out a quick gasp as all his muscles apparently jumped.

"Sorry. I didn't mean to scare you," I said, walking into the room. "This is where you scurry off to in the afternoon to be a mad scientist?"

"You know it!" Talgat said, beaming. "Welcome to my little kingdom. Want the two-cent tour?"

"Sure," I said, giving him a fake little bow, to which he rolled his eyes and gestured for me to follow him. The lab reminded me of the chemistry labs I'd sat through in high school and college, but this one didn't have as up-to-date equipment. The lab was filled with beakers, growers, a microscope and a whole slew of chemicals I couldn't pronounce.

"Agricultural biotechnology or genetically modified foods always sounds scary to people, but we've been doing it for a long time. Most people immediately think of Frank-N-Foods when they about these, but most of the time it's about figuring out which genes from two or more plants can make each other stronger."

"Okay, but how do you sell it to the public? I mean, we're an organic farm, so how does that jibe with our mission?"

"I don't want to be a total science geek, but the father of genetics, Johann Gregor Mendel, conceived of the idea of genetics by examining plants. He realized that if you grew two plants side-by-side, they would adapt, and future generations would be a mixed-hybrid of both. And in the farming industry in the US, we've been using techniques of growing different strains of a species side-by-side to create stronger, more durable offspring since the nineteen-fifties, if not earlier."

"Really?" I must have sounded more skeptical than I'd intended because Talgat spun and regarded me with his intense stare.

"Really. Farmers could test a lot of those genetics theories long before we had gene splicers. Dating back the mid-nineteen-sixties, we farmers were already growing different strands of wheat side-by-side an in effort to produce wheat that was more resistant to the environment and could fend off insects."

"Okay," I said, putting my hands up in mock surrender, "I believe you. So, why do people freak out about genetically modified foods?"

Talgat leaned against the back wall of the lab as he thought for a second. I took in the room and wondered what our customers would think if they saw this lab. Would they run in fear? Or would they be intrigued and want to learn about what's going on? Honestly, I wasn't sure yet what I thought about all this myself.

"I think there are a few reasons. There have been some big, corporate players in the market who have created a new species of plants that have done ecological damage, which is one reason the Food and Drug Administration requires the registration and oversight of all genetically modified foods. You don't want to create wheat that ends up killing bees. There are no studies that show this happens, but I've seen some conspiracy theories that genetically modified plants are killing bees, butterflies, et cetera. And I think people freak out when they hear 'genetically modified'. I don't think most people are even aware they're eating GM plants. For example, eighty percent of corn, cotton and soybeans in the US are some kind of GM plant. Chances are if you eat something that has corn, cornstarch or high fructose corn syrup, you're taking in a GM plant."

I nodded as he then dove into a lecture on how people are worried about modern technology in genesplicing that happens in big agricultural genetics labs than the more traditional GM plans.

"Sadly, I don't think most people," Talgat said, ending his impromptu presentation, "realize the difference between more traditional cross-bred genetically modified plants and those that occur through laboratory genesplicing. As you can see, I don't have the equipment to consider genesplicing in here. I'm doing my research the way Mendel did it back in the eighteen-eighties."

"Woo-hoo, go genetically modified plants," I said, doing my best impersonation of a cheerleader, complete with fake pom-poms and a high kick for added emphasis. Talgat didn't seem to appreciate my impromptu cheer and rolled his eyes, drawing his mouth in a thin line. Though I would swear one corner of his lips was battling to turn up.

"I wasn't prepared for Bio 101 today. I didn't take notes, and I didn't bring my number two pencil. I hope there's not a test."

"I'll show you a test," Talgat said, a mischievous smile crossing his face. He reached out and poked the side of my stomach, and I involuntarily let out a giggle like the Pillsbury Dough Boy. "You're ticklish—"

"Don't you even think about it," I said as I took a step backward.

"Think about what?" He took a step forward into my personal space. He acted like he was going to poke me in the side with the same hand, so I maneuvered to avoid him, only to be surprised when he got me on the other side. I let out a little squeal. Before I knew it, it was full-on war as I tried to tickle him back.

"Yeah, I'm not ticklish," Talgat said, grinning. "I never have been."

"Bastard!" I barked right before he got me again.

"Oh, dear God! Would you two fuck and get it over with already?" a loud voice barked from the doorway.

I spun my head to see who the new intruder was. In the doorway stood Jordan and Rasul. Each had a smirk on their face. I pulled away from Talgat and mindlessly went about smoothing back down my shirt.

"We weren't— I wasn't— He wasn't," I stammered out.

"Is this some kind of gay courting dance?" Rasul asked Jordan.

"Not one I've seen," Jordan smirked. "But then, I'm still young and haven't seen all the mating habits of my people yet."

"Make this stop," Talgat said, turning a color of red that mirrored the apples he was working on.

I hate admitting it but watching Talgat's ribbing from his brother and Jordan and Talgat's obvious discomfort of the whole situation made me want to bust out of laughing. In fact, it took all my control not to laugh. I could feel my body visibly shaking as I tried to hold it together. I knew that if I didn't let it out, and soon, I was probably going to pee my pants, so I burst out laughing.

Talgat spun to glare at me and saw me convulsing with laughter. I saw something flash on Talgat's face. At first, I thought it was anger, but the twinkle in his eyes and the ends of his lips curving into a wicked smile gave me a moment's notice before he launched himself at me.

"Shit!" I said, trying to put a table between Talgat and me. "Oh no, you don't," I squealed, pointing at the wiggling fingers on both of his hands.

Talgat dove to the right, trying to catch me off guard. But I saw the twitch in his muscles as he moved, so I spun to the left to keep him out of reach and the table between us.

"I'm sure there's a policy somewhere against tickling in the HR manual," I said. I shot him an innocent puppy-dog look before adding, "I'd hate to report you to HR."

"Wait! I think *I'm* HR on the farm," Talgat responded, as his smile grew and resembled the Cheshire Cat's.

"Get a room already," Rasul yelled at the two of us. "No offense, but I don't want to see the mating habits of my older brother."

"I'm not normally a voyeur," Jordan said, "but I would totally watch."

"Eww…" Rasul said, scrunching his face in disgust. "Bad mental picture, bad mental picture. I'm not going to be able to wash this out of my head." With that, Rasul turned and walked away, but not before he yelled back, "I'm so telling Ayala on both of you."

Jordan glanced between the two of us and motioned for us to continue. "Don't let me interrupt," he said, grinning broadly as he tilted his head to the side and leaned against the door frame. "This is the most action I've seen in ages—though I would recommend you two go on a date first."

The first thought that ran through my head was, *this is completely inappropriate*. The second thought I had was, *why the hell not?* I tried to gauge Talgat's facial expression to see what he was thinking, but his face was completely masked.

The silence permeated through the room. "Do I have to do everything for you two?" Jordan said. "Talgat, do you want to go on a date with Dale?" I watched as Talgat's eyes grew bug-eyed. I expected Talgat to run screaming from the room, but he surprised me and stayed in his spot. Jordan then swiveled his head to me, "Dale, do you want to go on a date with Talgat?"

"Ye…yes," I stammered out.

"Great! My job here is done." Jordan gave us a quick bow before adding, "Please hold your applause." He then spun around and left the lab, making sure he shut the door when he left.

I took in a deep breath and let it out before looking over at Talgat, who was eyeing me warily.

"You don't have to go out with me," I said, breaking the silence that followed. "I won't be offended."

"I'm not against going on a date with you," Talgat said slowly.

"Thanks for the vote of confidence," I said without meaning as much sarcasm as came out of my mouth.

"No," Talgat said. "I got that wrong. I don't want you to feel you were pressured into going on a date with me."

"If you know anything about me, it should be that I don't get pressured into doing anything I don't want to do."

"Really?" Talgat replied, his face scrunching. "Remind me how you ended up on a farm in the first place?"

"Okay," I said, putting my hands up again in mock surrender. "Let me rephrase. I don't get pressured into doing anything, except by my granddad. That man scares me. I love him, but he scares me."

"He scares me, too," Talgat admitted. "But wouldn't this be a conflict of interest? I won't lie. I like you, Dale, as a friend and a colleague. I don't want to fuck that up. The farm is my life. I won't do anything that puts this job in jeopardy."

I regarded Talgat for a moment before saying, "So, I may have checked into the policy on this subject."

"You did?" Talgat asked, a bit surprised by my admission.

"Yes, I admit I did. It was after you were at my house for dinner with your family. When you left, you put your hand on my chest and the tip of one of your fingers touched my skin. I practically melted." I couldn't believe I was letting the words roll out of my mouth. I then quickly added, "I'm sure you don't even remember doing it."

"I do," Talgat said, grinning. "I hadn't meant to do that. But once my hand was there, I left it there a few seconds longer than I should have. Nice pecs, by the way."

"Thank you," I said, doing my best not to grin. "So, what now?"

"Now, you properly ask me on a date, Mr. Dale Devereux."

"Talgat Kudaibergen, will you go to the school dance with me?" I joked.

"Only if it's a sock hop," he joked back.

"Perfect. Pick you up at seven?"

"Tonight?" Talgat asked quickly.

"No better time than the present," I said sheepishly. I was doing my best to act all in-control and macho about all this, but I was turning into a pile of mush standing before him.

Talgat took a deep breath in through his nose and exhaled through his mouth before saying, "Seven it—"

There was a pause, and I was afraid that Talgat was about to back out of it.

"Seven works for me," Talgat said. "But why don't I pick you up? That way we can avoid my siblings grilling you about your intentions toward me."

I barked out a short laugh and said, "Perfect. I will be ready to be picked up at seven."

* * * *

Talgat

After agreeing to go on a date with me, Dale turned

and left my lab. I turned back to my current experiment. I was getting closer and closer to the cherry flavor I wanted in the apple, but it was still tasting more like cherry cough syrup than cherry pie. I thought I needed to add more Fuji to the mix to up the sweetness level on the next go-around. I jotted a quick note in my research log before closing up shop for the night.

After locking the lab, I headed back to the administration building. I noticed Dale's SUV had already left the parking lot. I walked inside and was immediately accosted by Ayala and Rasul, who started peppering me with a million questions before I even closed the door.

"Slow down. I can only answer one question at a time," I said.

"Is it true?" Ayala asked, her arms crossed across her chest. I wasn't sure if the crossed arms were a good thing or a bad thing.

I played it coy. "Is *what* true?"

"Don't play games with me, big brother," Ayala said, narrowing her eyes at me. "Are you going on a date with Dale?"

"Define 'date'," I said, deciding to be a bit of a cantankerous wanker for the fun of it.

"You know what I mean," she huffed out.

"Yes. I agreed to go on a date with Dale."

"Did *you* agree, or did *he* agree?" Rasul asked. "From what Jordan told me, you two were too chickenshit to actually do it, so he had to intervene."

"That's not exactly what happened," I said.

"So, what happened?" Ayala questioned.

Knowing that postponing the story was only going to make things worse, I replayed the conversation after Rasul had left my lab.

"And why isn't he picking you up?" Ayala asked.

I debated what to say but went with "Because I didn't want the two of you grilling my date."

The looks of indignation that crossed Ayala's and Rasul's faces made me bust out laughing.

"We would never—" Ayala said.

"What kind of people do you think we are?" Rasul said, interrupting her.

"Two giant busybodies," I said. "Now, I have a date to get ready for, so let's get out of here."

* * * *

I stared in the mirror for what felt like the fortieth time. I've been on dates before, obviously. But there was something about going on a date with Dale that had me a bit more worked up than usual. Maybe it was because I didn't know what to expect. We hadn't discussed where we'd go or what we'd do. *Do I offer to pay?* I didn't want him to think that I was only using him for his money. *Maybe we should go Dutch? And what do the Dutch have to do with dating in the first place? And is the phrase 'going Dutch' somehow racist?*

"Pull it together," I said, finally turning away from the mirror. I opted for a pair of slim-fit jeans and a green button-down shirt. It wasn't exactly my fanciest outfit, but I figured it was at least more put together than I am when I was on the farm. *I'm such a hick.*

"You're going to be fine," I heard Ayala's voice from my doorway.

"Why am I so nervous?" I asked, pleading with her for some kind of explanation.

"Maybe it's because this is a real adult date and not one of those kids barely out of high school you've dated in the past." I began to object, but she waved me off before I could say anything. "Or maybe it's because you like Dale and are afraid you'll screw it up. Either way, he already likes you. Remember that. Don't be someone you're not."

I let out a quick breath through my nose and put on my glasses.

"You're not wearing your contacts?" Ayala asked.

"They were bothering me, so I figured I might as well go full-on nerd look tonight," I said, gesturing to my ensemble.

"At least you have the hot gay nerd vibe down," Ayala said with a wink. "You'll be fine. Try to loosen up and have fun."

"And don't give it up on your first date," Rasul yelled from somewhere down the hall.

"Eavesdropping much?" Ayala said, turning her head and yelling back.

"The walls in the place are paper thin. It's not my fault I can hear everything you two say," Rasul responded.

"Okay," I cut in before the two started a spat that I would have to referee. "If I don't leave now, I'm going to be late."

I reached out, hugged Ayala and whispered into her ear that I loved her. She whispered, "I love you, too."

"I can still hear you!" Rasul said.

"Well, I love you, too!" I yelled back.

"Gross! Keep that kind of talk for your boyfriend…Da-ale," Rasul said in a sing-songy voice as he drew out Dale's name.

I wanted to contradict Rasul about using the 'b' word, but I knew he was trying to get a rise out of me, so I didn't respond. It was one of the few times I purposefully tried to be an adult with Rasul.

I bounded down the stairs and left with one last goodbye before leaving the house. I hopped in the truck and pointed it in the direction of Dale's house. I mindlessly watched the familiar scenery pass by. Before I realized what happened, I was pulling up in front of Dale's house.

Dale was waiting on the front porch when I pulled up. He was wearing a pair of slim-fit blue jeans and a red button-down shirt that made his green eyes pop. I hadn't realized how tall he was before. I mean, I knew Dale was tall, but his slender, lanky self was at least six-foot-four, if not six-foot-five. *The next time he stands next to my brother, I'll see if they're the same height or which ones is taller. Dear God, sex with him would be like a Great Dane fucking a Chihuahua.*

I must have made some kind of face because Dale looked at me and said, "What?" after opening the door.

"Nothing," I said, trying to reassure him. "Just a random thought that ran through my head."

He gave me a sideways glance and shot me one of his winning smiles. "If you say so."

"We never discussed what we were going to do tonight," I said.

"Yeah, I realized that, too. I'm open to suggestions, but nothing that involves farms."

"Well, what type of food do you like?"

"I'm pretty open, but I have been craving seafood. Know anywhere?"

"Not locally, but there's a decent place down on the Rondout Creek in Kingston."

"Please tell me they don't actually get the fish out of the creek or the Hudson River."

"No worries," I said with a laugh. "They get it delivered daily from the fish market down in the city, like anyone else. I don't think anyone wants to eat a three-headed fish from the Hudson River."

"They don't have three heads, do they?" The quizzical expression on Dale's face made me laugh.

"I seriously doubt it, but it wouldn't surprise me, either. Don't get me wrong, the Hudson River is cleaner today than it ever was in the past—well, maybe not as clean as it was before Europeans settled and created New York City."

I pointed the truck toward Kingston. Twenty-five minutes later, I parked in the lot across from the fish restaurant. We walked in through the front doors, and since it was a weeknight, the place was busy but far from packed. We waited for only a couple of minutes before we were shown to our table. When I stepped to follow the hostess, I felt Dale's hand on the small of my back. It was a tiny gesture, but I practically swooned. Had it been so long since I'd had intimate contact with a guy that something as simple as a touch to my lower back was ready to make me rip off my clothes in public?

We were seated at a booth and both inspected our menus. Once we were alone, Dale peered over his menu at me and said, "I don't want this to be awkward, but I know it's going to be. So, I'm going to put this out there, and you're not going to talk for a second."

"Okay?" I questioned, a bit taken aback by the ominous statement.

"I'm paying for dinner. Don't try to stop me. I don't care."

"Okay," I said with no emotion. *Thank God that decision's over.*

"I hate talking about money."

"It's—"

"Let me get this out there," Dale interrupted. "I've always had money. I've come from money, and I realize that I have come from a world of privilege few know in our society. Hell, few people in the world come from the privileged background I have. And I know that it makes me completely out of touch with the 'real' world, because it's not the experience I've had."

"Uh-huh," I said, urging him to get it all out.

"I like you, and I think you know it. And I think you like me."

"I do," I admitted.

"I don't want money to become a thing, though I know it will. How can it not? It's just that I've dated guys before who only wanted me for my money and guys who felt they had to go above and beyond the call to duty to show me that my money doesn't matter. I want to be loved for me. Is that something so hard to ask for?"

I didn't know what to say to Dale. I sat there listening to him ramble on about his money issues and dating and did the only thing I could think of that would get him to shut up. I stood, reached across the table, grabbed the back of his head and pressed my lips against his. I felt the intake of his breath as I caught him by surprise. I was afraid he was going to resist and maybe even freak out since we were in public, but I felt the tension release out of him in that one moment. After a few seconds, I removed my hand from the back of his head and sat down.

Dale was speechless. It may have been the first time in his life when he was stunned into silence. It looked good on him. There was a hint of shock and desire that washed over him.

"What would you like to drink?" the server said, interrupting the silence at the table.

"Huh?" Dale mumbled.

I grinned and ordered a beer. "Whatever's on tap and a glass of water." I check on Dale, who hadn't gotten himself put back together. "He'll have vodka — whatever's on your top shelf."

The server wrote it down and said, "Be back in a minute to tell you about the specials and take your order."

When the server left the table, Dale studied me and finally uttered, "You kissed me?"

"Congratulations," I said. "I'm so happy you figured that out. Oh, and in case you're wondering, you kissed me back."

I kind of liked this flustered version of Dale. He was so used to having the upper hand in life. I enjoyed doing something that would both tantalize and shock him.

"Why?" Dale finally got out of his mouth. "Not that I minded," he added.

"Why? Because I thought it was the only way I could get you to stop talking…and it worked."

I reached out my hand and grabbed Dale's. I knew it was an intimate gesture, but I wanted to reassure him. "We both know you come from money, and we both know I come from a middle-income family who has worked very hard to get everything we have. The Kudaibergens are a true rags-to-riches American immigrant story. And I get you grew up in a world that is as unfamiliar to me as my world is to you. And I've watched as you made inroads into my world. And while your world scares me more than I'll admit, I'm willing to let you guide me into it. I want to know what it's like to be Dale — the good, the bad and the ugly."

"Where does this leave us?"

"Well, you're definitely paying for dinner," I said with a wink. "After that, we play it by ear. Let's have fun tonight. Let's just be Dale and Talgat, two grown-ass gay men who are on a date. Then we can figure the rest out tomorrow."

Before Dale could respond, the server was putting our drinks before us. "You ready to order?" the server asked then recited the night's specials.

"I think we still need a couple of minutes," I said.

"Sure thing, flag me down when you're ready." The server walked away, leaving Dale and me alone.

Dale lifted his vodka to his lips. "Hmm...not bad. What is it?"

"I don't know," I admitted. "I said for them to give you the top shelf."

Dale barked out a brief laugh. "See? You do already know me. The important things, at least."

"To us," I said, lifting my glass in Dale's direction.

"To us," he responded as we clinked our glasses.

* * * *

Dale

I was still reeling from the kiss by the time we finished dinner. I remembered shoveling food into my mouth, but I couldn't tell you what it was or what it tasted like. I could, however, still smell Talgat's cologne and relish the taste of his breath in my mouth. His lips had been so smooth against mine. If I hadn't been so shocked in that moment, I might have ripped his clothes off right there in the restaurant and had my way with him. By the time we left the restaurant it was a little after ten-thirty, so we headed back up the mountain to Woodstock.

We held hands the entire ride back up. If I thought he would have let me get away with it, I would have unbuckled my seatbelt and nestled in beside him, but I knew he would demand safety first. I guessed that meant road head was out of the question, too. In the dark, I rubbed my thumb across the back of Talgat's hand and wondered what it would be like to taste more of him...to taste all of him. I could feel my cock straining against my skinny jeans. *Thank God it's dark in here.*

I studied him and the sharp angle of his chin in the little moonlight that was coming through the driver's side window. He caught me looking, and with a quick sideways glance said, "What?"

"Nothing. I'm staring at your awesomely chiseled features. That Adam's apple looks like it could slice open a melon."

"What?" This time he said it while trying not to laugh.

"Okay, so that expression kind of sucked. I've always been horrible at flirting," I admitted. "I've spent more time bedding guys and getting their phone numbers."

"Oh, really?" Talgat said, a sense of mirth in his voice. "Well, Rasul told me not to put out on the first date."

I laughed at the thought of Rasul giving Talgat dating advice.

"I don't want to be crude or anything, but what do you like?" I asked.

"Wow, you put that right out there," Talgat replied.

"Not that I'm planning on seducing you — at least, not tonight," I said, adding as much of a sultry tone to my voice as possible, which ultimately caused Talgat to bust out laughing.

When he finally caught his breath, he said. "I guess we're both kind of bad at this. As for what I like, I like normal things."

"Define *normal*," I said. "There's a broad spectrum of normal in the gay community."

"Isn't that the truth," Talgat said with a grin I could barely make out. "As for normal to me, I guess I'm game for anything that's safe, sane, consensual and fun."

"That leaves things pretty open. Maybe I should ask what you don't like?"

"The usuals, I guess… Pain, marks, things that aren't sanitary. You?"

"I've explored my sexuality a bit. I always joke that you should try everything at least once — twice to make sure you didn't like it the first time. But I'm not a big fan of bodily fluids. Well, besides cum. I like cum a lot."

"You do, do you?"

Even though I couldn't see his face, I could make out the raised eyebrows in my mind's eye. "But I don't like it on me for very long, and I can't sleep in sheets that I've had sex on. I know that makes me weird, but I like to clean up afterward."

"I'll jot that down," Talgat said. "Always shower after sex with Dale. Okay, noted."

"Cheeky," I said. "Besides, what makes you think I'd shower with you?"

"I've seen that shower of yours. There's enough room for a small army. Plenty of room for the two of us," Talgat said as he squeezed my hand.

"So, are you more of a pitcher or a catcher?"

"Wow, that wasn't a smooth transition at all. I'm surprised you didn't say top or bottom —"

"I'm sorry. I shouldn't have —"

"Calm down, Dale, I'm fucking with ya. As to the question, I'm vers. You?"

"Likewise. I top more, but that's because there are so many bottoms in the city. I can't tell you the number of guys I've picked up who said they were tops, only to get them home, have them take one peek at my cock and hop on it like it's a pogo stick."

"Well then..." Talgat replied.

"Wow, that makes me sound like a slut. I mean, I went through my slut phase. Okay, I had a very long slut phase."

"We've all had them. Mine happened while I was in school. My best friend and I used to joke, *'a different night, a different hole'* as we'd pick someone up at the local gay bar."

We sat in silence for a few seconds. I stared at Talgat's profile. *Will I see all of him tonight?*

There was a sudden braking. The forward momentum pushed me roughly into the seatbelt straps before I was flung backward against the headrest, snapping me out of any revelry.

"What happened?" I gasped.

"Fucking deer!" Talgat said, gesturing out of the front window. Sure enough, a giant buck stood in the middle of the road. "Sorry about braking so fast. I crested the hill, and he was standing right there looking at me."

Talgat laid on the horn a few times before the deer finally turned and sauntered across the road. With the deer out of the way, Talgat started driving again.

"You okay?" he asked.

"More shook up than anything else."

"How's your neck? Think you have whiplash?"

"How would I know?" I asked.

"Wiggle your head and neck carefully. Any pain?"

I bent my head from side-to-side then front-to-back. Then I moved it in a circle. I didn't feel any pain anywhere. "Not that I can tell," I said.

"Then you're probably okay." We sat in silence for a few more minutes as we drove through the main street in Woodstock before taking the turn off toward my place. "And that, Dale, is why we wear our seatbelts," Talgat said.

I smiled in the dark but didn't respond. Admittedly, several snappy comebacks were floating around in my head. I had to acknowledge that if I had done what I'd wanted to do, I would probably be dead or seriously injured right now.

Talgat pulled up in front of my house, threw the truck into park and unbuckled his seat belt. I barely had mine off before his body was on top of mine, pressing into me. I felt the heaving of his chest against mine as he wove his hands behind my head and pressed our lips together. I send my hands exploring while we kissed. His back and the muscles strained against his shirt. I moved my hands down, touching his thighs before grabbing handfuls of his ass. A little moan escaped him as I grabbed him and pulled him into me. I could feel both of us growing beneath our jeans.

He drew back and ogled me before he unbuttoned my shirt, one seductive button at a time. With each new button free, he let his hand roam over what was visible. When my shirt was finally parted, he leaned down and teased my nipple with his tongue, causing me to gasp and have a minor convulsion that ran through my entire body.

He was about to unbutton my jeans, but I wasn't ready for him to go there yet. Instead, I reached down and pulled him up so I could plant my face against his. Our lips and tongues danced. After what seemed like a lifetime, he pulled away and rested his head between my nipples...his ear pressed against my skin.

"Whoa, your heart is racing," Talgat said, as one of his fingers slowly raked over my abs, causing me to shudder with each touch.

"Would you like to come inside?"

"Yes," Talgat responded immediately. "But I know I shouldn't. I don't want this to be another trick —"

"I don't think of you that way —"

"And I don't think of you that way. But after our conversation, we've both had our fair share of one-night stands. And I don't want you to be another notch on my belt."

"I get it."

"Really?"

I thought about it for a second before replying, "I get it. Am I horny and want to jump your bones for all their worth? Yes. If you don't believe me, feel my cock pressed against you."

In response, Talgat made a humping motion with his hips that almost had me coming in my jeans. I gasped, and he sat up.

"Besides, the best things come to those who wait," Talgat said.

"Blue balls come to those who wait," I responded. Thankfully, Talgat took the joke the way it was intended and laughed.

He reached over, patted my erect penis and said, "It's okay, little guy. We'll get you to come out and play soon."

"He ain't that little," I said, winking at him, then realized he probably couldn't see the wink in the darkened truck.

"I can tell," Talgat shot back. With a disgruntled sigh, he added, "I should get going. If I stay here too much longer, I won't make it home. And it's a work night, so we both have to be up early in the morning. And the last thing I want to do is give my siblings more ammunition."

I threw my head back and laughed. "I can only imagine."

"Oh, don't worry. I have no doubt that they'll be tormenting you before long, as well."

I leaned over and placed my hand against the side of his head and drew him in for one last kiss. This time, when he lifted his hand and placed it on my chest, he only touched skin.

When I pulled away, I opened the door, squinting quickly at the intrusive light. I said goodnight as I shut the truck door. I walked up the stairs and across the porch and unlocked the house.

"Alexa, turn on living room," I said. The lights in the house flared to life. I leaned against the door frame, my shirt untucked, open and blowing in the gentle breeze as I watched Talgat's rear lights fade in the distance. I couldn't see him, but I knew he was probably watching me in his rearview mirror.

Chapter Twelve

I lay in bed after my iPhone went off the next morning. I wasn't used to enjoying a date the way I had with Talgat. From the moment he had picked me up wearing that green button-down shirt till he had left me with my shirt dangling open in the night breeze, it had been magical. As I lay there, I got hard thinking about him straddling me. *Gotta love morning wood.* God, Talgat had been hot last night, the way he'd straddled me. He had been a combination of adorable, sexy, sensual and caring, all rolled up into one compact and gorgeous package. Part of me wished Talgat were in bed with me right now to take care of my growing problem, but another part of me was glad that we hadn't jumped into the sack after the first date. I've done that entirely too many times, so I know it's not necessarily the best way to start a relationship. I teased one of my nipples, remembering when Talgat's tongue and teeth had played with it the night before. Since I was alone in bed, I took matters into my own hand.

After a brief episode of flying solo, the orgasm I had was crazy intense. The first spurt caught me in the chin and the second hit the headboard behind me. I kept flying until everything was out before melting into the bed for a few seconds. As I came down from the brief high, my whole body shuddered. *Damn! If that's just my fantasies, imagine what the real thing will be like.* I grabbed the cloth I kept near my bed for these purposes and wiped myself and the spot on the headboard down. *Yeah, I'll need to clean that better later.*

Feeling invigorated for the day, I threw on my exercise clothes and headed down to my in-home gym.

* * * *

When I'd gotten to work, the place was still quiet, so I locked myself away in my office to get things done that morning. I knew it was going to be hard, if not impossible, to concentrate on the work I had to get done if I saw Talgat. I turned on my computer and waited for it to boot. I pulled out my iPhone and checked my messages. I had nothing that seemed too urgent until I saw an email from Granddad saying "CALL ME." *Great, this can't be good.*

I picked up the phone and dialed the office number. Even though I was his grandson, I still had to go through Molly — like everyone else did.

"Good morning, Devereux Farms. Jameson Devereux's office," Molly's chipper voice said.

"Good morning, Molly. Granddad asked me to call. Is he available?"

"Oh yes, he told me to patch you through as soon as you called. Give me one moment."

There was a brief pause as an audio recorded voice extolled the history of Devereux Farms. I'd heard this recorded message so many times I could say it by heart.

"Dale, you're getting to the office a bit late," Granddad said as he picked up the line.

"Actually," I said, "I'm early. We don't open the Administrative Office until nine a.m., and it's only eight-forty-five. Things are a bit different up here in Woodstock."

Granddad grumbled something unintelligible. In my mind, I filled in the words with "*kids these days have no work ethic*" or "*what am I going to do with him?*"

"So," I said, breaking the silence that followed, "what was so urgent?"

"How did you know it was urgent?" Granddad asked.

"You rarely send me emails with a subject line of 'call me' in all capital letters."

"Oh, I guess that makes sense," Granddad grumbled. "Well, I'm glad you thought it was urgent, because I'm afraid it is."

"Okay?" My computer finished booting, and I logged into my corporate email account, sensing Granddad was going to be sending me something—if he hadn't already.

"Well, Molly and I have been going through the financials of Devereux Farms after our last conversation." I didn't like the seriousness the tone of his voice took. "We know there is some kind of embezzling going on. We're still trying to figure out what is happening, but things don't look good."

"You don't think one of the Kudaibergens is involved. Do you?"

"Well…" Granddad's voice trailed off.

"That's ridiculous. There's no way. How could they do it with the current accounting structure?"

"We're still trying to figure that out," Granddad said flatly. "Now, pull yourself together, Dale. I understand you like the Kudaibergens, but you need be objective." I wanted to say something snippy, but I held it in and let Granddad continue uninterrupted...for now. "After going through piles of reports from the last decade, it appears the embezzling started about three years ago."

"When Ayala took over the accounting…"

"Sadly, that is what our analysis says."

"What are you going to do?" I asked.

"Well, embezzling is a serious crime," Granddad said. "I wouldn't be doing my job as CEO of Devereux Farms if I didn't report this to the FBI."

I ran my hand through my hair as my body went limp. In my heart of hearts, I couldn't imagine that Ayala was involved in a criminal conspiracy, but I had to be objective. As much as I liked the Kudaibergens, I hadn't known them that long. As much as this was going to hurt, I had to be unbiased and evaluate Granddad's evidence.

"Can you send me what you've put together?"

"Of course. I'll have Molly email it to you as soon as we get off the phone."

I thought about it for a few seconds. "Can you give me forty-eight hours before you call the FBI?"

There was a brief pause on the other end of the line. "Why?" was all he said.

"I want to dig into things from my end. If my findings support your embezzlement case, then I'll add more evidence for the FBI investigation."

"That makes sense to me. It's always important to get our ducks in a row. Due diligence and all."

"But, if what I find doesn't support your assumptions, will you be open to hearing my case?"

I heard Granddad let out a slow breath on the other end of the phone. "I'll be honest, I doubt it. Your evidence would have to be pretty solid for me not to report this to the FBI, but I'll give you until Monday morning. That leaves you a little over forty-eight hours and not a second longer."

"Thanks," I said. "If I have something sooner, I'll let you know."

"Be careful," Granddad said. "If you are dealing with a criminal conspiracy up there, they may not take too kindly if they catch you poking around into their affairs."

"Understood."

We then said our goodbyes. I sat in front of my computer waiting for the email from Molly. I had a ton of other things on my agenda today, but this had to take priority.

* * * *

Talgat

I had gotten home the previous night to find my brother and sister waiting for me. Thank God I had decided to not stay the night with Dale. I'm betting those two would have called the cops to hunt us down. I told them about the G-rated parts of the date before heading up to bed. I don't want to sound like a crazed teenager falling in love, but I dreamed about Dale. And let's say that my dreams included everything we hadn't done in the truck the last night. I was falling for him…hard.

By the time I got to work the next morning, Dale was already holed up in his office with the door shut. I could hear him talking, so I figured he was on the phone already. As much as it pained me to say it, he had been good for the farm. We were already doing a bang-up job with what we had, but Dale had taken the entire operation to a new level. I walked out to the lab to check in on my latest round of growth to see if any of them were faring better than the ones I'd seen the day before. I logged some notes, watered my babies and turned on the sun lamp in the grow shed, then headed back to the administration building.

I caught sight of Rasul, Jordan and a couple other farm hands out in the fields pruning the trees. People don't understand but getting apple trees to grow takes a lot more work than the public thinks. Plus, we have to spray all the time to make sure that the various insects, birds and other mammals don't run off with our crops.

I walked into the cool admin office, glad to be out of the heat of the September afternoon. I poked my head into Ayala's office, only to find that she wasn't there, so I headed upstairs to see if she was meeting with Dale. *God, I hope she can keep her mouth shut and not interrogate him about last night.* Ayala and Dale were in the conference room at opposite ends of the table. They hadn't bothered to shut the blinds, so it was obvious that neither of them were happy. I thought about heading to my office and staying out of it, but I'm a big brother and my protective instincts took over, so I poked my head in.

"How's everyone doing in here?" I asked.

"Fine," they both said in perfect unison. It didn't take a genius to know they were both lying through their teeth.

"What's wrong?" I asked.

"Dale here thinks I'm embezzling from the farm," Ayala stated matter-of-factly.

"That's not what I said," Dale countered. "I asked about several wire transfers that have been tied back to various accounts."

"Back up," I cut in. "Start at the beginning."

Dale took a long, slow breath in, so I pulled out a chair in the middle of the table and waited. I listened to Dale's story about his meeting with his granddad that morning and the allegations Ayala was facing.

"Here's what we know," Dale surmised. "Starting roughly three years ago, a bank account that was originally registered by Safiya Kudaibergen started sending small amounts of funds to a series of off-shore bank accounts."

"How is my mother involved?" I asked. "I'm not seeing the connection here. She was dead three years ago."

"Exactly. The question becomes, who had access to her account? And it seems like Ayala did, at one point."

"Who else had access to that account?" I asked.

"As far as we know, no one did or does. That account should have been shut down upon your mother's death, so we don't even know how that has slipped through the system. And to be perfectly honest, I'm not supposed to be telling you this."

"Why?"

"Because my granddad told me not to. He basically said, *'you haven't known them that long, so don't trust them,'*" Dale said in a voice mimicking the elder

Devereux. "I have less than forty-eight hours to figure this out before Granddad calls in the FBI."

"Holy shit." I heard leave my mouth as my brain tried to process what Dale had just told me.

"And right now," Dale continued, "the only suspect they have is Ayala. So, if I can't come up with a miracle, your sister is getting arrested and charged with embezzlement later this week." As if to emphasize his point, Dale threw the stack of papers he was holding down on the table, and they scattered halfway down the slick surface.

"How can we help?" I asked. "There has to be something we can do."

"We were discussing options before you got here," Ayala chimed in. "I know Dale won't believe me," she said, glaring daggers at my might-be boyfriend. "But you have to believe me Talgat, I would never…" Her voice trailed off. She put her head into her hands and cried.

I wanted to throw my arms around her and tell her it was going to be okay, but I honestly didn't know if that were true. Clearly, someone was setting Ayala up to take the fall, but who? I was stumped. And the longer I stood watching my baby sister cry, the rage inside me boiled. I sat there replaying the conversation and finally remembered something Ayala said.

"What do you mean, 'Dale won't believe you'?"

"It's not that I don't believe her. I want to believe her. God knows I want to believe her, but the evidence paints a radically different picture," Dale said, his eyes pleading with me to understand.

"No," I said, with no emotion. "Belief is trusting someone, having faith in someone. You want evidence. You want a logical explanation with a bow on top. And right now, we don't have one. How could we? We just found out about this ourselves. So no, you don't believe her. You don't believe in any of us. You never have. Neither has your granddad."

"Not fair," Dale said, his eyes narrowing as his leg bounced up and down on the ball of his left foot.

"Whatever," I said flippantly. "You and *your* kind have always seen us as gutter trash immigrants from Kazakhstan. Of course, it's one of us who is embezzling, because it's always the dirty immigrants."

"I never said that," Dale said, his own voice rising.

"Really? You people immediately assume that we're all about money because we don't come from it ourselves. Well guess what, pretty boy? We care about things beyond money. Frankly, it's *your* kind who only thinks about money and power and not people."

"And what about your kind?" Dale snapped. "You always look down your nose at those of us who have money. You covet our money. You wish you were one of us."

"Really? And which one of us was the one to bring up money almost immediately into our first date," I spat back at him.

"Get the fuck out," Dale said. His face turning a color of red I don't think I've seen on someone before. "Get the fuck *out!*" Dale yelled as he swiped the papers in front of him in every direction. "You and your entire family are not welcome here anymore. You're all fired."

I looked at Ayala, and the look of pure horror that swept over her face as she said, "You can't do that."

"As your brother so nicely pointed out, my kind only thinks about money and power. I have both. I want you off my property...*now.*"

I could tell that Ayala wanted to balk and argue, but I knew in that instant, Dale was a lost cause. I stood up and walked over to Ayala and helped her stand. She could barely hold herself up, but I helped her toward the conference room door. Dale spun around in his chair to put his back to us as we left.

"You can all leave your keys on the front desk. Please take any personal items with you today." Dale's voice was barely a whisper as he added, "I never want to see you again."

Once Ayala was out of the room, I had to leave him with one last piece of my mind.

"Last night you said you wanted someone to love you for you. Well, if this is the real you, it's no surprise you've never found someone to love you. Because this person, this 'whatever it is that you are', is not able to love or be loved." I heard Dale huff as I turned to leave the room. I placed my hand on the doorknob as I stepped through. Without looking back, I added, "I hope you learn money isn't everything, Dale, because it's not. Family, friends…boyfriends, those can't be bought…not really." I didn't wait to hear if he had a retort. I shut the door.

Chapter Thirteen

Dale

I walked over to the window that overlooked the small parking area and watched as the Kudaibergen siblings left my farm. I could hear Rasul the moment Talgat went to him and told him what had happened. He was the only one who stared up at me as he flipped me off. I had no doubt that he would be kicking the shit out of me right now if it wasn't for his brother.

I watched as the truck pulled away and headed down the drive to the farm entrance. I was still standing at the window ten minutes later when there was a knock on the glass door to the office. I spun my head quickly to see who it was and found Jordan standing outside. I motioned for him to come in as I got down and started picking up the mess I'd made during my little tantrum.

"Mr. Devereux?" Jordan said hesitantly.

"Please, call me Dale."

"Okay, Dale," Jordan replied, clearly still not sure of himself. "Do you have a moment?"

"Sure," I said, before gesturing to one of the chairs. "Take a seat."

Jordan regarded me, staring me up and down. It was almost like he was trying to peer into me. Something about his dark brooding eyes made me feel laid bare.

I laid out a sigh and asked, "What can I do for you?"

"First, tell me to butt out if it's none of my business," Jordan hesitated, "but what the fuck just happened?"

"You're right. It's none of your business," I said. Jordan started to rise, but I motioned for him to sit back down. "But it's going to come out eventually, so I might as well tell you directly." I steepled my hands under my chin and tried to figure out what to tell him exactly. "Simply put, someone has been embezzling funds from the farm. All the evidence points to Ayala Kudaibergen. As you can imagine, none of them took the accusation very well. And they're not going to take it well when the FBI comes to arrest her in a few days."

"Whoa," Jordan said. The way Jordan slumped into the chair made it look like he'd been hit by a two-by-four. "You're sure?"

"I wish I wasn't, but all the evidence points in her direction. And neither Talgat nor I took that well. We had a bit of a blowup, which is why they're no longer here and no longer allowed on farm property. My granddad gave me forty-eight hours to show it couldn't have been Ayala, but everything I found points to her. I'm going to have Granddad call the FBI and let the investigators figure this mess out. If she's innocent, they'll prove it. I'm not a forensic accountant."

"For what it's worth, I don't believe she did it." I began to object, but Jordan waved me off. "I know, I know. You're looking at the facts. You're looking at the evidence, the paper trail. I'm staring at the people. The Kudaibergens are some of the most honorable people I know. And their mother and father were more honorable than them. They've busted their asses for everything they've ever earned, and they've done this proudly. Sure, they can be one stubborn-ass bunch, but they wouldn't steal from you, from this farm. This farm gave them life here in America. That may not mean much to the likes of you and me who were born and raised here, but they're not like us."

I sat there, staring off into space. I guess Jordan felt he'd said his piece, because he got up and left. I sat there for what seemed like forever. Before I knew it, the sun had set, and I was left sitting in the dark. Only when I realized I was utterly alone did I let the emotion of the entire afternoon hit me. The tears flowed. I felt their wet presence, first on my cheeks then on my shirt. For the first time since my own parents' funeral, I sobbed uncontrollably.

When I finally stopped, an idea rushed into my head as if it were given to me by the gods on high. I mentioned in my yelling match with Talgat that I wasn't a forensic accountant, but I had one on speed dial. I picked up my phone and called Grayson.

"Grayson Jackson," a rushed voice said on the other end of the line.

"Gray, it's Dale. Do you have a moment?"

"Not really. Can you make it quick?"

"Probably not."

"Dammit. I'm already running behind to a date. Let me text her and let her know I'm going to be late. I'll call you right back."

Before I could say okay, Grayson hung up the phone. I decided it was time to stand and at least head back into my office. My eyes had adjusted to the dark long ago, so I didn't need to turn any light on until I was in the office.

I flipped on the lights in my office as the phone chirped.

"It's me," I said into the phone.

"Okay, I only have a few minutes. What's the situation?"

I swiftly outlined everything that happened that afternoon. Grayson had me pause and asked for clarifications a few times while I was telling the story.

"Do you think she did it?" Grayson asked me bluntly.

"No. I don't think she did. And I was an ass for questioning that for a second."

"Okay, so see this from a fresh vantage point. You spent the entire day evaluating evidence that she committed the crime. Flip it. Find evidence that she couldn't have committed the crime. One thing I've seen with a lot of these cases is that when people are set up to take the fall, there is some piece of evidence that simply stands out as impossible. You need to find that one thread. Once you have that thread, pull on it and keep pulling until you see what happens."

"Got it," I said. "Find the thread and yank that motherfucker."

"Not quite what I said, but you get the point," Grayson said. I could hear him laughing over the sounds of horns and traffic in the background. I hated admitting it, but all that traffic just sounded noisy after living up here for a few months. "I'll call you after my date. Okay?"

"Sounds good to me."

I hung up the phone and gathered all the files I had. I grabbed a couple of boxes and every financial file I could find in the administrative building. It was time to eat some crow.

I found the Kudaibergens' address and headed over there. If I was going to piece this together, I needed their help. There was no way around it. Sure, I'm certain it was the last thing my lawyers would tell me to do, but I didn't care. My granddad didn't know these people like I did. Sure, I may not have known them that long, but I had no doubts that Ayala was innocent. More than that, I should never have had any doubts.

On the way over, I grabbed four large pizzas and three two-liter bottles of sodas. I figured I needed to at least show up with a peace offering.

I parked my car on the street and walked up the sidewalk to their front porch. Their house was in the middle of a residential area, so they had neighbors close by. *Hey, at least this way it will be harder for Rasul to hide my body.* Juggling the pizzas and sodas, I pushed the doorbell next to the front door.

I waited for a few seconds, then heard shuffling behind the front door.

"Who is it?" Talgat yelled through the peephole.

"Pizza delivery," I said, blocking my face with the four boxes.

"We didn't order pizza."

"Talgat, it's me, Dale. Open up."

"Fuck off," he replied.

"Talgat?" I said in response. "Talgat? We need to talk."

"Why would I want to talk to you?"

"Because if we don't talk, how are we going to prove your sister's innocence?"

I heard the locking mechanism slide open as he cracked the door. He blocked the view into the house with his body.

"What made you change your mind?" Talgat questioned skeptically.

"I had time to think. Plus, Jordan came by and made me realize what a royal ass I'd been."

"See? I told you he'd come around," I heard Jordan's voice hail from inside the Kudaibergen house.

"Jordan's here?"

"Yep, he dropped by to see how we were doing and to tell us about your conversation."

"Can you let me in? These pizzas won't eat themselves. If after I've said my piece, you want me to leave, I'll go."

Talgat said nothing, but he opened the door and pointed the way to the living room. I took in the living room. There were a couple of couches and a couple of recliners. A coffee table sat in the middle. A giant bookcase expanded the width of one wall. There was some original artwork on the other walls. I let my head swivel as I took it all in, and I placed the pizzas on the coffee table.

"Who was it?" I heard Rasul yell from upstairs.

"Dale Devereux," Talgat replied.

The way he said my full name made me cringe. The sound of feet flying down the stairs drew my attention in time to see Rasul fly into the living room and come at me with full force. Thankfully, Talgat grabbed his brother around the waist before Rasul got to me.

"You fucking little prick motherfucker!" Rasul yelled in my direction. "I'm going to kill you. How dare you come here after what you did to my family?"

I held my hands up in surrender and said, "You're right. I was an absolute jerk today, and you have every right to hate me right now. And if it will make you feel better, I'll gladly let you beat the crap out of me. But first, we need to prove your sister was framed."

Maybe it was my words or the determination on my face, but something I said seemed to take some of the wind out of Rasul's sails. He turned and said, "Talk."

I quickly outlined the conversation I'd had with Grayson.

"So, you believe me now?" Ayala said, coming into the living room. Her face was red and puffy, and I could tell she'd been crying, which caused my heart to break a little. Even worse, she was crying because of me.

"I believe you. I should have always believed you," I said. "Now, we need to figure out how to get other people to believe you, too."

"What do we need to do?" Talgat asked.

"We need to find the thread."

* * * *

Talgat

I hated admitting that I was leery of Dale after our blowup that afternoon, but there were some things said that couldn't be unsaid. Even if he was going to help us prove Ayala's innocence, I wasn't sure what to make of him at this point. I decided a direct approach was going to be best. When he asked if someone would help him cart in boxes from his SUV, I volunteered.

The night was already dark, and the streetlamps added a hazy glow. There was a hint of crispness in the air and the upcoming fall that we were on cusp of. I spotted Dale's SUV pretty easily because it's a large vehicle and kind of hard to miss. I swear he asked the dealer for the biggest one on the lot that wasn't a minivan.

"I'm sorry," he said as we were walking down the street. "I blew up at you today. I said some things…"

I didn't know what he wanted from me. And I was still trying to figure out what I thought.

When I didn't respond, Dale continued. "You're wrong, though—"

"How so?" I said with a bit more bite than I'd intended.

"You said that I didn't believe in any of you, and that's not true. I believe in your entire family. I believe in you. I have since I got up here and realized you three were the heart and soul of the farm."

I had pulled a little ahead of Dale on the sidewalk. He could have kept pace with me if he'd wanted to with those lanky, long legs of his. Instead, he reached out, grabbed me and spun me around. Part of me flinched and my fists clenched involuntarily. Dale clearly saw the tension in my body and jerked his hand away from me like he'd been scalded.

"And what I said about you wanting my money. That was a low blow. I know it was. In that moment I dug for the one thing I thought would hurt you, and it clearly did. I was such a complete ass."

This time I found my hand reaching out to grab his. I hadn't intended to offer him solace in that moment.

Hell, I wasn't even sure what I thought of him yet. But whether I wanted to or not, I still had feelings for Dale.

"You hurt me today," I said. "You hurt my family. And while I can tell you're trying to make that right, I can't pretend it didn't happen."

"I'm not asking you to." Dale absently rubbed his thumb over the back of my hand.

Let go of his hand, a voice inside my head said, but I couldn't do it. I wanted to feel his touch. I wanted him to reassure me it was going to be okay — that Ayala was going to be okay, that *we* would be okay.

"I shouldn't have said what I said to you, either. I got protective of Ayala, and I took some potshots at you I knew would hurt. I'm…I'm sorry, too."

"But you weren't completely wrong," Dale admitted. "I've grown up in a world where anytime there's a problem, we throw money at it. If that doesn't fix it, throw more money. And for most of my life, money has been the center of my relationships. I hate admitting it, but my family's wealth opened doors to personal and professional circles. I sat in the office after you left, trying to argue against what you said, but I couldn't."

"Dale—"

"No, you were right. I don't even know how to have relationships that aren't centered on money."

"What about Grayson?" I interjected.

"We're friends because our families were rich enough to send us to a prep school. And we stayed friends because our lives intersected in the same social circles. The difference between Grayson and me is that Grayson always wanted to be more than his family's money. He could have been a high-powered, ridiculously rich partner at a law firm, but he opted to work for the district attorney's office."

"And you went and worked on Wall Street," I concluded for him. Dale let out a sigh. I could see his breath in the cool air. In the dim light, I could make out a single tear falling. I reached up with my hand and wiped it away. "You are more than your money. And you have so much more to offer the world."

Dale drew me into him and wrapped his arms around me. I laid my head on his chest and could hear the pounding of his heart. I wrapped my arms around him and pulled him close to me for all it was worth. I willed myself not to cry. I didn't have time for crying.

I broke the hug and gazed into Dale's face. "We've got to save her. I don't know what I would do if I lost her."

"We will. And we'll make whoever did this to her pay dearly."

The determination in Dale's eyes gave me a sense of comfort I hadn't had since the blowup that afternoon.

"Okay, enough of this," I said. "We've got work to do."

I heard the telltale beeping sound of Dale's SUV doors opening as he pushed the button on the fob. I took in all the boxes Dale had in the SUV.

"Oh geez, this is going to take us a few trips."

Chapter Fourteen

Dale

After Talgat and I had unloaded all the boxes into the house, we had divvied them up. Each of us had taken a specific pile. I had given Ayala the information my granddad sent me. If anyone could find the needle in the haystack there, it was her. I had given Talgat the personnel files to go through. I'm sure I was breaking some employment law by giving Talgat those files, but I figured I'd deal with that problem later. I took the company's information files. Jordan had opted to help Ayala, and Rasul had volunteered to make coffee and get anything we needed. I knew diving into the files was going to be a bit much for Rasul's ADHD, so I had been glad to see that he was chipping in where he could.

I sat down on the floor and started going to town on the box. Without realizing it, Talgat positioned himself behind me and our backs were touching. Even in this endeavor, it was like we were propping each other up, giving each other emotional and physical support.

At some point, Talgat went upstairs and came back down wearing his glasses. When I looked at him, he said, "My eyes were growing tired of the contacts."

"No worries," I said. "I think you're sexy in glasses."

In the corner, I heard Rasul make a barfing noise.

I watched as Talgat shot Rasul a looking, saying, "*Bokshil!*"

"*Zhopoyeb!*"

"Only if he's lucky," Talgat said, motioning in my direction. I wasn't sure what was said, but the abject horror that crossed Rasul's face made me wonder what had just happened.

Ayala, who had been watching the exchange, giggled and said, "*Dolbaebs*, thick-headed fools," before turning back to her stack.

"Do I want to know what just happened?" I asked Talgat as he sat back down.

He smiled at me for a second, then grabbed the back of my head and drew me in for a quick kiss.

"Get back to work," Talgat said with a wink before turning around to his own stack.

We spent the next few hours going over and over the information in the boxes. I surveyed the room and saw everyone was yawning. Rasul had passed out in the corner. His gentle snoring was almost peaceful.

Periodically, one of us would ask a question or try to clarify information from someone else in the group. But it felt like we were spinning our wheels. A little after midnight, Talgat asked his sister, "When did you finish your degree?"

"Three years ago. Why?" Ayala responded.

"And you graduated in May, right?"

"Yep. Then started working in June." Suddenly, excitement crossed her face as she said, "Holy shit."

I peered over to see a flurry of work as she started digging through the papers sitting in front of her.

"We found the thread," Ayala said, looking like she was about to burst into tears.

"What?" I questioned. "I'm missing something."

She walked over to us with a stack of papers. Jordan followed and stood hovering behind the three of us as she laid it out.

"Notice the date of the first transfer. It was shortly after my mother's death but before I graduated from college."

"Okay," Jordan said behind me. "And what does that get us?"

"How could I have made the transfer if I wasn't employed by the farm? I didn't have access to anything at that point."

I thought about it for a moment. "Now, I don't want to be an ass," I said, which garnered me a glare from Talgat, "but won't they argue that you had access to your mother's information?"

"No. Company policy is that an individual's access is immediately shut down to the bank accounts upon their death. I wouldn't have been able to log into the bank with her information, even if I had tried."

I thought about it for a moment. "Let me call Grayson," I said. I pulled out my phone and searched for his name and hit call.

"Dale, it's late," Grayson said, answering the phone. "This better be good."

I quickly broke down what we'd found. When I finished laying out the evidence, there was a pause on the other end of the line.

"I think you found your thread," Grayson said. "Now, we need to pull on it. To do that, we'll need access to Devereux Farms' accounts. What's the likelihood that we can get access?"

"I can get us access," I said reassuringly. "Meet me at the office around eleven tomorrow?"

"I can be there," Grayson responded. "Let's see where this leads us."

As soon as I hung up the phone, everyone looked at me expectantly. "Grayson thinks we've found the thread. I need to get down to the city. I'm going to meet him at the corporate headquarters at eleven a.m. I don't know how I'm going to get access to the files, but I'm going to do it."

"Give me a minute to throw some things in a bag," Talgat said. "I'm going with you."

"Me, too," Ayala chimed in.

I thought about it for a second before saying, "Ayala, I actually need you here. In case we need information from this end, I need your help to find it and get it to us. You can always Zoom with us. Is that okay?"

I could tell she wanted to balk, but she realized it made sense. I stretched out my leg and dug into my pocket, pulling out three sets of keys.

"I believe these belong to you." I handed Ayala and Talgat their keys back. Somehow Rasul had slept through all this, so I gave Ayala his.

"I'll get them to him when he wakes up."

I turned to Talgat. "Go. Pack. As it is, we won't get to the city until three a.m."

* * * *

Talgat

Dale had agreed to let me drive the first half of the trip down into the city. Thankfully, in the middle of the night, there hadn't been much traffic as we traveled down I-87. We had watched the night sky fly by us. By the time we had gotten out of Woodstock, it was almost one-thirty, which should put us at Dale's place in a little over a couple of hours. He'd offered to put me up in a hotel room, but I told him I could sleep on the couch. Honestly, I've slept in worse places. When I'd been younger, dad would 'let' us sleep over in the barn on the farm.

"Trust me, if I could survive making a bed from straw, I think I can handle a night on a fancy couch."

"Who said it's fancy?" Dale asked.

"Umm." I looked him up and down. "I know who I'm talking to," I said, with a slight roll of my eyes. Not a full-on eye roll, but a good three-fourths of one for added emphasis.

We had crossed into New Jersey, and I knew I was going to need to let Dale take over driving. I had peeked at the passenger seat, but he had been dead to the world. Surprisingly, the coffee that we'd gotten at QuickChek had been enough of a pick me up. I didn't feel too tired yet. Admittedly, after getting fired yesterday, well today… *Dear God, how long has it been since all that craziness went down?* I steered the car onto New Jersey Highway 17 toward Ft. Lee, New Jersey, a town made famous by Bridge Gate, a recent political scandal.

As with most political drama, it showed that the rich and powerful knew how to play the system and were usually the ones who can't be taken down. Where I had been born in Kazakhstan, most people are Sunni Muslims of the Hanafi school. When we had immigrated to the US, my parents had taken a decidedly non-religious approach to life. We had been encouraged to explore all religions and religious traditions as kids. All three of us kids had ended up decidedly non-religious.

So, there I was in this thing called Sunday School, which confused me. Why would anyone invite a peer to go to a special school on Sunday was beyond me, but my friend told me it would be fun. And the Sunday I had agreed to go, I learned the Jewish story of David and Goliath. I had liked the idea. A simple small man, probably a teenager at that time, had taken on some fantasy action-figure giant and downed his ass with a single rock and a slingshot. I love a good fantasy novel as much as the next person, but this was some Tolkienesque shit going on.

Sadly, I'd learned over the years that David rarely takes on Goliath in the real world. And when the opportunity for David to take on Goliath arises, rarely does David succeed. Our modern world is designed to stamp out David and ensure that Goliath gets larger and more powerful. As I crossed over the George Washington Bridge, I wondered to myself if Ayala was David and our legal system was Goliath in my metaphor. Hell, maybe I was David and the Devereuxs were Goliath. Only time would tell, I guessed.

There was a stirring next to me in the SUV as I turned south onto Harlem River Drive.

"Where are we?" Dale asked, rubbing his eyes as he did a quick stretch in the seat.

"Harlem, I think."

"You were supposed to let me drive half the way," Dale complained.

"I know. I wasn't tired, and you were all cute sitting over of there in your chair, completely oblivious to the world passing you by."

"How much longer?"

"GPS says thirty minutes till we get to your building."

"Are you sure you don't want me to take over?" Dale asked.

"Nah. We're this close. Let's get there, park and get to bed."

Dale reached out, put his hand on the back of my neck and rubbed it for a second. It felt good. "If you keep that up, I'm going to fall to sleep."

"I'm sure there's something else I could rub that would help wake you up." I didn't need to look over at him to know he had a mischievous grin on his face.

"Need I remind you," I said, "that distracting the driver from what's going on while driving is never a good idea?"

"You're no fun."

"Not while driving, I'm not. When I'm not driving, you do not know how much fun I can be."

There was a brief pause on Dale's part, so I wasn't sure if he was mulling over my flirtatious behavior or coming up with a good comeback. Instead, he said, "I look forward to finding out."

So did I.

Before we knew it, we were pulling up in front of Dale's building.

"Where do we park?" I asked.

"There's a parking garage. The entrance is around the corner. And I know it says it doesn't open until six a.m., but residents have twenty-four-hour access with a keycard." I watched while Dale stretched his legs out against his seatbelt as he stuck his hand into his pocket. He removed his billfold and a keycard. When I got to the parking garage, he handed me the card, the barrier lifted and he helped me navigate the parking structure.

"I believe my parking space is four-hundred-one, from what I remember."

"Wait a second," I said, realizing something. "You had a parking space, but you didn't have a car?"

"When I got the apartment, I thought about getting a car. And you may not realize it, but parking spaces are at a premium in this city, so it was much easier to get the parking space at the same time I signed my lease. If I had waited and gotten the car then tried to get a parking space, I might have run into a problem." He shot me a side look and could probably tell from my scrunched-up face that I was trying to make sense of what the hell he'd said. "Basically, it's easier to get the parking space when you can than need it and not have it."

"I don't think I will ever get city life," I admitted.

We drove the through the garage, finally found Dale's parking space, and I parked the vehicle. He placed his garage ID card on the dashboard so the parking people wouldn't have the vehicle towed. I got out and stretched as soon as my feet hit the concrete. I then opened the back door, grabbed my duffel bag and walked around to the back of the SUV, where I handed Dale his keys back and followed him to the elevator bay in the garage.

The elevators took us to the lobby of the building. I was taken aback when the elevator opened up from the bowels of the garage into the marble foyer of his building. I took in the high-vaulted ceilings with glass chandeliers overhead.

"Mr. Devereux," a voice off to the left said, "it has been a while."

I watched as Dale turned his head to see who said his name. "Oh, hey, Charlie. Been living up in Woodstock for a few months. Sadly, I'm down for a couple of days. Everything around here been good?"

"Same old, same old," the security guard said. "Have a good night."

Dale crossed the lobby and punched a different elevator button. Thankfully, there was an elevator already on the ground floor, so the doors immediately slid open, and we got in. I didn't pay attention to what button Dale had pushed, as my exhaustion settled in. Instead, I leaned against the side wall, forcing my eyes to stay open.

"You okay?" Dale asked.

"Just exhausted. I can't wait to hit the hay."

"Well, you'll be glad to know that there is no hay whatsoever in my apartment," he replied with a quirk of lips.

"I am way too tired to respond to jokes right now," I said as I shot him my own grin.

The elevator dinged as the doors opened, and he led me down to the hall to his apartment. He pulled out a different keycard, which led us into the apartment itself. He held the door open for me and said, "Make yourself at home."

I walked in and took in everything. Basically, it was very Dale. It was clean, sleek and modern. He told me to put my bag on the island in the kitchen, then gave me the quick tour. The place wasn't very big. Heck, the first floor of my house was probably twice the size of the entire apartment. But, I guess, by city standards, this place was nice and spacious. It had a second room and everything. Of course, they call it a second room, but you could only put a twin bed in there. Anything larger and you couldn't walk around the area.

Dale's bedroom, on the other hand, was decently spacious and had enough room for a king-size bed. I put my hand on the bed and pushed it up and down a couple of times to see how much give the bed had.

"It's one of those beds that conforms to your body. I saw the commercial on TV where someone was jumping up and down on the bed without knocking over a glass of wine. That sold me," Dale admitted. "I kind of went through an infomercial junky phase. I wasn't sleeping very well, so I spent way too much time watching late-night infomercials and buying a ton of crap I didn't need."

"I think we've all been suckered in by a good infomercial," I said. "If you don't mind, I want to brush my teeth and go to bed." I then shot narrowed my eyes at Dale before adding, "One of us didn't get a nap on the way down here."

He scrunched his face and tried to shoot me a mean look, but then smiled instead. "You know," Dale said, "this bed is large. You don't have to sleep on the couch."

"Are you sure? I don't want to encroach on your space. And, I am looking to sleep right now, so I don't want to give you the wrong idea. Not that I wouldn't mind fooling around with you over and over again, but not right now. I'm way too tired to be at the top of my game, and we still have what will probably be a long day ahead of us."

"Got it, no hanky-panky tonight…just sleep," Dale said. "And you're right. Today is going to be long. And we're probably only going to get five hours of sleep, so we should hop into bed and crash."

"Sounds like a plan."

I walked back out into the kitchen and grabbed my duffel. I then brushed my teeth and headed into the bedroom to find Dale already in bed.

"I hope you're okay with me sleeping naked?" Dale asked, an innocent look flashing on his face. Apparently, the surprise must have flashed on my face, because it made Dale laugh. "I'm messing with you. I sleep in my boxers."

I let out a short-whistled breath before saying, "Me, too." I quickly stripped down and climbed into bed with Dale. "We may not get to hanky-panky tonight, but I'm totally calling little spoon."

"Alexa, turn off bedroom lights," Dale said. The lights went off, and I felt him squeeze in behind me and wrap his arm around my mid-section.

I don't know how long I lasted before sleep took me, but I remember the light kiss on the back of my neck as Dale said, "Good night."

Chapter Fifteen

Dale

Gloria Gaynor's *I Will Survive* invaded the dream I was having, but my body quickly transitioned to the real world, and I reached for my iPhone, only to find Talgat lying in front of me waking up himself.

"Wow," Talgat said. "I think that's the gayest thing I've ever woken to."

"Hey," I said, with a gentle poke to his side. "At least it's classically gay and not *Bad Romance*. Besides, is that the gayest thing you've ever woken up to?" I said, as I prodded my morning wood against him.

"What is that? Did you bring a pencil to bed with you?" Talgat joked as he ground backward. "I take it someone's happy to see me this morning?"

I lowered my arm that was resting on Talgat's midriff, finding my own erect joystick to play with. "I'm not the only one who's happy this morning."

Talgat rolled over to his back, and I could see the full extent of his erection under the covers. Mine was now draped over his right leg. I twitched it to say hello and grazed it off Talgat's own cock.

"God! This is killing me," I spat out between my gritted teeth. "I would like nothing more than to ravage your entire body, but we don't have time."

"Quicky?" Talgat said, with a mischievous smile crossing his lips. "Besides, I don't think this is going away on its own."

I wanted to call attention to the fact that it was Talgat's sister's freedom that was in jeopardy, but he was definitely in a frisky mood. And I didn't want to be a rude host. I pulled the covers back from both of us and saw that both of our cocks had escaped our boxers. Talgat's was about seven inches and thick. We're talking can of soda thick. Mine was a little over eight inches but was only about as thick as a remote control. I sat there looking at his hard cock standing up between his boxers, and I couldn't help myself. I let my tongue lance out at Talgat's right nipple, then licked him all the way down to the top of his hipbone and traced my tongue down the inguinal crease leading right to his shaft. I gazed up and saw Talgat staring down at me. He reached behind him and added another pillow behind his head to make it easier to see what I was doing.

I started by running my tongue around the base before slowly licking from the base to the top of his uncut cock. Talgat shuddered slightly and thrust upward with his hips. I wasn't ready to take him completely inside me yet. Instead, I took my tongue and let it explore inside Talgat's foreskin. I wormed my tongue in between the skin and the head and circled around, fully exploring him. The taste of human skin mixed with salty pre-cum filled my mouth as Talgat squirmed beneath me.

After he couldn't take any more of my teasing, I opened my mouth and sucked him to the base. Thankfully, I have a big mouth, and it was coming in handy as I deepthroated his cock and started building up a steady rhythm. He reached to either side of my shoulder before grabbing the hair on the back of my head. He pumped my throat faster and faster. I was timing my breathing to make sure I could keep going without choking or passing out from oxygen deprivation.

"I'm gonna come," he blurted. He began to pull out of my mouth, but I wouldn't have any of that, so I bobbed up and down faster and faster until the warm rush filled my mouth, and I swallowed as more erupted into me. I gulped in satisfaction. When he finally let out a labored breath and I felt his muscles relax under me, I let myself surface for air.

As I pulled off him, I saw a smile on his face.

"Damn, you're fucking good at that," he said between breaths.

I pulled myself up the length of his body and lay next to him. I was still flying at full mast, and he peered at me hungrily and said, "Let me take care of that."

"No time," I said. "I take forever to come when someone else tries to get me off. For now, I'm going to quickly jack off, but you can help."

"Tell me what to do."

"Kiss me."

Talgat rolled over and pressed his lips to mine as I grabbed my throbbing cock in my hand and worked my fingers rapidly against the frenulum. My whole shaft is sensitive, but the fast way to make myself cum was pressure and vibration to the underside of my cockhead.

Our lips moved together in synchrony as he darted his tongue inside my mouth or mine inside his. As I got closer, I needed Talgat's lips more intensely. I bit the underside of his lip slightly as I ejaculated between us, my cum coating both of our flat stomachs as I kept going to make sure I got every last drop.

When I had the last of my cum spurt out of me, I flopped onto my back and let out a fast breath. "God, I needed that." I glanced at the clock and realized we only had an hour to get up and get to the office.

"Damn," I said, finally turning my head to look at Talgat, who was now propped up on one of his arms, staring at me.

"What?" he said, looking from my chest down to my now-flaccid cock.

"We're going to have to shower together to save time. We've got to get moving." I sat up to get off the bed.

"Well, it's always better to shower together, anyway," Talgat responded. "You know, conserve water. It's good for the environment."

Talgat

Dale walked around the end of the bed and headed out of his bedroom. I stared at his ass, wishing I'd tasted it this morning. Don't get me wrong, unexpected morning head is fucking amazing, but I wanted to pound Dale's ass so hard it was driving me crazy. Looking at his ass as he walked away brought new life into my cock.

"Are you coming?" Dale said, turning in my direction. He caught site of my growing appendage and added, "Someone's ready for round two." He turned away from me and headed out the door, adding, "I have a bottle of lube in the shower – if you're interested." He slapped his left ass cheek for emphasis.

I didn't need to be asked twice. I was out of that bed so fast. By the time I got into the bathroom, Dale had already turned on the shower. He had one of those fountain showers that flowed from overhead, with additional shower heads shooting water at you from three different sides. Once the temperature was to his liking, Dale stepped in, grabbed my hand and dragged me into the shower with him. We stood in the middle kissing and running our hands all over each other's bodies. Dale's muscles felt amazing beneath my fingers. It wasn't long before he was as hard as I was.

Dale nodded at a bottle in the corner of the shower, and I knew exactly what it was and didn't have to be told twice. I reached over, grabbed the lube and squirted out a healthy amount into my hand as I lathered up my hard cock.

Dale leaned against the back wall of the shower with his forearms pressed against the wall, angling himself so his ass was at the right height for me.

I put some lube on a finger and ran it around the outside of his hole before gently pressing in. Dale's stomach muscles flexed slightly as he took in a breath then eased against me. I stepped to his side so my hand could work in and out of him. First one, then two fingers. I nibbled on his earlobe, teasing him.

"I want you in me. I want you to fuck me so hard that I'll remember it for the rest of the week. Then, I'm going to bend you over and return the favor twice as hard."

Challenge accepted, I thought to myself as I centered myself back between his legs. I felt for his hole with my index finger and gently guided myself inside. I pushed ever so slightly, knowing that the girth of my cock was hard for some guys to take. Dale reached his hand around and pressed against my stomach as he let his sphincter relax. When he was ready, he pushed back against me until my pelvis pushed against his ass cheeks. I then pulled out and thrust back in slowly. After two or three slower thrusts, I started building momentum, becoming a human jackhammer going in and out of him, faster and faster. I reached my arms around and held on to him like a drowning man holding onto a life preserver.

"Where do you want me to cum?" I asked between labored breaths.

"In me," he groaned.

So, I did.

When I pulled out, Dale turned around, and I could see the mischievous smile on his face as he glanced down at the raging boner between his legs. If anything, I swear the thing was longer now than when I'd seen it earlier.

He reached for the lube and got himself ready. I steadied myself for what was about to come. Instead of fucking me doggy-style standing, he lifted me up off the ground with my back against the wall. I wrapped my legs around him as he explored my hole with his fingers. He entered me, and my entire body shuddered. It had been so long since I'd felt another guy's finger up my ass. Then there were two.

"Damn, you're tight," Dale said, before pressing his lips against mine. We kissed, and he kept going in and out of me with his fingers, loosening me up.

He finally broke away and asked, "Are you ready?"

I whispered a low, "Fuck me."

He lowered me slightly against the back wall of the shower, and I felt his cock there. He lowered me a bit more, and his cockhead entered me. Even after his fingers, I wasn't quite ready for the size of it. I let out a brief gasp.

"Breathe," Dale said, staring into my eyes. I responded by locking my legs around him tighter and pulling his neck down so his face could meet mine as he entered me. Before long, he was all the way inside, and I gasped as our mouths and tongues danced. The warm water rushed over us as he thrust upward into me repeatedly.

He only broke away to ask me where I wanted to him to cum and I told him, "Wherever you want."

A few minutes later Dale's heart was racing, and my ass was getting more of a workout than it ever had before. I knew the moment he filled me because his eyes rolled into the back of his head slightly as he tossed his neck backward in a series of pounding thrusts.

When he was done coming inside me, he left his cock there as he leaned over and kissed me some more. It had been a long time since some guy had bred me. And as his cock finally slipped out, I knew this wouldn't be the last time I'd have this experience.

Dale let out a low gasp and said, "Well, that was a fucking workout. Now we gotta clean up."

He grabbed a loofah and some bath gel. He cleaned my entire body with the loofah except for my face and hair, which he let me do myself. I then returned the favor. I may have slipped a finger inside him while I was supposed to be cleaning. I couldn't help myself.

After the shower, we finished getting ready and Dale called a car service to come pick us up. I peeked at the clock, which already read eleven a.m. Fuck! We were already late.

As I finished putting on my pants, I could still feel the space left by Dale's cock. I had a sneaking suspicion both of us were going to be feeling that morning's workout for the rest of the day any time we moved. I smiled at the thought.

Chapter Sixteen

Dale

I texted Grayson to let him know we were running behind as we rode the elevator down to the lobby of my building. I was sort of sorry that we were running late, but not that much. I could tell that both Talgat and I were feeling much better after the couple of rounds of fun we'd had that morning. Not only was the sex amazing, but it had seemed almost effortless. Despite the height difference, we had seemed to fit together nicely. I had especially enjoyed having him riding me in midair against the wall of the shower. Even thinking about it made wish we had time for round three right there in the elevator. Admittedly, the elderly woman standing in the opposite corner of us would probably have had a problem with that.

The door opened, and I gestured for the old lady and her ankle-biting dog to exit the elevator first.

"Do you know her?" Talgat asked.

"Not really," I admitted. "I've seen her around."

"Oh. I thought she hated you or something from the look on her face."

"I think she has permanent resting bitch face."

"I could plant her on the farm, and she'd scare animals and small children alike."

The image of the older woman standing on a stake in the middle of the orchard made me grin as we walked through the lobby. The building had a new doorwoman I'd never met before, opening the door for residents this morning. I read her name tag, 'Jill', and thanked her by name as Talgat and I left the building. I said her name a few more times in my head, trying to learn it.

"What are you doing?" Talgat asked.

"Memorizing the woman's name."

"The woman who held the door open?"

"Yep. She's new. Granddad taught me long ago that it's very important to learn the names of everyone who works for you, especially those most people overlook. 'Because everyone's a human and deserves respect for a job well done.'" The last part, I said in my best Granddad voice.

I stared ahead and saw my car service arrive. An older gentleman hopped out of the car and immediately opened the back door for us.

"Mr. Devereux, it's been a long time."

"I've been living upstate for a while."

"Becoming a weekender?" the driver asked.

"Not exactly. One of the family farms is up there, and I've been working with its farm manager here, Mr. Talgat Kudaibergen," I said, gesturing to Talgat, "to make it more profitable than it already is." I then turned to Talgat and said, "Talgat, this is Roland Sypher. He's one of my regular drivers."

Talgat shot out his hand for a handshake. The driver accepted Talgat's hand, but I saw the flash of confusion on the man's face and the slight hesitation when Talgat had first offered it, though. I then slipped into the car and scooched across the back leather seat to let Talgat get in.

"Why do you slide across like that?" Talgat asked. "I could go around the car in get in on the other side."

"Only if you want to get hit by an oncoming car or bike messenger," I said jokingly. "Here in NYC, you always enter a car from the curbside and exit the car from the curbside. It's safer that way."

"I don't know if I could ever get used to living down here."

"I said the same thing when I moved to Woodstock."

We spent the next few minutes in traffic and were quickly at the Bush Tower. The driver pulled right up, and we exited. "Call the service when you're ready to go somewhere else," the driver said as I shut the door.

"Thanks for the ride," I said, nodding my head to show I'd heard the comment about calling when I was ready to go.

"Do you need to give him a tip?" Talgat asked in hushed tones.

"It's automatically built into the system. One thing about the service is that it's completely electronic, so I never need to have cash on me when I call. At the end of the month, I get a bill and I add an automatic twenty percent that goes to the drivers I've used over the course of the month. It's quite efficient. Occasionally, I'll tip them some extra cash if they've done something above and beyond what they normally do."

I grabbed Talgat's hand and dragged him toward the entrance to the Bush Tower. I noticed how he gaped up at the tower in awe, like he'd never been there before.

"I know, I know," he said. "I look like a tourist. I just can't get over how tall the buildings are in this town."

"Maybe it's how short the buildings are in Woodstock," I joked.

"Whatever," Talgat said, rolling his eyes over-enthusiastically.

I opened the door to the building and waved at the security guard. I couldn't remember his name, but he clearly recognized me and didn't try to stop me from heading to the elevator bank.

On the way up to the corporate offices, I ask Talgat, "Are you ready for this?"

"As ready as I can be," he said.

I could tell he was getting more nervous as we ascended with each floor. I reached out and grabbed both sides of his face with my hands and said, "We've got this," before kissing him lightly and engulfing him in a bear hug.

When I heard the ding of the elevator and the doors slid open, I let go of him and put on my professional veneer. Talgat's eyes went wide as he saw the sudden change in my posture and facial expression. I turned my head and whispered, "It's my professional face. It's my 'don't fuck with me I know what I'm doing' look. I mastered it working on Wall Street," I said with what I hope would be a reassuring wink.

I walked the short distance to the office door and found it locked, so I pulled out my keys and let us in. I left it unlocked so Grayson could get in when he got here. I walked through the office and noticed most of the lights were off.

"Are you sure your granddad is here?"

"Trust me. He's here." I walked into the outer office where Molly was stationed during the regular work week and saw that the light underneath my granddad's inner-sanctum was on. I knocked on the door three times.

There was a shuffling sound on the other side of the door before I heard my granddad's voice say, "It had better be good," as he opened the door.

"Is that any way to greet your favorite grandson?"

"You're my *only* grandson," he replied. "You're my favorite by default." He then reached out and patted me on both shoulders. "You look good. Apparently, country living suits you," he said with a smirk. If he was surprised by Talgat and me, Granddad didn't let on. He extended his hand and said, "Mr. Kudaibergen, it's good to see you. Thanks for taking care of my grandson." Granddad then opened the door wider and motioned for us to come in.

Saying nothing, I sat down at the conference table in the office and motioned for Talgat to do the same.

"First," I admitted, "I know you're going to be upset, but I fully disclosed the situation to the Kudaibergen siblings. I felt they had a right to know."

Granddad sat down at the table, placed his elbows on the table and steepled his hands under his chin. Granddad's face was completely void of any emotion as he said, "Indeed."

"And it's a good thing I did. Without their help, I wouldn't have found a problem with the original theory that Ayala Kudaibergen was embezzling money from the company."

I spent the next thirty minutes laying out the process we had gone through the previous evening to find the one piece of evidence that was out of place. When I had told Granddad about the date problem, he lowered his hands from his chin and strummed his fingers slowly over the wood. This was the motion he often made when he was puzzling over a situation in his head, which was a good sign. If he hadn't done that, it would have meant that he outright didn't buy the additional evidence.

When I had finished my case, Granddad focused on me intently and took a second to respond. From the look in his eyes, I could tell he was carefully putting together what he would say.

"I won't say I'm overwhelmed by the evidence, but it's enough to make me pause…seriously pause. What do you suggest we do now?"

As if on cue, there was a knock on the door. Granddad's gaze shot to the door, and he slowly rose. I motioned for him to sit back down, saying, "This is my proposal." I walked over to the door and let Grayson inside. He was wearing a three-piece suit. *Why the fuck is he wearing a suit on a Saturday?*

"Grayson," Granddad said, a smile pulling at the corners of his lips, "it's been too long." Granddad shot Talgat a quick glance before saying, "I wish it was under better circumstances."

Grayson walked over to where Granddad was sitting and held out his hand. "Mr. Devereux, it has been entirely too long." The two shook hands, and Grayson walked around to the other side of the table and sat down.

"So," Granddad said, "how did Dale rope you into this?"

"Well, sir," Grayson said, "I don't know if you're aware of my position, but I currently work for the Accounting Fraud Division for the Manhattan District Attorney's Office."

I knew my granddad already knew this, but he smiled and nodded politely, saying, "Congratulations."

"Eventually, this case would end up on my desk, anyway. I would then coordinate efforts with the FBI when we brought it before a grand jury and indictments would be made. Depending on the state of the crime, then it would either be tried in New York State or the Federal Court. From what I know so far, this looks like it would end up as a federal indictment."

Talgat fidgeted next to me in his chair. Under the table, I laid a hand on his knee and squeezed it. I knew we had this. I got his nerves, though, because Grayson was talking about the case in clearly dispassionate terms.

"And what are your thoughts?" Granddad asked.

"Well, after talking with Dale, I encouraged him to find the piece of thread that doesn't fit. In my experience, when someone is being set up as the patsy for a crime, there's always some piece of evidence the real criminal misses. When Dale told me what they found, it sounded like the thread we could start pulling on to see what else unravels."

From the glare Granddad shot me, I could tell he was not thrilled I'd already brought in Grayson without telling him first. "Before you get upset, Granddad, hear me out on this. Grayson has been my best friend for as long as I can remember. When I called him to talk, I did so first as a friend, trying to figure out what to do. Thankfully, he was the right person to call. Now, I knew when I called him back to let him know what we found that I was calling him back in a capacity that would force his hand professionally. You gave me forty-eight hours, and Grayson is part of my forty-eight hours."

"I must add, though," Grayson said, "that my boss knows I'm here. He doesn't know all the ins and outs of the case, because honestly, I still don't, but I had to make sure I did this as above board as possible to avoid any problems if this case goes to trial." This last part was news to me. I did my best to make my face impassive as Grayson turned to stare at me.

"So," Granddad said after an awkward silence, "what do we do now?"

Grayson broke my eye contact to look back at my granddad. "Now, we dig—with your permission, of course."

"Be honest with me, boy," Granddad said, narrowing his eyes as Grayson. "Do I need to bring in my own lawyers?"

"Before I answer that, let me take off my DA Office hat, metaphorically speaking. As Dale's best friend, I think getting to the bottom of things yourself before bringing in your lawyers is a smart move. The more we can piece things together unofficially, the smoother the official process will be. If we open this to a full forensic accounting audit conducted by the FBI, anything and everything that's ever happened with your finances will be laid bare."

"I have nothing to hide," Granddad said.

"I'm sure you don't. But my friends at the FBI will pull at every string to see if moves. The process is lengthy and can make you appear guilty, even if there's nothing going on. And if they get a whiff of impropriety, they could freeze your finances. If, on the other hand, you supply them with a simple, tidy case that clearly points to a suspect, they'll happily take the win in court."

"Okay," Granddad said.

"Putting back on my DA hat. It's always in your best interest to retain counsel and discuss these matters with them directly."

I leaned back in my chair, waiting to see what Granddad would say. Honestly, I did not know what direction he was going to go here. Finally, resolve crossed his face, and I knew his decision was made. All he said was, "Let's get to work."

Chapter Seventeen

Talgat

Sadly, I felt very much out of my element. If you want to discuss the relative benefits of different fertilizer, I'm your guy. If you want me to stare at a computer screen for hours on end or try to read a spreadsheet, I'm going to want to gouge my eyes out before too long. Thankfully, the other three men in the room rolled up their sleeves and got to work.

Dale had produced a thumb drive at some point that had all the files he'd gotten from the office. I didn't know that information was digital. If we had it on a computer somewhere, why did we have so many boxes of paper that we'd gone through last night at my place?

One of the first things the three men did was start comparing the profit-and-loss statements from the farm that had been put together by Ayala and those on official record with Devereux Farms. It didn't take a math genius to figure out there was a huge discrepancy. The three were going over the files when Dale turned to me.

"Text Ayala. It's time to rope her in. If she's not at the office already, tell her to get there." Without skipping a beat, Dale went back to his conversation with the other three men. I was happy to let them figure this out without me.

I stepped out of the office and pulled out my phone. I called Ayala instead.

"What's up?" Ayala asked.

"Dale needs you to get to the office."

"I'm already there. You may have forgotten, but it is Saturday, so things are a bit hectic around here without all this going on," she responded. "But in between handling farm emergencies, I've been waiting for the call. I thought it would come sooner, so I was getting worried."

"Dale and I were late getting to the offices."

"You two were late? You're never late." There was a brief pause before she said, "Unless…"

"Unless what?" I blurted. Maybe a little too quickly.

"Dear God! You did! Rasul," I heard Ayala yell. "Talgat got laid. Woot!"

I was so glad I was standing in the outer office alone. I could feel myself turning hot. I was glad there were no mirrors there because I'm sure I was turning the shade of a red delicious.

"It's about fucking time!" I heard Rasul yell.

"We can talk about my sex life at another time," I groused. "We have more important things to discuss than the multiple times I had sex this morning." I couldn't help myself. I knew hearing that would scandalize both of them, and the silence at the other end of the line made me smile.

"Eww," Rasul said first. "I could have gone my entire day without hearing that. Hell, I could go my entire life without knowing that."

I could see the color draining from Rasul's face in my mind, and it made my smile bigger, so I hung up on them and walked back into the office.

"Everything okay?" Dale asked without looking up from the stack of spreadsheets he was pouring over.

"Ayala is already in the office waiting for your call." Dale finally looked over at me as I sat back down at the table. He narrowed his eyes when he saw the goofy-ass grin on my face.

Instead of saying anything, I pulled my phone and texted Dale a quick message.

The little brats guessed about our morning playtime.

I heard the soft vibration of Dale's iPhone on the table. He picked it up and read the message. For the first time since entering the Bush Tower, Dale grinned then immediately wiped it off his face. I glanced over as Grayson cocked his head slightly, clearly wondering what was going on between Dale and me.

My phone buzzed as Dale put his iPhone back on the table.

Can't wait for a repeat performance.

I did my best to focus all my attention on the screen of my phone. I watched as Dale got up and turned on the conference equipment in the room. Before long, I saw the smiling face of Ayala.

"Where's Rasul?" Dale asked.

"He was here a bit ago," she said with a smile. "He felt the need to go do something manly like chopping wood, planting seed or installing a fence post in a hole on the back part of the property."

I shivered with laughter, but I held it in. Dale grabbed my knee and clamped down on it hard, as he obviously did everything in his power not to laugh, although he was turning red. Thankfully, Mr. Devereux seemed oblivious, but Grayson raised one of his eyebrows when I peeked at him. I gave him a tight-lipped smile.

"So, young lady," Mr. Devereux said, "I wish we could talk under better circumstances, but I need you to walk me through the step-by-step accounting processes of the farm."

I glanced down at my watch and saw that it was already nearing five p.m. I could tell this was going to take a while. "Before you get started, why don't I go get us something to eat?" I offered to the small group.

Mr. Devereux said nothing, but he walked over to his desk and grabbed a menu from the top drawer. "This place is open on Saturdays and isn't too far from here. We can phone in an order and Mr. Kudaibergen can pick it up."

I mouthed "sorry," to Ayala as the room ordered the food. As soon as we got off the phone, Mr. Devereux handed me two cards and a key.

"This card," he said, gesturing to the top white card, "will get you into the building. This card will pay for the food and the key will let you back into the offices. I think they've been unlocked since you got here. Let's get them locked again."

"I'll be back shortly." I pocketed the three items in my pocket.

I walked out of the office and heard Dale say, "Wait a second." I turned around, still in the outer office, when Dale grabbed me and planted a kiss on my face.

"It's going to be okay. Trust me. Granddad wouldn't consider talking to Grayson or Ayala if he still believed she had anything to do with it. I know he keeps a steely facade, but he's a mushy softy at heart. I hope you'll get to see that one day."

"I needed to hear that." I turned around to leave as Dale swatted me on the ass.

Chapter Eighteen

Dale

Ayala took the time to walk Granddad through what she'd told Grayson and me the previous night, so I decided now was a good time to run to the bathroom. I also figured I could warm up the coffee maker. I had a sneaking suspicion it was going to be a long night.

I had finished getting those last few drops out before putting my dick back in my pants when I heard the door to the restroom open. I zipped up and watched as Grayson walked over to one of the other urinals.

I turned my attention to washing my hands. Part of me always feels weird being in the restroom with people I know. As a gay man, I've seen a lot of cocks in my life. Hell, I've seen Grayson's cock, and he admittedly has a nice one. I saw it in all its glory once when I accidentally walked in on him and his then-girlfriend having sex. In my defense, I had knocked and heard something that I thought sounded like, "Come in." In reality, it was either a low moan or Grayson saying, "Go away." But there I was, standing in the doorway with light flooding in, shining a spotlight on Grayson banging away. To his credit, he didn't stop or bother looking at me. He said, "Dale, go away! And shut the door."

I finished washing my hands and pulled out a couple of paper towels as I heard Grayson zipping up his fly. "So, you and Talgat? How long has this been going on?"

I watched as he put soap on his hands and started washing him.

"We've flirted for a while, and we had a date earlier this week. Then all hell broke loose, and I acted like a royal ass. Then I figured out how to save his sister, thanks to you. And he stayed with me last night. We both passed out. But this morning we got a little distracted when we woke up, which was why we were late getting here."

Grayson barked out a short laugh as he finished washing his hands. "Dear God, is your dating timing always this bad?"

"Seems like it."

"What about Avery?"

"I haven't spoken to him since he sexually assaulted Jordan. I think that was the final straw for me."

"About fucking time. Honestly, I was tired of pretending I liked that prick. I always thought you could do way better than him."

"Oh really? And why didn't you say anything?"

"You never asked. And I didn't think it was my place to insert myself into your love life. You're my best friend. You're also one of the most stubborn people I know. If I said something bad about Avery, it might have pushed you into his arms more. I figured eventually you'd tire of Avery or Avery would show his true colors."

"You think you're pretty smart, don't you?"

"I know I am," Grayson said, grabbing a couple of paper towels. "I also know that you are. It may take you a bit longer some days, but you always get there."

"What do you think of Talgat?"

"I don't know him that well, but he seems like the kind of guy I always hoped you'd end up with."

"What's that supposed to mean?"

"I always hoped you'd find someone who could ground you, someone who would show you a world different from the one we grew up in. Let's face it. We are two privileged motherfuckers, and it's easy for us to take that for granted. I hoped, and still do hope, that you'll meet a guy who isn't from our world."

"Whoa. I can tell you've thought about this a lot."

"Not for you, but for me, too. I've had half the girls we went to school with throw themselves at me. I don't want to date someone who complains that her twelve-hundred-dollar pair of shoes got scuffed on the street or is more disappointed that her daddy took the private jet to the Bahamas and she had to fly first class to Cabo. We both know those women. I would much rather meet someone who thinks I'm a boring middle-class tax accountant lawyer, who thinks I buy my suits off the rack at Macy's."

"I hate to break it to you, Gray, but that suit is tailored within an inch of its life to fit you perfectly. There's no way in hell that suit was bought off a rack anywhere."

Grayson smiled at that one. "I like my clothes. I know I'm gorgeous in a suit."

"You are. You always have been," I admitted.

"Yeah, you've always liked my ass in a suit," Grayson joked.

"Sorry, but Talgat's ass is much nicer than yours," I shot back. "And the things he can do with it," I added.

Grayson stuck his fingers in his ears and started saying, "La, I can't hear you," which made me bust out laughing. "You always have to go there."

"Yep! If there's a line, I want to do a disco jig right over that fucker."

"What are we going to do with you?"

"Love me?" I said with a sheepish grin.

"Always," Grayson said, before giving me a big bear hug. "We better get back to your granddad. I don't want him to scare Ayala off."

We were leaving the restroom as the elevator door opened and Talgat walked out, carrying our dinner.

"What were you doing?" he asked, giving us a strange look.

"Powdering our noses," Grayson joked.

"Ayala is explaining the financial process to Granddad, so we ran to the restroom."

We headed back into the office. Talgat locked the door behind us. Once back in the room, Granddad turned and said, "We think we have a theory."

"Okay?" I questioned. I took the bags from Talgat, opened them and handed out everyone's orders. I watched as Talgat walked over to Granddad and handed him the cards and key.

"Keep the keys, Mr. Kudaibergen, you're going to need them. Besides, you may not have noticed, but the black one already has your name on it."

Talgat flipped the credit card over and his eyebrows shot up. "Thank you, sir. I don't know what to say."

"Nothing. You've earned them." Granddad then shot me a glance before he added, "Even though this one over here was all up in your business making your life hard."

I scrunched my face and wanted to stick my tongue out at the old man, but held it in. Instead, I said, "You think you're so funny, old man. I have three words for you, 'involuntary commitment laws.'"

"You wouldn't dare," Granddad said, narrowing his eyes at me.

"Don't try me, old man," I said before grinning at him.

I looked to the side and saw Grayson and Talgat with looks of shock on their faces. Only then did I realize how that conversation must sound to outsiders. "It's a joke. I've been threatening to have Granddad committed since I was like eleven."

"And I threatened to send him to military school. I guess I can't use that one anymore," Granddad joked.

Talgat leaned over. "I'm gonna run to the restroom. Be right back." With that, he headed out of the office.

"So, what's this theory of yours?" Grayson asked, sitting down again and opening his food.

"There are only a few people who have access to the financials and the information someone would need in HR to able to pull this off. We have a list of about a dozen names. We need to narrow it down," Ayala said.

"Do you have a list of dates and times when these transactions were made?"

"Yes," Granddad said. "What are you thinking?"

"If we know the transactions can be limited to a few people, we can start conducting an IP search for the dates and times. It's a shot in the dark, but if we can match all the transfers to specific Internet usage, then we may find our suspect."

"How long will that take?" I asked.

"Depends on the nature of the transactions, the foreign banks and the speed of the cyber forensics professional."

"Have anyone in mind?" I asked.

"As a matter of fact, I do. Can I bring her in?" Grayson asked, looking between Granddad and me.

I deferred to Granddad's judgment on this one. He said nothing but nodded his agreement. Grayson took a bite of the steak he had in front of him before grabbing his phone and heading back into the outer office.

"Mr. Devereux?" Ayala asked.

"Yes?" both Granddad and I said at the same time.

"I'm going to log out for now. Rasul, my brother," she added for Granddad's clarification, "just got back with dinner here, too. Call me if you need anything."

"Thank you, young lady. I'm sorry for all the stress this has caused you. I can tell that you are truly an amazing asset to this company. When the dust settles, we should have a conversation about your future within the company and what you want out of life."

"Thank you, sir." Ayala was clearly taken aback by Granddad's words. "I look forward to that conversation." She then glanced at me and said, "Tell Talgat to check his phone."

For the first time that day, I found myself in the room with Granddad by myself. "I'm sorry I threw all this at you today, Granddad. I didn't know how else to do this."

"I think you're doing fine. And, despite what you may think, I do trust your judgment."

"Thanks. That means a lot coming from you. And I may not always show it, but I do respect and love you, even when you exiled me to Woodstock."

"Ha!" Granddad laughed.

I smiled and grabbed the bottle of Coke I'd ordered with dinner. I uncapped it and let out a sigh before drinking a mouthful.

"So, how long have you and Talgat been seeing each other?"

I spat my drink across the table before looking at Granddad. My professional facade completely crumbled.

"How'd you—?"

"I'm old, not blind. I saw how he looks at you and how you peek at him. I also saw your hand sneaking under the table every so often."

"It's new," I said, leveling my eyes at Granddad. I grabbed a few napkins from the table and started to wipe up the mess I'd made.

"What do you think HR would say about that?"

"I researched the issue before I considered it," I admitted. "Technically, I'm out of the hierarchy, so the way policy is written doesn't apply to me at all. And if it did, there are provisions for dating relationships."

"Oh, really?"

"Someone taught me to always read the policy and stick to the letter of the law."

"Must have been a very wise man," Granddad said, knowing full well I was talking about him.

"So, what did I miss?" Talgat said, as he entered the room.

"Dale was telling me about his new boyfriend," Granddad said. If Talgat's eyebrows could have left his forehead in that moment, they would have. "Don't keep your mouth open like that, Mr. Kudaibergen. You don't want a fly to land in there."

"It's cool," I said, reassuring Talgat. "He figured it out all on his own."

"How?" Talgat squeaked out as he sat down in his chair.

"Because you and my grandson are not nearly as sneaky as you two think you are. I've been around the block a few times. It's hard to pull a fast one on me." Granddad picked up his knife and started slicing off a piece of the porkchop he'd ordered before placing it in his mouth. Talgat was still slack-jawed when I glanced at him.

"Where'd Ayala go?" Talgat asked, finally realizing that she wasn't on the screen anymore.

"She's having dinner. Rasul showed up with it. But she said to check your texts," I said.

Talgat pulled out his phone and laughed.

"What?" I asked.

He turned it to me and there was a peach and eggplant emoji on the screen, which caused me to smile.

"I'm beginning to think not having siblings may have been a good thing," I joked.

"What did it say?" Granddad asked.

I knew not telling him wasn't an option, so I told him as plainly as possible. "It was two pictures, nothing big. It's related to farming. There was a picture of Georgia peach and an eggplant."

"Ahh," Granddad said, shoveling a bite of his baked potato into his mouth. I watched as he mulled it over and I took another drink of my Coke. "She assumes you two are going to have sex later."

For the second time, I spat across the table. This time, it also came out of my nose.

Chapter Nineteen

Talgat

Watching the horrified expression on Dale's face as Mr. Devereux made it clear he understood emojis was probably the funniest thing I'd seen in a long time. I helped Dale clean up the Coke. Although Mr. Devereux hadn't laughed, the look on his face told me he was pleased with himself. I think I was finally beginning to put my finger on Dale and his grandfather's relationship. They each had a tendency of underestimating the other one, but then they both relished showing each other up.

I cut into the chicken I had ordered and found it to be one of the moistest chickens I'd ever eaten. I chewed the meat and let the flavor swirl in my mouth. I didn't know what the chef did, but this was by far the best damn chicken I'd ever tasted. I wouldn't tell Dale this, but it definitely tasted better than him. It was like my mouth was having an orgasm with each bite.

I was so enthralled with my meal that I didn't realize Grayson had come back into the room until I heard Mr. Devereux say, "So, did you know these two were dating?"

Grayson shot a sideways glance at Dale before saying, "For about an hour now. I picked up on some nonverbal cues earlier, but only had it confirmed for an hour or so."

"That makes two of us," Mr. Devereux said, as he pointed his fork at Dale. "As I said, who did you two think you were fooling?"

"I guess we were fooling ourselves," Dale said in between bites of his grilled swordfish. "And it's still relatively new, so let's not go broadcasting to everyone that we're dating, shall we?"

Instinctively, I reached out and patted Dale under the table. "See? Right there. It's that kind of under the table stuff you two kept doing that gave it away," Mr. Devereux said.

I shot my hand back above the table so fast, which caused Grayson to laugh. "I'm not averse to affection, Mr. Kudaibergen. Just no hanky-panky in the offices or while on the job."

"Yes, sir," I said. I shot a glance and Dale that hopefully screamed, "Save me."

"Grayson," Dale said, steering the conversation in a different direction, "what did you learn from your friend?"

"She's on it. She got the info from my phone for your Wi-Fi account and backdoored her way into your system. She's currently checking all the IP addresses and hopes to run a search once she's mapped it out. She said she'd have it back in a few hours."

The rest of dinner went without incident. The evening wore on and was quickly heading into the early morning. I called Ayala and Rasul shortly before midnight and told them to get some sleep. I promised I'd call them if we heard anything.

We'd all talked about heading home to bed, but none of us wanted to leave until we had an answer. By two a.m., Jameson Devereux had fallen to sleep on a fold-out cot he kept in his office.

When he started snoring, Dale, Grayson and I headed out into the office and chitchatted for another hour before Grayson found a piece of floor to lie on and Dale and I did the same thing.

The next thing I knew, I was being shaken gently.

"Dale, we have an answer," I heard a voice saying.

I opened my eyes to see Grayson shaking Dale's shoulder, but since I was once again playing little spoon, I was getting rocked, too.

"Give me a second," Dale said as he slowly sat up and yawned. His hair was going in several directions, but he was still so cute.

"Morning, sleepyhead," I said, as I rolled over and stared up at him. I then forced myself into a sitting position and stared at Grayson. "Did you wake Mr. Devereux yet?"

"No," Grayson said. "I think you'll want to hear this first," he added, looking at Dale.

I didn't know Grayson that well, but the serious expression he was wearing wasn't good. Just staring at him woke me wide awake.

Now that we were all focused, Grayson told us, "The IP address that made the wire transfers starting after Mrs. Kudaibergen's death all came from this office, like we suspected. But, more specifically, the terminal that conducted those transfers can all be traced to the computer in your granddad's office."

"What?" I spat out. "How the hell?"

"You think Mr. Devereux did this?" Talgat asked, his voice clearly dripping with doubt.

"Not necessarily him, but someone who had access to his computer." Grayson then looked at Dale directly and asked, "Who has access to his computer?"

"There are only two people who have access to my computer," Mr. Devereux said, looming over us. "Myself and Molly Frone."

"What?" Dale gasped. I could tell from the shock on his face that this was not what he'd expected to hear. I'd only met Molly a few times, and she seemed like a perfectly pleasant person.

"She's been like a grandmother to me," I heard Dale say. "It can't be her," he added, shaking his head. He glanced up at his granddad. There was a look that almost pleaded with the old man for him to tell Dale he was wrong.

I helped Dale to his feet, and we walked back into Mr. Devereux's office. "Are you okay?" I asked Dale.

"No. I'm just shocked." Dale stared at his grandfather. "Why aren't you shocked?"

"I am. I'm better at hiding it than you are," Mr. Devereux said, his voice void of any emotion.

Grayson picked up his phone, dialed a number and spoke to someone on the other end. "The name is Molly Frone. Do a deep dive and see what you can find." When Grayson hung up the phone, he reached out, squeezed Dale on the shoulder and tried to give him his best reassuring look. "I hate leaving all of you like this, but it's at the point where I need to fully rope in my boss. We'll be back in a bit to start this investigation officially."

"Okay," Dale got out of his mouth. "Thanks… Thanks for everything." Dale shot Grayson a small smile that didn't make it anywhere near his eyes.

I wished I knew how to help Dale. I could tell that Molly's criminal activity was breaking him. I hoped there was another mistake, like the one pointing in Ayala's direction…for Dale's sake.

"Why don't you sit down?" I said to Dale, as I pulled out a chair. Dale flopped into it in a daze.

Mr. Devereux glanced at me, saying, "Let's get him a bottle of water. We have them in the breakroom area. Follow me."

I could tell from his tone of voice that this was not a request, so I squeezed Dale's shoulder once and followed Mr. Devereux out of the office.

"You see," Mr. Devereux explained as we walked through the office space, "after Dale's parents died, Molly was a huge stabilizing influence in his life. I wasn't always the best granddad to the boy. I did my best. I'd raised my own son, and I never thought I'd be trying to be Dad and Granddad to another one. Molly was always there. She planned his birthday parties and our holidays. She has always been there."

"So, why weren't you surprised the way Dale was?"

"Dale saw what she did for him, but he never saw her. She was a perfectly adequate assistant. She wasn't great by any stretch of the imagination. I thought about firing her many times, but I couldn't bring myself to do it because of the relationship she had with Dale. I cynically wondered if she didn't establish that relationship knowing that it would make her untouchable."

"Wow," I said. "And you never told Dale?"

"I never felt the need. If she made him happy, that made me happy. Did I think she was altruistic? Never. She was an employee. And no offense to you and your siblings, but I keep my employees at arm's length for a reason."

"None taken. I get it. As the CEO, you must make tough decisions. And if you saw everyone as a family member or friend, it would be hard to make those decisions."

"That was my fear when Dale started defending Ayala. I was afraid he'd fallen for your family and couldn't see what was going on in front of his face." Mr. Devereux reached out and grabbed my forearm, which caused me to turn and lock eyes with him. "I'm glad that I was wrong. I've watched Dale grow a lot over the last few months. And I think most of that has to do with you. He may not realize it, but you've been a transforming influence in his life. And when he finally takes over the reins of Devereux Farms, he's going to be a far better leader from having known you."

"I'm not going anywhere," I said almost a bit more confrontationally than I'd intended.

"I hope you don't," Mr. Devereux reassured, releasing my arm after a gentle squeeze. "I want you to know that I've already seen an enormous change in Dale, and I can't wait to see how that change grows more because you're in each other's lives. I think your parents would be very proud of the young man you've become, Talgat. I want you to know that."

I stood there doing my best to hold it together. Somewhere deep inside me, I'd needed to hear that my parents would be proud of me. And it was gratifying to know that Mr. Devereux knew my first name.

Mr. Devereux led me into the breakroom and said, "Now, let's get Dale that bottle of water."

* * * *

Dale

I was shaken. I'm talking shaken to my core, shaken. I couldn't believe that Molly Frone was the one who'd set up Ayala. I saw Granddad's face when he'd learned Molly was the likely suspect. He wasn't surprised. I, on the other hand, couldn't believe it. There was a rustling sound in the outer office. I was going to stand and investigate, but I didn't have the energy for it.

"Mr. Devereux," a voice said in the outer office. "I'm surprised to see you here so early on a Sunday morning. Don't you take any days off?"

She poked her head in and I glanced up from my seat and said, "Good morning, Molly."

She took one look at me and said, "Did you and Talgat break up?"

"How did you—?"

"I figured you two were bound to end up together at some point this summer. I also assumed if it ended in disaster, you'd come running back to the city. What did he do to you?"

"Nothing," I said, the wheels in my mind spinning on overload.

"It's okay. You can tell me." She sat down across the table from me, reached out one of her manicured hands and grabbed my hand gently. It took every ounce of control in my body not to flinch at her touch. Part of me wanted to scream at her. Part of me wanted to beg her to tell me it wasn't true. Part of me wanted to see her cuffed and being perp-walked out of the building.

"You're right. You always knew me too well. We had a blow up yesterday," which was technically true. I left off the part about us making up. "Ayala, Talgat's sister, has been stealing from the company. I confronted her, and he didn't like it." Again, all this was true, so it was easy to keep a straight face.

"Oh, honey," Molly said, her face showing a level of concern only a mother shows for her children. "Maybe you and that nice Avery guy can give it a real go this time."

Molly knew that I had an on-again, off-again relationship with Avery, so I wasn't surprised that she said that.

"Yeah, he's dead to me."

"Oh?"

"He forced himself on someone sexually and refused to apologize for his poor behavior. I felt it was time to cut him loose."

"Oh dear," Molly said. "When it rains, it pours."

"What are you doing here?" Granddad growled from the doorway. "Get away from my grandson."

Molly seemed taken aback until she saw Talgat standing behind Granddad. In that instant, that mask of motherly care dropped.

"Holy fuck," I said as I saw the handgun suddenly pointed in my direction. Instinctively, I jumped up from the table and knocked the chair I was sitting in over as Molly leveled her gun at me. "Molly?" I gasped.

She rolled her eyes. "You can cut the shit, kid."

I felt myself stand a little taller as I put back on my professional facade and said, "So it's true?"

"Depends on what you're talking about?"

"You've been embezzling from Devereux Farms for years and tried to pin it on Ayala Kudaibergen."

Her hand clutched at her nonexistent pearls. "I would never," she said a bit too dramatically to have any hint of sincerity behind the words.

"I wish I could say I was surprised," Granddad cut in, "but I'm not."

"Oh, Jameson, you've known I was up to something for years but couldn't figure out how to prove it. And as long as I kept little Daley here in my good graces, you wouldn't touch me."

"You used me?" I asked.

"Well, duh. You think I wanted to waste my time on birthdays and holidays of a spoiled, rich brat? No. Trust me, I had better things to do with my life. But this place was my cash cow, so I plastered on the fakest smile humanly possible and hugged you next to my breast. Honestly, you were the easiest mark of all time."

"You've done this before?" Talgat said, entering the conversation for the first time.

"Oh look, the dirt farmer is the first one to put it together," Molly said.

"You're a grifter, a con artist," Granddad said matter-of-factly.

The smile that stretched over Molly's face was sinister, and I almost expected her to take a bow for her acting prowess. "Well, this has been fun boys, but I have somewhere else I need to be."

"You're not going to —"

"Get away with this?" she responded to me. "I already have. And I know you probably think I'm a huge monster right now, but you will always hold a special place in my heart, Dale. You really will. You've been my meal ticket for a couple of decades. I won't soon forget that. So, I will not shoot you," she said as she swiveled the gun in her hand as she pointed it at Talgat.

I screamed as Talgat's eyes grew. The sound from the small firearm reverberated off the walls. The world slowed and everything happened at a speed that approached the pace of a snail. I started toward Talgat and watched as Granddad shoved Talgat out of the way, putting himself between the bullet and Talgat.

Granddad spun, flailing his arms out to his sides like a ballerina on a bender.

I screamed again.

Chapter Twenty

"FBI," a voice screamed over the chaos, "put your hands up." Three people in black windbreakers and baseball caps rolled into the room as Granddad hit the ground. I was kneeling beside him moments later. Talgat was shielding me from the FBI agents with his body.

"Put the weapon down," a voice barked. I looked up to see Molly raise her gun, then then the sound of three shots fired reverberated around the enclosed office. I did my best to protect my granddad's body with mine as Talgat held me tighter, protecting me from the chaos going on around me.

"Sir?" a voice said. "Are you okay? Have you been shot?"

"No, not me. His granddad. He threw himself in front of the bullet meant for me," Talgat said as if I were hearing it underwater.

"Medics!" someone yelled.

"Sir," I felt a pair of muscular arms on my shoulders, trying to pull me away from Granddad. I pushed against the hands, still trying to protect my granddad. "Sir, you need to let the EMTs do their job."

"Dale, it's okay," Talgat said. This time, I knew it was him lifting me off the ground. I stood and buried myself in his chest. Hot tears were falling from my eyes, dampening Talgat's shirt beneath me.

I felt Talgat's hand on the back of my head. I stared into his eyes, put my hands on either side of his face and kissed him. I then blanched as I realized I'd probably gotten blood on his face. I pulled my hands away and gaped at them.

"What's wrong?" Talgat asked.

"Where's the blood? I saw Granddad get shot. I should have blood on my hands. Where's the blood?" A normal person would think that the lack of blood on their hands was a good thing, but in that moment, I was like a reverse Lady Macbeth. The lack of blood was going to drive me insane.

"Stop your blabbering, boy," Granddad said as the EMTs lifted the gurney. "It's going to take a lot more than pesky little bullet to get rid of me."

"How?" I stammered out of my mouth.

"She missed," Granddad said matter-of-factly.

Only then did I see a group of agents looking at a bullet lodged in the opposite wall. Not only had she missed, she'd missed by a lot.

"It's a two-millimeter Kolibri, boy," Granddad said, looking up from the gurney. He let out a little chuckle, which threw me. "I bought it for her as a birthday present a few years ago. The German hummingbirds are novelty items and gun enthusiasts collect them, but they're actually shit as guns. The bullets from those things have practically no spin or velocity."

"Then what happened to you?"

"I think I twisted my ankle when I pushed Talgat out of the way. I didn't think she could hit the broadside of the barn with that thing, but…just in case."

I looked to the EMT that was standing there. "Is he all right?"

"Seems to be. We're going to take him to the hospital to make sure he broke nothing. At his age, a fall can be terrible."

"At my age?" Granddad yelled as the EMT rolled him away. I could still hear Granddad laying into the poor EMT for the age comment.

With Granddad safely out of the office, I glanced at where Molly Frone's dead body lay. Although her gun may not have been great for accuracy, the ones the FBI agents had definitely were.

"Can I get the two of you to follow me?" an agent asked.

"Sure," Talgat said as he gently guided me out of the office. I shot one last glance down at Molly's corpse and a genuine sense of loss tugged at me. Not the loss of a life, though. As far as I was concerned, that old bag got everything she deserved. But a different Molly also died in that office — the Molly I thought cared about me, that Molly. The Molly who made me smile… The Molly who taught me to love. That Molly might have been a mirage, but I still mourned the passing of that Molly.

"I'm Supervisory Special Agent Aaron Massey," the young-looking agent said. For the first time I looked at the man and realized, *Damn, he's fucking hot*. As if Talgat could hear my thoughts, I felt his arm gently worm its way over my shoulders and bring me closer to him. I settled my head on it.

I listened to the agent's questions and answered them the best I could. He also asked Talgat questions, and I didn't listen to those answers because they were identical to mine.

"Dale!" a voice yelled over the crowd in the room. I glanced over to see Grayson heading in my direction. "I heard someone was shot. Are you okay?" I watched as Grayson swiveled his head around, then realization hit him. "Your granddad? Oh my God, I'm so sorry, Dale. If there's anything I can do for you—"

"It's okay, Granddad is okay. He wasn't shot. He twisted his ankle, and the EMTs took him to the hospital to make sure it wasn't broken."

"What happened?" Grayson asked.

"Excuse me," the FBI Agent broken in. "And you are?"

"Grayson Jackson, friend of the family and Assistant DA. I've been working on this case for the Manhattan District Attorney's Office. I'm the one who called this in."

"Called what in?" I asked.

"Well, I wanted to be ready to go as soon as we got the warrant signed off on. I let the FBI know what was going on and who our suspect was."

"Okay," the agent said. "The DA's office faxed us a copy of the woman's driver's license. We were stationed outside the building ready to come up when the warrant was ready. When we saw the woman go into the building, we felt obliged to follow."

"So, that's how you got here so fast," Talgat muttered. "I'm glad you did. I don't know what she would have done if she'd realized her first shot didn't hit anyone."

We spent the rest of the day sitting in the outer office, repeating our stories. I called Granddad's driver to let him know what had happened. He said he was going to check on him in the hospital for me since I was stuck answering questions. I got a text that everything was fine with Granddad and that he promised to call me later.

After who knows how long, I asked Grayson, "Can we go yet?"

"Yeah, you two have had a long day. Get out of here. I'm sure you're going to need to come sit for a formal interview in the next couple of days. I'll have someone in my office reach out and schedule it."

"I want to go home and sleep for like a week," I said, leaning against Talgat.

"Which home?" Grayson asked.

Without looking at each other, Talgat and I answered in unison, "Woodstock."

Want to see more from this author?
Here's a taster for you to enjoy!

Up on the Farm:
Bewitched by the Barista
Jason Wrench

Excerpt

Christmas music filled the elevator as I rode in silence up to our apartment, thankful my new client had signed on the dotted line with little fuss. I think we had both been trying to get home for the holidays. Nothing sped up the process like a late afternoon meeting on the day before Christmas, I guessed.

The elevator doors opened, and I stepped out into the empty hallway. Even on busy days, people in our building were quiet, respectful and kept to themselves, which was how I liked it. My fiancé, Jeremy, wasn't expecting me for at least another couple of hours. I kind of looked forward to surprising him. We had reservations at nine for dinner, so it would be nice to chill out, maybe throw on some news before we headed into the frosty night. Well, for New York City, it wasn't the coldest Christmas I'd seen. In fact, it was downright seasonal.

I pulled my keys out of my pocket and slipped the right one into the lock before turning it clockwise and pushing open the door. I stepped in and was immediately surprised by the dimmed lights and a handful of lit candles glowing inside. Sometimes, Jeremy takes relaxing baths. I opted not to yell out and didn't want to break his mood. *Hell, if I'm lucky, maybe I'll slip into the tub and join him.*

I hung up my coat on the hook near the door and set my briefcase down on the counter. I walked into the living room and immediately saw clothes strewn about the apartment. *Well then*, I thought to myself. *If that's how he wants this evening, I don't want to disappoint him.* We'd played this little game before. I'd come home, Jeremy would have stripped and had been waiting for me on our bed. Once, for Valentine's Day, he'd had a trail of rose petals leading me into the bedroom.

Without thinking, I shrugged out of my suit coat, laying it over the back of the sofa. I kicked off my loafers and made quick work of my tie. Before long, I was naked as the day I'd been born. I stared down at my washboard stomach. Not as flat as when I'd been a teenager, but I still looked pretty damn hot. Just staring at my nude body and its tightly manscaped features had me growing in anticipation.

The bedroom door was closed. I reached out, grabbed the handle and twisted it. I pushed it open quietly, just in case Jeremy had fallen asleep while he was waiting for me. The thought of walking in on a nude Jeremy lying on our bed facedown definitely caused my cock to twitch. I looked down at all eight inches of me standing as straight and hard as a ship's mast.

It took a second for my eyes to adjust.

"What the fuck!" I yelled.

Jeremy was mid-thrust into some young twink's ass.

He whipped his head in my direction. "Roger," Jeremy started, his voice trailing off.

I stared in disbelief as Jeremy's cock sat nestled in the guy. The twink, whose face was shoved into the mattress, lifted his head and looked at me.

"Oh...hey, Roger," Avery said. "Wanna join?" He winked at me and licked the top of his lip.

Part of me wanted to go over and shove something between those lips to see if he'd choke on it. But with my luck, he'd have no gag reflex. Instead, I narrowed my eyes and said, "Avery Addington." I sounded like a principal who wasn't too surprised to see a pupil in the main office. "What the fuck are you doing here?"

Avery looked at me with a 'are you fucking kidding me' look, before he said, "Uh...having a good time."

My nails bit into my palms in clenched fists. Jeremy sat there with his cock still sitting inside the kid. Then he slowly slid out.

"And you're not wearing a condom!" I was pretty sure neighbors up and down the hall heard that one.

"Don't worry, daddy," Avery said, drawing out the word 'daddy' like it was some kind of badge of honor for reaching the ancient age of forty. "I'm totally on PrEP."

"I'm. No. One's. Father."

I knew if I didn't get out of there, I was going to say a few things I wouldn't want to repeat in polite company, not that Avery was polite. Avery was one of those kids who had a reputation, and now I saw the reputation in all its glory splayed out on my bed...and on the sheets I'd bought!

I shut the door.

I looked out at the living room. Only then did I notice that there'd been two pairs of pants on the floor. *How had I been so blind?*

I walked over to where I'd discarded my clothes and heard the bedroom door open.

"You don't get the right to be angry with me," Jeremy said.

"What?" I spun around and looked at Jeremy. "I'm not the one who was fucking around on my fiancé…on Christmas Eve!"

"Well, if you weren't working all the time…"

"I work all the time so we can afford to live here, so we can afford that dream wedding you've been wanting."

"Hey! It's not my fault I'm having a problem landing a job."

"Jeremy," I said, trying to keep the venom out of my voice as much as possible, "you've been having a problem landing work for years. When are you going to realize that you're a two-bit hack of an actor who will never make it big? Sure, you're hot, but you don't have any fucking talent." As soon as the words were out of my mouth, I kind of regretted them — but not really.

"Well… How long have you been holding that in?"

I breathed in through my nose and let it out. "This is neither the time nor the place to have this conversation."

"Oh, and why not?"

"You're naked. I'm naked. And that two-bit hustling twink is in *my* bedroom."

"*Our* bedroom."

"As if that makes it better?" I groused.

Avery chose that moment to make his appearance. He reached up and rested his arm on Jeremy's shoulder as he draped himself around my fiancé. I couldn't help but focus downward, seeing that Avery was the only one in the room who was on full alert.

"I am not a hustler," Avery said.

"You're what? Twelve—?"

"I'm twenty-five, I'll have you know."

"And yet you act like you're a child. You're the fucking gay version of Peter Pan. All the rumors about you are true, aren't they?"

"I don't pay attention to rumors. Anyone who has a problem with me isn't my problem."

"What the fuck ever," I said. "I just can't—"

"We need to talk about this," Jeremy said, cutting into my dressing down of Avery.

"Talk about *what*?" I asked. In the flickering candlelight, I realized that all three of us were standing there stark naked. I was so mad at Jeremy that I hadn't thought about the fact that I was letting an absolute stranger stare at my naked body. "I can't talk to you now…not like this—"

"Roger—"

"Don't, *Roger*, me." I found my underwear on the ground, reached down, grabbed them and pulled them up. When I was finally covered, I looked back up at Avery and Jeremy. "I hope you two are happy together."

"Oh, I'm not looking for a relationship," Avery said, with almost a hint of disgust at the thought of it. "I found him on Grindr and thought he looked like fun."

"Grindr!" I yelled again. "You're on Grindr?"

"It's not like that—"

"Like *what*? Like you created a profile on a dating app behind my back." Only then did I realize what other implications this had. "Is Avery even the first?"

The look on Jeremy's face was all I needed to see. Avery clearly wasn't the first. My face went slack.

"Roger…"

I couldn't say anything. I didn't know what to say. I'd never felt more betrayed by anyone in my entire life.

"Roger!"

I got dressed. I heard Jeremy's voice in the background, but I'd honestly stopped listening. At some point, Avery had slunk back into the bedroom. I looked up at one point and could see the kid acting like he owned the place. Avery was propped up with his arms crossed behind his head. The light from the living room provided me enough to see the smug look on the little prick's face.

I laced up my shoes, stood, walked to the front door, grabbed my briefcase, pulled down my coat and left.

Even as I shut the door behind myself, I could hear Jeremy calling after me. I walked in a haze to the elevator. A happy, smiling couple stood in the small box hand-in-hand when the doors opened. *That should have been me*. As much as I wanted to make a snide comment about how love was fake, I plastered on a smile and turned my back to the couple. On the ride down, a tear fell down my cheek.

I walked through the lobby and quickly realized I did not know where I was going. Out in the cold air, I pulled out my phone and pulled up my favorite hotel app. On Christmas Eve, there wasn't exactly much availability, and the prices for booking this late made my eyes bulge. I found a hotel I'd always wanted to stay at and booked it. I had the money in my savings, so I might as well enjoy the stay. I booked for three nights. I needed distance. I needed to figure out what my next move was.

Fuck! I have nothing with me. Thankfully, Duane Reade was always open, so I could get my necessities there. If I hurried, I could buy some new clothes for a few days. At least, I hoped I could find a department store still open. I hailed the first cab I saw and said, "Take me to Macy's Harold Square."

The guy got a weary look on his face before saying, "Whatever. It's your funeral."

I leaned back and stared at my reflection in the cab's window as we passed the familiar sights of the city. *What am I going to do now?*

* * * *

I got out of the cab at Macy's Harold Square. I looked down at my watch and saw I had about twenty-five minutes to get inside, make purchases and get out before the place closed at six p.m. I looked at the throngs of people through the windows, took a deep breath and walked in.

I hadn't stepped foot inside a department store in years. Jeremy always shopped for me. I never quite trusted my style choices, so it was nice to have a boyfriend, then fiancé, who enjoyed doing that. I looked at the map and realized I had to get to five floors. I wouldn't have time to try on anything. *This should be fun.* I rode the escalator up to the mezzanine and grabbed some sportswear, so I could still hit the gym. I dashed up to the second floor for casual pants, then to the third for a couple of pairs of jeans. On to the fourth, I stocked up on underwear. Last, I ended up on the fifth floor and picked out three dress shirts, a sports coat, two pairs of slacks and two ties. I looked at my now-overflowing bag of stuff and tried to figure out how much this crazy shopping spree was going to set me back.

I found a checkout line and stood in it with the rest of the impatient holiday shoppers. I let out a breath. The intercom system warned shoppers that the store would close in five minutes, so people needed to make their final selections. The queue was already long, but more and more people seemed to pile in behind me. I guess there were a lot of last-minute Christmas shoppers in the world. Thankfully, the people behind the counter clearly wanted to get out of work as much as the holiday shoppers wanted to make their purchases and be on their way.

A mother in front of me was trying to juggle a bag of stuff, two kids and a baby. I did my best to keep the baby entertained by making faces at it, which made the time fly by faster.

"Next customer," a chipper voice said when it was my turn. I was directed to a clerk in the middle who wore a pair of reindeer antlers with twinkling Christmas lights.

I hoisted my bag of purchases onto the counter.

"Oh dear," the clerk said, "did an airline lose your luggage? I hate it when that happens. You'd be amazed at how many people I see come through here in a hurry, needing to purchase a new wardrobe like this." She kept chatting away as she scanned the barcodes and removed the RFID anti-theft security tags from my purchases. "That'll be thirteen-hundred, seventy-nine dollars and twenty-seven cents. I sure hope the airline is paying for all this. Can I charge this to your Macy's card?"

"I don't have one," I responded.

"Would you like to open one today?" the clerk asked.

"Probably not today. You are busy," I said, looking back at the long line of people still waiting to check out. I pulled out my wallet from my back pocket, flipped through the cards and laid down my platinum American Express Card.

"Thank you," the clerk said as she swiped the card, handed me my receipt and asked me to sign the store copy. Once I had put my John Hancock on the bottom line, she packaged all my new purchases into giant Macy's bags and handed them to me. "Have a Merry Christmas," she said with a huge smile.

"Thanks. You, too," I replied almost automatically.

I grabbed my purchases and followed the path to the nearest exit. A security guard stood next to the door. I wasn't sure if he was there to make sure no one was shoplifting or keep any other customers from sneaking in. I nodded as I walked up. The guard opened the door for me, and I stepped back into the cold air.

With clothing in hand, I knew I needed to go buy the rest of my essentials. I shifted my bags into one hand so I could pull out my phone. I quickly searched for the nearest Duane Reade's and headed off in that direction.

The streets were quieter than they would have been on an ordinary evening. I followed the map to the closest store, which was less than a block north of Macy's, right on Sixth Avenue. I walked in and found it busy, but not nearly the chaos I'd just gotten out of. I grabbed a basket and made my way through the store. I picked up shaving cream and a razor, toothpaste and a toothbrush, gel and a comb, deodorant, bodywash and a small bottle of cologne that I hoped wouldn't make me smell like a teenager going on his first date. I also picked up some food essentials — and by essentials, I mean I bought a shit-ton of comfort food. By the time

I got out of Duane Reade's, I had spent almost one hundred and twenty dollars. I looked down at all my bags and made my way to the hotel.

I'd never stayed at The Time New York before, but I'd heard good things about the upscale hotel. I thought about hailing a cab but ended up walking the twenty minutes to West Forty-Ninth Street — quite the feat with the load I was juggling.

My mind was a jumble of thoughts. I wanted to talk to someone, but the last thing I wanted to do was bring my drama into someone's life on Christmas Eve. It wasn't anyone else's fault that Jeremy had imploded my life with one trick.

The snow crunched beneath my loafers as I walked. Along the way, I passed a few restaurants that were still open, serving customers who either didn't want to stay at home on Christmas Eve or didn't celebrate the holiday at all. That's one thing I can say about New York City. There is always something open, since we have so many faiths represented. Many years ago, before I'd met Jeremy, I remembered hanging out with my Jewish friends on Christmas Day. Their tradition was to go to a nice Chinese restaurant then to a movie. Maybe I'd drag myself out of the hotel tomorrow and find a Chinese place…or at least get delivery.

I made it to the hotel, got checked in with no problems and took the elevator up to my room. It was modern but small. There was a king-sized bed and a small writing table, but that was about it for the main part. The bathroom was also pretty small, but it had all the necessities.

I took a shower then pulled the tags off the new pajamas I'd bought and lay down on the bed. For the first time since I'd walked in on Jeremy, I let myself soak in everything that had happened to me that evening. I was numb. Trying to think made me a little lightheaded. I sat cross-legged and let myself cry. At first, the tears came one at a time. But once the flood works opened, I was a waterfall of pain. After I finished my first emotional catharsis of the weekend—I was sure there would be more—I washed my face to take some of the puffiness out. I called down to the hotel restaurant, Serafina, and ordered lasagna al forno. I wanted carbs, carbs and nothing but carbs. I also ordered a bottle of Seravino, Malbec, Antigal Uno, Mendoza. I'd learned a long time ago that I love a good Malbec wine, and the only good Malbecs were the ones straight from Argentina. None of those fake American Malbecs for me. I didn't need to order dessert, since I'd already splurged on comfort food at Duane Reade's, but I ordered the tiramisu, anyway.

I grabbed the remote control from the bedside table and turned on the TV. I flipped around a few channels but wasn't paying attention to what was on the screen. The simple act of flipping channels was enough to occupy my mind for the moment. Part of me wanted to roll up into a little ball and go to sleep, but I knew that would be a bad idea with my room service heading up. I kept channel surfing.

The sudden knocking on the door drew me out of my weird zombie-like funk. I forced myself off the bed and answered the door. The guy on the other side saw my shadow because he said, "Room service," right as I looked out of the peephole. I opened the door.

"Good evening, sir," a handsome young Italian man said in a thick Brooklyn accent. He may have had all the Italian genes in the world, but he was clearly a New Yorker. "Want me to put this on the desk?" he asked, motioning with his head down toward the tray he was holding.

I stared into the man's chiseled face and into the dark brown, almost black, eyes. "Huh?" I heard myself ask in a dazed and confused voice.

"Your food? Would you like me to put it on the desk, then open your bottle of wine?"

"Yes," I said, snapping out of it. "Thanks. Sorry, just a bit slow tonight," I said with a thousand-watt smile. I'd learned years ago how to put on the fake show-smile for clients, so it came almost second nature. I stood out of the way and held the door open for the young man, who quickly entered the room and set down the tray. He made quick work with the wine opener.

"One glass or two?" the guy asked.

Such a simple question with such huge implications. "Just one," I said, casting my eyes down to avoid breaking down in front of this guy—not that it mattered, because it wasn't like I was ever going to see him again. He poured a small amount into one glass and handed it to me to smell and taste. I swirled the wine around in the glass. I noticed the legs sticking to the top of the wine glass before slowly sliding back down, indicating a fuller, richer wine experience with a higher alcohol proof. The Malbec had a bold and spicy aroma with hints of blackberries and plum. I lifted the glass to my lips and took a sip. *Damn! This is good.* But at seventy dollars a bottle, it should have been pretty decent.

"Thanks," I said. The server filled the rest of my glass, then recorked the bottle before setting it back on the desk.

While he did that, I pulled out my wallet and found I had no cash on me but a couple of fifties and a one-hundred-dollar bill. *Oh well, at least someone will have a nice Christmas.* I pulled out the hundred and handed it over to the man.

"I can't," the man said.

I waved him off with a "Merry Christmas."

He thanked me again before letting me know to call down if I needed anything else. I assured him I wouldn't, but I promised to call if I did. I showed him out of the room and turned on the 'Do not disturb' sign when he left.

Once the waiter was gone, I grabbed the tray and moved it from the desk to the middle of the bed. I decided dinner in bed was just what the doctor ordered. Before I dug into the food, I drank my first glass of wine, then topped it off while I tried to once again find something to watch on television. I finally settled in on *A Diva's Christmas Carol*. It was a two-thousand film starring Vanessa Williams as Ebony Scrooge. Part of me preferred the nineteen-thirty-eight black-and-white film, but I never pass up an opportunity to watch Vanessa Williams.

With Vanessa on the television, I dove into my lasagna and enjoyed every carb-alicious, cheesy-drenched morsel. I also finished a couple more glasses of wine. By the time I'd finished dinner, I only had enough wine for half a glass of the tasty red stuff. *Too bad you can't lick inside a wine bottle*, I thought to myself. I also considered ordering another bottle but thought that would probably be a bad idea.

Instead, I made the insta-coffee in the hotel room and served it up with my tiramisu. During all this, Vanessa Williams was replaced with a more recent remake of Dickens' classic novel, where Ebenezer Scrooge was played by Sir Patrick Stewart. When I finished my dessert, I left the dishes in the hall outside my door. The movie played on in the background as I brushed my teeth. I curled back up on the bed and sighed. I can't even remember which Ghost of Christmas Past, Present or Future I'd gotten to before I passed out from emotional exhaustion.

About the Author

Jason Wrench is a professor in the Department of Communication at SUNY New Paltz and has authored/edited 15+ books and over 35 academic research articles. He is also an avid reader and regularly reviews books for publishers in a wide number of genres.

Jason loves to hear from readers. You can find his contact information, website details and author profile page at https://www.pride-publishing.com

PUBLISHING

Sign up for our newsletter and find out about all our romance book releases, eBook sales and promotions, sneak peeks and FREE romance books!